PATH TO HONOR

Knights Of Honor
Book Nine

Alexa Aston

Copyright © 2018 by Alexa Aston
Print Edition

Published by Dragonblade Publishing, an imprint of Kathryn Le Veque Novels, Inc

All rights reserved. No part of this book may be used or reproduced in any manner whatsoever without written permission, except in the case of brief quotations embodied in critical articles or reviews.

Books from Dragonblade Publishing

Dangerous Lords Series by Maggi Andersen
The Baron's Betrothal
Seducing the Earl
The Viscount's Widowed Lady

Also from Maggi Andersen
The Marquess Meets His Match

Knights of Honor Series by Alexa Aston
Word of Honor
Marked by Honor
Code of Honor
Journey to Honor
Heart of Honor
Bold in Honor
Love and Honor
Gift of Honor
Path to Honor

Legends of Love Series by Avril Borthiry
The Wishing Well
Isolated Hearts
Sentinel

The Lost Lords Series by Chasity Bowlin
The Lost Lord of Castle Black
The Vanishing of Lord Vale
The Missing Marquess of Althorn
The Resurrection of Lady Ramsleigh

By Elizabeth Ellen Carter
Captive of the Corsairs, *Heart of the Corsairs Series*
Revenge of the Corsairs, *Heart of the Corsairs Series*
Shadow of the Corsairs, *Heart of the Corsairs Series*
Dark Heart

Knight Everlasting Series by Cassidy Cayman
Endearing
Enchanted
Evermore

Midnight Meetings Series by Gina Conkle
Meet a Rogue at Midnight, book 4

Second Chance Series by Jessica Jefferson
Second Chance Marquess

Imperial Season Series by Mary Lancaster
Vienna Waltz
Vienna Woods
Vienna Dawn

Blackhaven Brides Series by Mary Lancaster
The Wicked Baron
The Wicked Lady
The Wicked Rebel
The Wicked Husband
The Wicked Marquis
The Wicked Governess
The Wicked Spy
The Wicked Gypsy

Highland Loves Series by Melissa Limoges
My Reckless Love
My Steadfast Love

Clash of the Tartans Series by Anna Markland
Kilty Secrets
Kilted at the Altar
Kilty Pleasures

Queen of Thieves Series by Andy Peloquin
Child of the Night Guild
Thief of the Night Guild
Queen of the Night Guild

Dark Gardens Series by Meara Platt
Garden of Shadows
Garden of Light
Garden of Dragons
Garden of Destiny

Rulers of the Sky Series by Paula Quinn
Scorched
Ember
White Hot

Highlands Forever Series by Violetta Rand
Unbreakable
Undeniable

Viking's Fury Series by Violetta Rand
Love's Fury
Desire's Fury
Passion's Fury

Also from Violetta Rand
Viking Hearts

The Sons of Scotland Series by Victoria Vane
Virtue
Valor

Dry Bayou Brides Series by Lynn Winchester
The Shepherd's Daughter
The Seamstress
The Widow

Men of Blood Series by Rosamund Winchester
The Blood & The Bloom

Table of Contents

Prologue 1
Chapter 1 9
Chapter 2 18
Chapter 3 28
Chapter 4 37
Chapter 5 44
Chapter 6 54
Chapter 7 62
Chapter 8 72
Chapter 9 83
Chapter 10 93
Chapter 11 101
Chapter 12 107
Chapter 13 118
Chapter 14 128
Chapter 15 137
Chapter 16 146
Chapter 17 154
Chapter 18 162
Chapter 19 170
Chapter 20 179
Chapter 21 185
Chapter 22 193
Chapter 23 204
Chapter 24 213
Epilogue 222
About the Author 227

PROLOGUE

Kinwick Castle—July, 1376

NAN DE MONTFORT held the tip of her wooden sword to Drewett Stollars' throat, daring the page to move. He lay flat on his back, his face red from anger and exertion. She had a feeling that he might begin to cry if she did not let him sit up soon. It would serve him right for all the taunts he'd thrown her way since he'd come to foster at Kinwick last autumn. Drewett had returned early from his summer visit to his home and already she wished him gone again.

"You're a cheater, Nan," he loudly complained as his eyes darted around to see if anyone within hearing distance might be listening to his accusation and come to his aid.

The sound of clanging steel continued around them. Nan gave Drewett a triumphant smile, knowing none of the pairs of soldiers in the training yard would come to the grumbling boy's rescue.

A shadow fell across Drewett. "What have we here?"

Nan recognized Gilbert's voice but refused to acknowledge his interruption. The murderous look in Drewett's eyes told her that she didn't dare look away for even a moment.

"I bested him," she said with confidence, making sure not to sound as if she bragged. She knew the captain of Kinwick's guard would be proud of her. She'd overheard Gilbert confiding to her father how lazy and untrustworthy Drewett remained, despite everything Gilbert had tried to teach the young boy.

"Let this page up," Lord Geoffrey de Montfort instructed as he joined Gilbert.

Reluctantly, Nan took a small step back and let her sword hang at her side. With her father present, she knew Drewett wouldn't try anything foolish—but she would have to remain on her guard for the next few days. The page had a long memory and a short fuse and would do what he could to make Nan pay for embarrassing him, even though she doubted any man in the training yard had paid a bit of attention to the two tussling seven year olds.

"Stand alongside one another," her father instructed as Drewett rolled to his feet and reclaimed his sword that lay in the dirt where she had kicked it beyond his reach.

Nan held her ground, which made Drewett have to come to her. He stood so close that their shoulders almost touched. She knew the boy wanted to intimidate her. Little did he know that nothing he could do could ever intimidate her. Growing up with three older brothers had already taught her to be fearless and strong. Besides, she was a de Montfort. De Montforts never feared others. They created fear instead.

"She cheated, Lord Geoffrey," whined Drewett.

Nan cringed inside, knowing her father hated anyone telling tales. She almost felt sorry for the boy standing beside her.

Almost.

When Geoffrey remained silent, Drewett continued. "I know Lady Anne is your daughter but she does not fight fair. Knights are supposed to be fair." The page glanced in her direction and sneered. "You can't even be a knight. You're just a girl. You have no idea what fairness is about."

Nan didn't know what irked her more—hearing herself called Anne or having Drewett point out that she was a girl. She never went by Anne.

And she was a girl who could do anything a boy could. Even be a knight if she put her mind to it.

"Aye, Drewett, knights do act honorably," Geoffrey agreed pleasantly as he came to stand in front of the pair, towering over them. Then the warmth left his voice. "But in war, all is fair. You have a definite height advantage over Nan. A longer reach, as well. You also outweigh her and might have worn her down in time."

Nan bit her tongue to keep from speaking. She could have danced circles around this stupid boy for hours if need be. Though irritated, she allowed the lesson her father was trying to teach the fool continue to unfold.

"Nan, what did you do to secure such an advantage over Drewett? When I arrived, your opponent had a sword at his throat and his weapon was well out of reach."

Keeping a smile from her face, Nan solemnly replied, "I snaked my foot around his ankle in order to trip him, Father."

Geoffrey also kept a stern look on his face but Nan knew he was secretly pleased. He directed his next words to the fostering page.

"You must always fight to win, Drewett. 'Tis important not only to protect yourself but those around you. Moreover, you must be able to count on the man next to you. These are important things to remember."

"But *she* isn't a man, my lord," the boy huffed. "*She* shouldn't even be in the training yard. Lady Anne will never be a knight. I don't see why I have to partner with her."

Nan froze at the page's words. She wanted to turn and shake some sense into him.

Geoffrey knelt so that his eyes were level with Drewett's. Nan glanced at her father and saw the ice in his hazel eyes, which now burned bright green as he glared at the boy.

"Lady Nan has more integrity and honor in her smallest toe than you do running through your entire body, Drewett Stollars."

His tone was ever so soft but one that frightened Nan. She'd only heard it on a few occasions and vowed never to do anything to disappoint her father so that he used it with her.

"Today is a turning point in your young life," he told the trembling page. "Either you will move forward and choose to become the best man you can be from this moment on—or you will go elsewhere. I'll not have someone I'm responsible for with such an abysmal attitude.

"The choice is yours."

Nan held her breath, wondering what Drewett would do.

The boy turned to face her. She saw both misery and regret mingling on his features and knew it was time for her to take the high road. Nan gave him an encouraging smile. She saw him relax and heard the long breath he exhaled.

"Lady Nan," he began, "I am sorry that I have offended you in the past."

She noted the use of her preferred name and inclined her head slightly in acknowledgement of it and their unpleasant encounters over the past several months.

"You are not a cheater. You are an excellent sparring partner and I can learn much from you. Will you accept my humble apology?"

The hungry look in his eyes begged not only for forgiveness—but acceptance. Nan decided that, mayhap, she had intimidated this boy and he now offered her an olive branch.

"I will," she assured him. "I hope that we can be not only sparring partners but also friends."

For the first time since he'd arrived at Kinwick, Drewett Stollars smiled. Nan beamed at him. He gave her a stiff bow and she returned it. A glow filled her. She believed that she had made a friend.

"Well done," pronounced Geoffrey as he rose to his full height. "Gilbert, will you see young Drewett has something to occupy him. I am in need of time with my daughter." He smiled at her. "Let's walk, Nan."

"I'll care for your sword, my lady," Drewett said eagerly and reached out.

Nan passed the weapon to him, amazed at the change that had come over the boy. Her father took her small hand in his large one and they set out from the training yard. These were the hours Nan cherished most. Geoffrey de Montfort was a busy man so when he made time to spend just with her, she treasured every moment. He'd recently returned from London, where he'd left her brother Ancel to protect Richard, the king's grandson, so this was the first day since he'd come back that they'd been alone together.

They walked in companionable silence through the castle grounds and out the gates. Geoffrey headed toward the meadow. Nan had roamed the estate since she could walk and knew more about it than anyone except her father. She often brought things to his attention that she had noticed, whether it was a fence needing repair or how a tree was growing.

Finally, he spoke.

"King Edward has died. I received a missive from court this morning. It happened a little over a week ago."

It saddened Nan to think the old king had passed. He had come to Kinwick on summer progress several times. Though she could only recall a vague image of the monarch, she remembered him being kind to her, even slipping her a sweetmeat when no one was looking. He teased about how they both had a sweet tooth and that one day, he would be successful in stealing Cook away from Kinwick. He would bring the servant to the Palace of Westminster and be able to eat her fruit tarts every day.

"That means Richard is our new king? Even though he's so young?" she asked.

"Aye. The old king had an idea he would not last long. 'Tis why he requested I bring Ancel to London to watch over his grandson. Your brother will be a member of King Richard's royal guard. Richard knows how loyal de Montforts are to the crown and that Ancel will look out for him and always keep his best interests at heart."

Nan would miss Ancel. Living in London or at the other royal residences, he wouldn't be able to come home very often. At least she still had Hal and Edward with her. They fostered at Winterbourne, which was directly to the north of Kinwick, and both brothers were home now on their summer break. Nan had begged Hal to teach her how to shoot a bow and arrow yesterday and he'd promised they would start their lessons this afternoon. Excitement filled her at the idea of learning how to use a new, powerful weapon.

"Have you thought anymore about fostering?" her father asked.

"Only if Lord Hardwin lets me serve as his page," she promptly replied.

At seven, Nan could leave Kinwick to foster. Boys always did and sometimes girls did, as well. But Nan wasn't interested in learning anything some older noblewoman might try to teach her. She'd never been interested in anything remotely involving a castle, unless it was in regard to its defense. Who cared about how to make candles or scent rushes?

"Fostering with Hardie is not a choice for you, Nan. Nor is being a page at any nobleman's estate." He paused. "Mayhap your mother and I should send you to court for a few years as we did Alys."

"No," Nan said forcefully. "Besides, Alys only stayed at court until the queen died. Then she was allowed to come home."

Geoffrey squeezed her hand. "I suppose we could come to a compromise and allow you to stay at Kinwick. I will teach you what I can and your mother could do the same."

Nan stopped and tugged on him. "You've already talked about this with Mother, haven't you?" she asked.

He grinned. "How did you become so clever? You must take after Merryn." He searched her face. "This will give you the best of both worlds."

Nan decided she could tolerate whatever her mother wished her to learn. She even promised herself she would do it with a smile on her face because she would still have plenty of time to learn what she really cared about—everything Geoffrey de Montfort could teach her. He was a great soldier and nobleman. He had been to the wars in France and advised the king at court. She would soak up everything he shared with her—and still learn how to make those stupid candles.

"So, Happy Wanderer, what do I need to know?"

She loved her father's pet name for her. Every time he used it, she stood taller and radiated happiness.

"I think we should go see Joseph," she suggested, knowing the falconer always looked forward to showing off his raptors to the earl. "He has been training three new eyases. You will be surprised how much they've grown, Father, since the last time you saw them."

"An excellent idea," Geoffrey proclaimed.

They crossed the meadow and headed toward the road. From there, they would cut through the woods to reach the falconer's cottage where he trained Kinwick's peregrines.

As they left the road to enter the woods, an odd sound brought both of them to a halt. Nan cocked her ear upward, listening.

A faint cry sounded. She wondered if it belonged to some animal in a trap, yet something told her it was no animal.

It was human.

"This way," she said, pulling on her father's hand and walking rapidly.

Nan spied a basket and slowed. Another tiny mewl sounded. She broke away and ran toward it. The basket was large and had a tall handle. Cushioned in the bottom was a wool blanket of dull brown. Atop the blanket lay a small babe. Its bare feet kicked out. Nan had seen a few babes around the estate when she had been dragged along by her mother to visit tenants, but as the youngest of the de Montfort children, she had no experience being around any.

She gently touched the babe's head and a coo came from the infant. Nan would have sworn the babe actually smiled at her. She took its tiny hand in hers and was surprised by the strong grip as the littlest fingers she'd ever seen wrapped around one of hers.

Her father knelt beside the basket and smiled. He lifted the babe and brought it to his chest.

"What are you doing here all alone, little one?" he asked softly and brushed his lips against the blond fuzz of the child's head.

A sick feeling overwhelmed Nan. "Someone left it here."

Geoffrey nodded. "Her," he said. "'Tis a girl."

"Why would someone do that?" Nan asked, anguish filling her. Then anger replaced it. "She could have died out here, Father."

"But she didn't." He paused. "We will do our best to find her parents but if we can't—or if they don't wish to be found?" He smiled at the child, whose feet continued to dance back and forth. "Merryn and I will take you in," he promised the child.

He placed the girl gently back into the basket and rose. Nan wrapped the blanket around her protectively.

"Something tells me that you have found the newest de Montfort, Nan. This child will be your sister. You've been close to Hal and Edward since they were near your age and they've influenced you quite a bit. I think 'twill be good for you to have a sister to care for."

Nan knew how much her mother loved babes. Her parents had recently returned from visiting their first grandchildren, Philippa and Wyatt. Her sister, Alys, had given birth to the twins in March and had begged them to visit. Nan had chosen to remain at Kinwick, having no interest in people who couldn't talk or walk, much less how all the conversations her mother and Alys had seemed to revolve around herbs and healing.

But this babe called out to something deep within her. Though she had no interest in the womanly arts, Nan felt a strong pull toward this child.

"If we cannot find her parents, can I name her?" she asked.

Geoffrey lifted the basket by its handle and smiled down at the babe. "I think she'd like that."

"Jessimond," Nan said. "I want to call her Jessimond."

CHAPTER I

Sandbourne—April, 1388

TRISTAN THEROLDE URGED his horse on, impatient to reach Sandbourne and see the horseflesh available there. He'd become interested in breeding horses and both Stephen and Toby encouraged him in this pursuit. He glanced to where both men rode to his left and right and tamped down the emotion that threatened to flare up. These two knights had fostered with him. They had known one another since they were boys polishing armor and running errands, as all pages did. Other than Dawkin, his captain of the guard at Thorpe Castle, these men were the only ones he trusted.

Life had taught him to be guarded.

"That should be it," called out Toby as he pointed straight ahead.

Tristan picked up the pace. The sooner they arrived at Sandbourne and he conducted his business, the sooner they could return to Leventhorpe lands. He never fully relaxed outside the walls of Thorpe Castle—and was only beginning to learn to do so inside them.

The trio approached the gates. Tristan spoke to the gatekeeper, who knew they were expected, and open the gates for them to enter. The outer bailey buzzed with activity as they passed from it into the inner bailey. He saw an elegantly dressed woman awaiting them at the keep and motioned for his men to follow him to where she stood.

As they approached, Tristan assessed her as he did everyone that crossed his path. She was taller than the average female, with a willowy frame and a long blond braid that skirted her waist. Mayhap two score or a bit more, her radiant beauty still shone brightly.

He dismounted and went to greet her as his knights remained in the saddle.

"Greetings, my lord," she said in a low voice. "I am Lady Elysande Devereux, Countess of Sandbourne. I assume you are Lord Tristan Therolde, Earl of Leventhorpe."

He kissed the proffered hand. "Aye, my lady, here to spend time with your husband and see his horses, which I hear are some of the best in southern England."

She laughed. "You mean *my* horses? And to be clear, my lord, they are the best in *all* of England."

Tristan frowned at her presumptuous words. "I corresponded with Lord Michael Devereux regarding the matter," he said curtly.

He recalled during a brief trip to London hearing that Sandbourne's horses were the best to be had but also something about the earl's wife knowing much about horses. Tristan had brushed that off as ignorant gossip. A woman knowing more than a man about anything bordered on the ridiculous.

"True," the noblewoman acknowledged. "You wrote to Michael and he respectfully answered your missive." Her eyes blazed. "But if you wish to discuss horses and consider purchasing any, you will deal directly with me, my lord."

His temper flared. "See here, Lady Elysande—"

She held up a hand and he bit back the unflattering words about to fly from his mouth. If these horses were as good as others claimed, it wouldn't do to insult Lord Michael's wife. Some women had wormed their way into their husband's heart and whispered into their ear in order to have their say. This lady seemed as one who might be one of those. Disappointment filled him, for he had been looking forward to meeting Devereux after hearing so many complimentary things about the nobleman.

A stern look crossed her face and color heightened her cheeks. "You are a guest, my lord, and will be accorded every courtesy, but one thing must remain perfectly clear from the start of our conversation. I will be the one who decides if you are worthy to purchase any horse from our stable. I am the one who breeds and trains every horse sired at Sandbourne. I have taught my husband much about horseflesh over the years, but he will be the one to confirm to you that I control everything regarding Sandbourne's stables."

Then she gave him a sweet smile. "I know many men do not hold women in high esteem, nor do they believe that a woman can be an expert on anything beyond birthing babes or weaving tapestries. You will find things very different at Sandbourne." She paused. "I hope we have not gotten off on the wrong foot, my lord. Why don't we take your horses to be watered and fed and you can look over some of our mounts? We can also go to the enclosure, where more of our horses are kept."

"As you wish, my lady."

Tristan had the good sense to offer her his arm while he kept his horse's reins in his free hand. He did not bother to glance at either Stephen or Toby, knowing both knights probably hid smiles after listening to him being dressed down by this woman. If he liked any of their available horses, he would see that he purchased them—even if he had to grovel to Lady Elysande.

He also had something else on his mind and would see if that, too, could be accomplished during this brief visit to Sandbourne. The time drew near for his sister to be betrothed and wed. At ten and seven, Gillian was already a grown woman, both beautiful and sweet-natured. Tristan rarely ventured from his estate and hadn't made the appropriate contacts necessary in order to arrange a desirable match for her. If Lord Michael had any sons that would make for a good husband, Tristan would discuss an agreement between them.

As they strolled to the stables, Lady Elysande pointed out things along the way and was greeted in a friendly manner by everyone they passed. Though she had been sharp with him, the noblewoman spoke to those working at the castle with kindness—and that courtesy was returned. It wasn't hard to see that she was beloved by her workers. That spoke in her favor. Still, it confused him why her husband would allow her to be in charge of such a vital part of his estate. Mayhap Lord

Michael simply let his wife think she was and fooled her into believing she had control over the horses they bred and sold.

A cheer went up as they came to the training yard. An archery contest appeared to be occurring in the sectioned off butts. Knowing how Toby enjoyed showing his prowess with a bow and arrow, he looked to his friend and saw a huge grin on his face.

Lady Elysande must have seen it, too, for she said, "If you wish, my lord, your men can allow our stable hands to care for their horses so they might remain in the training yard. Would you care to do so?" she asked his men.

"Aye, my lady," responded Toby with enthusiasm. "I am Sir Toby. This is Sir Stephen. We would very much like to watch—and mayhap participate—in this contest."

Tristan grimaced. He should have introduced his men when they arrived but Lady Elysande had thrown him so that he'd neglected his good manners. Not that he used them much anymore. He dined alone every meal and rarely met with others in the nobility. His manners had grown rusty with disuse. He hoped that wouldn't reflect upon him poorly when it came time to negotiate a price regarding horseflesh.

"I am pleased to meet you both," she said graciously. She lifted her hand from where it rested on Tristan's arm. "Give me your reins and tell me your horses' names. I will see they are cared for."

Both men introduced their horses to her as if they were allowing her to meet people for the first time. She stroked each horse and spoke directly to it and then asked the knights questions about their mounts. Satisfied with their answers, she dismissed them and they eagerly hurried to the butts.

As they led the three horses to the stables, she said, "And what of your horse, my lord? What can you tell me about him?"

Tristan groaned inwardly but pushed forward, intending to humor her. He told her the horse's name, making one up on the spot since he'd never bothered to name the creature before now. He shared where he'd bought the animal and a little about its sire and dam.

"But what else? What does he like to eat? What little treats do you spoil him with? Does he enjoy cantering or a full gallop? Are his bowel movements regular?"

Tristan looked blankly at her. He couldn't answer any of those questions.

Lady Elysande gave him a withering look. "I am not quite sure why you have come to Sandbourne, my lord. You say you are interested in breeding and training horses. I only sell a small part of my stock each year and then only to a select few. Why should I allow you to purchase any horse at all when you come to me so ill prepared?"

"Because I need something to occupy my time," he admitted gruffly. "I'm not much for being around people. I thought spending my time with horses would prove worthwhile."

Her whole being changed as she bestowed a radiant smile upon him. "That is the first honest thing that has come from you. Horses can do so much for humans. They can befriend us. Nurture us. Even heal us." She studied him for a long moment. "I think you have been deeply hurt, my lord. I promise you that working with horses will be the first step on your road to recovery."

He visibly cringed at her response.

"You may have revealed more to me than you would have chosen, Lord Tristan," she said softly, "but you have come to the right place. I hope you choose to spend some time at Sandbourne."

They led the horses to the entrance of the stables. Tristan remained silent, feeling naked after what had passed between them. Two lads met them and Lady Elysande instructed them on the names of each horse and the preferences she'd learned from Toby and Stephen before the boys led the three animals away.

"Let's start in the stables and then go to the meadow," she suggested.

Tristan let her lead him about, discovering she was a fount of knowledge. Within minutes, he learned that stallions usually would breed a mare in the summer and that the gestation lasted around eleven months, leading to foals being born in the spring and early summer. Though a stallion could breed as early as two years of age,

Lady Elysande recommended waiting until the male turned four because early breeding could affect the growth of any offspring. The same held true for mares, which could carry a foal by the time they turned eighteen months, but the noblewoman also liked to wait until they were more mature.

"Foals can walk and then even run a few hours after birth. Though they drink plenty of their mother's milk, they also might nibble at hay or grass," she shared.

"So this is a busy time of year for you," Tristan said. By now, he did not question that this woman knew exactly what she spoke of. He regretted questioning her authority and would do whatever it took to get in her good graces.

"Aye. I have spent several nights in the stables recently with mares ready to deliver or even with those in the enclosed meadow. Michael is good enough to wait with me each time. In fact, 'tis how we met. The first time we saw one another, I was helping to deliver a foal. Michael jumped right in without any previous experience." She smiled. "He has been by my side ever since."

They came to a large stall with a golden mare whose belly was so large that she looked ready to give birth at any moment. Beside her stood a tall man with dark hair, stroking the horse gently.

"That's a good girl," he crooned and then looked up. "Hello, Mother."

"Lord Tristan Therolde, I'd like you to meet my oldest child, David. He has recently been knighted and returned to live at Sandbourne."

"'Tis a pleasure to meet you, my lord. Mother says you've come to look at our horses."

"Aye, Sir David. And learn. I fear my knowledge regarding horses is limited."

The young knight laughed. "Mother has forgotten more than most people will ever know about horses. She will be an excellent tutor for you."

"David has been assisting me with the births since his return."

"And I plan on helping her to train the new foals, as well. I love horses as much as Mother does and that's saying quite a bit."

Tristan found himself drawn to the man's genial manner and smile. A handsome knight from a good family would be the perfect man for Gillian to partner with. Though Lady Elysande seemed a bit unconventional, Tristan knew she would be a welcoming mother-in-law. He would broach the issue when the time came and hope that David Devereux was not already betrothed or married.

"Send word if any difficulties arise. I'm going to escort Lord Tristan to the enclosure."

"It was a pleasure meeting you, my lord. I will see you at the evening meal," David told him. "That is, if this beautiful lady has given birth by that time." He gave the mare a fond pat.

Tristan and Lady Elysande left the stables. As they drew near the training yard, a loud series of cheers broke out, drawing his curiosity. He wondered if Toby had been able to participate in the contest.

"We can always visit the meadow later," the countess told him. "I hope you will remain at Sandbourne for a few weeks. Shall we see how the archery contest fares instead?"

"I would like that, my lady."

Tristan led her to the butts. A ring of soldiers encircled the area. He saw Toby with a bow in hand, determination on his face as he drew back the string and let the arrow sail. The arrow struck close to the center of the target and the men applauded his effort. A second man joined him and Toby stepped aside. His arrow also hit the target but landed almost dead center. More shouts of encouragement exploded.

He figured it came down to these two men as to which one might win the competition. After each one shot twice more, the Sandbourne man threw his bow to the ground and his hands in the air, happiness spreading across his lean face.

"It looks as if we have a new champion for this week. Well done, Hervey."

Tristan assumed the man speaking was the Earl of Sandbourne.

Well over six feet, he had broad shoulders and piercing blue eyes. Not much would get past this man, who looked to be two score and five.

"He's not a true champion," someone hollered from the crowd. "He ain't beat the de Montfort!"

At once, the name *de Montfort* began to be chanted by all those present. Calls for the de Montfort continued as men stomped their feet and clapped their hands.

"Enough!" cried Lord Michael, trying to hide a smile and losing that particular battle. He glanced to the crowd at his right. "Would you like to participate?"

A slightly built man stepped forward and nodded, his head down as if embarrassed at all of the sudden attention. Wild applause erupted as he stepped to where the soldier named Hervey stood. Tristan read the doubt creeping into the man's eyes. This de Montfort must be quite skilled to have the support of all those gathered and cause a skilled soldier who'd just won an archery contest to question himself.

Then the newcomer turned to pick up a bow. Tristan caught sight of a dark as night braid that whipped around.

A braid?

He studied the person more carefully and found it wasn't a man at all. It was a woman—dressed as a man. She wore an oversized tunic of dark brown and baggy black pants. She reached down and slipped off her shoes, tossing them and a blade aside. More cheers broke out as Tristan caught sight of a shapely ankle for a moment. Then she wiggled her toes and seemed to grip the very ground under her with them.

The group grew silent as a young boy wheeled out a new target. Concentration filled the woman's face as she studied it. Her slender body seemed as taut as the bowstring she pulled back. Without warning, her arrow flew through the air.

And hit dead center.

She gave a brief nod to the crowd acknowledging her effort and then stepped aside so her challenger could take his turn. They alternated until each had sent five arrows to the target, with the same boy hurrying out and moving the target further away after each shot an arrow. By the time the match ended, four of her arrows clustered together so tightly around the bullseye, Tristan didn't see how there could be any space between them. The fifth had split one of those arrows straight down the middle. Hervey, while coming close, never stood a chance against his competitor.

Chants of *de Montfort* began again. Tristan watched as the soldiers hoisted the woman up in the air and paraded her around the butts. He found himself breathing normally again after holding his breath each time she fired an arrow.

Then she passed by, high above him. She looked down and their eyes met. Hers were a startling blue, like two sapphires in her heart-shaped face. Tristan's heart slammed against his ribs as he watched the cheering men carry her off.

Turning to Lady Elysande, he asked, "Who was that?"

"My cousin. Nan de Montfort."

CHAPTER 2

Nan demanded that the soldiers return her to the ground since she had a low tolerance for being the center of attention. They did as she requested. A grinning page held up her boots and baselard. Nan accepted them and plopped on the ground in order to put the boots back on. By the time she stood and slipped her dagger into its resting place inside the boot, most of the men in the butts had scattered. They had gone back to their training exercises in the yard, paired off as they wielded swords and maces under the watchful eye of Michael and his captain of the guard. Two pages collected the targets that had been used in the archery contest, pulling the arrows from them. She gathered her own bow and set of arrows and decided to return to the keep.

Because she definitely wanted to meet the stranger that had stood next to Elysande.

It hadn't surprised Nan to see an unfamiliar face at Sandbourne. People constantly came and went at the estate, most of them interested in viewing the group of horses Elysande had assembled through years of buying and breeding. She and Michael had been wed over a score and had built what Nan heard many say was the finest stable in England. Consequently, many noblemen ventured to Sandbourne trying to purchase a Devereux horse.

The newcomer had to be one of those men.

Deciding to check on Nightfoot before she washed away the day's sweat and grime, Nan headed toward the stables. She found her horse hanging his head over the stall's door as he gazed at the horse directly across from him like some love-struck fool.

Laughing, she threw her arms around the stallion's neck and gave him a kiss. "How's my sweet Nightfoot? Have you made any progress with your new lady friend?" she asked playfully.

The horse snorted and she chuckled. Nan went inside the stall and brushed him for several minutes, promising to return tomorrow for a long ride.

As she left the stall, she heard a shout and went running. She found a stable hand already there and heard David telling the boy to fetch the countess at once. The boy ran off and Nan poked her head inside.

"Something wrong with Ginger?"

"She's in a bit of distress," her cousin shared. "Nothing I couldn't handle but you know how involved Mother is with her horses. If anything did go wrong during the birth and I'd neglected to summon her, it would be my head on a platter," he joked.

Nan opened the stall door and joined him, noting how restless Ginger seemed as she paced around the enlarged area. The horse's flanks glistened with sweat. She pawed the ground several times and then lay down, immediately rising and pacing again.

"I think I'll take her out to the pasture," David said. "I believe the open space would be beneficial to her, especially if there's a breeze outside. It might bring her some relief."

"Is she trying to position the foal?" Nan asked, having learned something about horses from Elysande over the years.

"Aye. It may calm her to have more room. Some horses like being out of doors when they give birth." He slid a rope around Ginger's neck and knotted it. "Come on, girl. Let's find you a place to have your little foal."

David led the mare from the stall. Nan made sure to give the two of them plenty of space to pass, knowing how temperamental a horse about to give birth could be.

"Will you tell Mother where we've gone?"

"I'll wait for her at the entrance to the stables to make sure I don't miss seeing her," she promised.

Nan stroked Ginger once as David slowly moved her along. She followed them from the stables and watched as they crossed the bailey and then took up her watch, waiting for Elysande. Within minutes, her cousin appeared.

"David took Ginger out to pasture," Nan explained. "Her waxing has begun but the membrane hadn't ruptured yet."

"Thank you for letting me know. Would you mind telling Michael where I am? I know he's busy with the men now but he will want to know."

"Of course." She paused. "And what of your visitor?"

Elysande frowned, distracted, and then said, "Oh, Lord Tristan. I told him where I'd be for the remainder of the day. He's a grown man and can entertain himself."

"Is he here to purchase a horse or two?"

Elysande's brows rose. "We'll see." She took off for the meadow in long strides.

Nan knew how those who came to purchase a Sandbourne horse had to win Elysande's trust before she would let any horse leave the estate. By the look on her cousin's face, this nobleman had yet to prove his worth. Shrugging to herself, Nan returned to the training yard and motioned Michael over.

"Something wrong?" he asked, alert to her mood.

"Ginger is having a bit of difficulty. David took her to the enclosure and Elysande is with them now. She wanted you to be aware of her location."

He laughed. "Because she'll want my company—and expects me to bring her food. Birthing a foal can take many hours. My wife has the patience of Job while she's with her horses but she never likes to miss a meal if she can help it."

Michael called over Sir Imbert. "Take over for me, Imbert," he told his captain of the guard. "Lady Elysande has a mare needing to foal. I will be with her for most of what is left of the day."

"Aye, my lord." Imbert flashed Nan a smile. "Nice shooting today, my lady."

"Thank you, Imbert. Hervey was quite good. He's made marked improvement in the last week since I've returned to Sandbourne."

"I'll tell him you said so." Imbert nodded and returned to the men.

Nan accompanied Michael back to the keep. They both went to the kitchens. The earl asked for a basket of food and wine to be prepared for a foaling and the kitchen maid knew exactly what to put inside. Nan knew this must be a frequent occurrence at Sandbourne. For herself, she asked for hot water to be sent up for a bath.

She went to her bedchamber and opened the small trunk that had accompanied her from Kinwick. It contained gypons in several colors and a few pairs of pants, along with a handful of cotehardies. She lifted one out, a pale blue that she had worn to Hal and Elinor's wedding not two weeks ago, and smiled. Her brother had fallen in love with a woman falconer. Hal had always attracted flocks of women with his good looks and easy charm, but Nan could see the difference in him whenever he was in Elinor's presence. Not only had he matured, but Hal was definitely a man in love.

For her part, Nan adored this new sister-in-law. Elinor had a gentle spirit and usually dressed as Nan herself did since it was easier to work with raptors in men's clothing than while wearing smocks and sideless surcoats. Before the wedding, she and Elinor had spent some time together and enjoyed one another's company immensely. Then the gaggle of de Montfort relatives had descended and Nan had seen Elinor swept away, each woman eagerly fighting to find time alone with the bride-to-be. Nan finally gave up and let the others dominate Elinor's time since she knew eventually all these women would go home. Once Nan returned to Kinwick, she wouldn't have to compete with everyone for a piece of Elinor.

Except for Hal, of course.

She loved all three of her brothers fiercely. Had actually worshipped Ancel as if he were a god. Ancel was a dozen years her senior and Nan thought he could do anything. She was closest in age to Edward, who was only three years older than she, and had begun following him around from the time she could walk. Since Edward forever shadowed Hal, Nan chased after them both. It had been Hal, five years her elder, who'd patiently taught both her and Edward everything important. How to fish. How to swim. How to hunt. How to whistle. Hal had told them both stories and even helped Nan learn how to read.

When she turned six and Raynor had crafted a wooden sword for her, as he did for every de Montfort child, Hal had been the one to patiently thrust and parry with her long after Raynor instructed her on the basics and returned home to Ashcroft. More importantly, Hal had been the brother who first put a bow in her hands. He had started her with a crossbow because it didn't require any upper body strength to shoot. Once Nan became proficient with it, Hal had moved on and had Nan take up a bow and arrow.

Life had never been the same since.

When she held the weapon in her hand, be it a regular bow or longbow, it brought her peace and a sense of power. Her bow and arrows had become her constant companions when Hal and Edward were both away fostering at Winterbourne. Nan had roamed Kinwick high and low with these in hand. She had devoted hours upon hours practicing until she could hit a target every time with confidence. And while she always looked forward to the summer break when Edward came home, it was Hal who Nan felt closest to.

Placing the sky blue cotehardie trimmed with gold on her bed, she chose a gold smock to place under it. She knew the color of the dress would enhance her eyes and she wanted to look her best tonight for this Lord Tristan. Why, she couldn't say. She hadn't spoken to him yet and had no idea where he lived or what he was like.

But something in his eyes intrigued her when she'd passed by him.

Mayhap it was the surprise that showed on his face. More than likely, he was one of those men who doubted a woman could do much of anything. For that alone, she wanted to look her best and show him how wrong he was. Yet Nan believed there was more to it. She'd always been good at reading people, as clearly as someone who might read a book. She could look at a person and make sense of him or her without ever having spoken to them.

When she glimpsed Lord Tristan for that brief moment, she saw he wore an air of deep sadness, much as if it wrapped about him like a cloak. Something made Nan want to bring him relief and put a smile on his face. His extremely handsome face.

Why on earth would she think of that?

True, the nobleman was attractive. No woman could miss that. But Nan wasn't most women. She never really looked at a man as other women did. She had never been interested in a man physically, other than to categorize his physical strengths and see how best to defeat him. Regularly, she beat soldiers using her bow and arrow and sometimes even her sword. She crushed them in playing games from skittles to tables to chess. It took her time to win over most males and when she did, they saw her as a comrade or even a little sister. Never once had she wondered about what it would be like to kiss a man.

Until now.

A knock on the chamber door startled her. "Come," she called.

Servants entered with buckets of hot water, pouring them into the small wooden tub one brought along. They left without asking if she needed assistance—because she never had accepted it. Nan was a woman who did everything for herself.

She went back to the trunk and lifted a vial her mother had given her from it. Returning to the tub, she opened the vial and poured in the freesia, stirring it with her fingers. Immediately, a gentle floral scent wafted up. Nan had never used any oils in her bath water. Mayhap, the time had come for her to do so regularly.

Disrobing, she eased herself into the hot water and gave herself up to the delicious feel of it for a few minutes before scrubbing her body clean. She dried herself and dressed in the smock and cotehardie. Having no mirror to inspect herself, she decided she could at least brush out her hair and rebraid it. She enjoyed the subtle scent of freesia that surrounded her and chuckled, knowing how delighted her mother would be that she'd finally given in to using it.

Funny how a little fragrance made her feel... feminine. She had never used that word to describe herself. Her mother, certainly. Merryn de Montfort was an elegant beauty who made decisions like a man but was feminine to her very core. Alys, her older sister and Ancel's twin, was merely a younger version of their mother, resembling Merryn in everything from looks to interests. Even young Jessimond, the last of the de Montfort siblings, was delicate and ladylike. Though seven years Nan's junior, Jessimond already seemed more womanly than Nan ever could be. She might grow into the most beautiful de Montfort woman of all.

Nan realized many years ago that she wasn't as comely as her mother and older sister and never would be. Years had to pass before she understood this was the reason she had pulled away from what her mother and Alys enjoyed and tried to make her own way in the world. Fortunately, she had learned a great deal from Merryn and no longer resented her or Alys for being so beautiful. And now that she was dressed as a lady and smelled divine, Nan felt a tiny bit pretty in her own right.

Leaving her chamber, she made her way down to the great hall for the evening meal. As she entered, she noticed the dais sat empty as workers pulled the trestle tables from the wall and began lining them up alongside benches. If Ginger's labor proved difficult, Elysande wouldn't consider leaving the mare—and that meant Michael would not leave her. Now that David was spending more of his time with the horses, Nan assumed he would also remain with his parents as they saw the foal into the world.

That meant she would be alone with Lord Tristan.

A feeling of trepidation mingled with excitement filled her as she went to the dais. Before she could climb upon it, a hand gently touched her elbow.

"May I assist you, my lady?"

Nan looked up to find deep brown eyes rimmed in gold staring at her in open admiration. Nan judged him to be right at six feet with a lean yet muscular build. Hair the color of warm sand complemented his tanned face, though a small, white scar that stood out on his chin spoke to some incident in his past.

"Thank you, my lord," she said demurely. She almost burst out laughing. She had never been demure in her entire life. Her brothers would have howled at her shy behavior.

The nobleman seated her and took the spot to her right. His thigh accidentally brushed against hers under the table, sending a delicious shimmer through her.

"I would like to introduce myself to you. I am Tristan Therolde, Earl of Leventhorpe. You may have met two of my knights today, Sir Stephen and Sir Toby."

"And I am Lady Nan de Montfort of Kinwick Castle, daughter of Lord Geoffrey and Lady Merryn. I saw Sir Stephen in the crowd but did not have the pleasure of conversing with him. Sir Toby, as you know, came close to winning the archery contest today. I definitely would like to spend time conversing with him."

Nan found her heart racing as she spoke. Her left hand clutched her right in her lap to keep them from wringing nervously.

"Wine, my lady?"

She turned and saw a servant in front of the dais. "Thank you, I would."

The woman poured the liquid into a cup and then did the same after Lord Tristan confirmed he also wanted some. Then another servant brought a trencher for them to share. Nan had eaten thousands of meals over the years and shared a trencher with everyone from her young nephew, Cyrus, to visitors Kinwick entertained that were old enough to be her great-grandfather.

None of them had looked like Tristan Therolde. Smelled like Tristan Therolde. Exuded a quiet power and strength as this nobleman did.

She wondered what he tasted like.

"What did you say?"

By the Christ—had she spoken aloud?

Glancing around, she sputtered, "What the venison tastes like. I asked what the venison might taste like. The last time 'twas a bit tough. Very unlike Cook. Usually, her meat is beyond tender and swimming in its juices."

"Ah." Lord Tristan nodded to himself and picked up his cup of wine.

Nan could not afford to be rattled around this man. She took a deep breath, something Hal long ago had taught her to do if she became frightened or flustered. Exhaling slowly, she felt more in control.

As another servant brought the tray of venison to them, Lord Tristan chose several pieces for them to share. A small round of cheese and fruit were also placed by their trencher. Nan bit into a pear and chewed it thoroughly, thinking how to make conversation. She was never at a loss when speaking to others and hadn't a clue why things had suddenly changed.

Swallowing, she asked, "Where do you reside, Lord Tristan? Is your home far from Sandbourne?"

He grew still. "Thorpe Castle lies in Essex."

Nan shivered involuntarily. Essex and Kent had been the site where the peasants' rebellion had begun a handful of years ago. Her sister-in-law, Margery, had lost her mother during the violent outbreak. The poor invalid had been murdered in her own bed while Margery remained hidden from sight, unable to save her own flesh and blood.

"Ancel, my eldest brother, was in the king's guard when the revolt began," she began. "He was sent to Essex to help quell it. I worried about him constantly."

"'Twas a difficult time for many," he commented brusquely.

Their conversation died after that. Though Nan tried several times to engage him in talk, the earl proved taciturn. Finally, she gave up and they ate in silence. At first, Nan felt she might have said something wrong but didn't know what. Surely, asking him where he lived wasn't too personal a question. She wondered how long he had been an earl. He looked to be a few years over a score. It could be that his father died young and Lord Tristan had heavy responsibilities thrust upon him at a young age, which might have made him grow serious. Or mayhap, he wasn't meant to be the earl originally. He could have had an older brother who laid claim to the title. Possibly, this brother had passed away and that's what made the nobleman so sad. As they ate, Nan spun stories about him in her head. She had always done so from the time she was young. Her parents had often laughed at her vivid imagination.

The trencher emptied. Nan saw the workers beginning to stand and return the trestle tables against the walls, signaling that the meal had come to an end.

Turning to her seatmate, she said, "I am afraid I failed miserably taking Elysande's place tonight. She is a gracious hostess and would have been here to entertain you if not for Ginger."

Lord Tristan's eyes flickered in interest. "The horse about to foal?"

"Aye," Nan said. "I see she told you. That is why she is absent from the meal tonight."

"But that was several hours ago," he pointed out.

"Oh, it might take all night before Ginger produces her foal," she confided. "Elysande is dedicated to her horses as much as her own children." She smiled. "And Michael is dedicated to his wife. They were a love match from the beginning."

He frowned in disapproval. "I don't believe in such things."

His firm tone surprised her. "You don't believe in love matches?"

"Nay. I don't believe in love."

CHAPTER 3

TRISTAN SAW LADY Nan's lips part, a quizzical look upon her face. He had to draw on all the willpower he held not to lean over and sink his teeth into her full, bottom lip. The maid had tempted him since they'd sat down to their meal. Even now, a tantalizing floral scent teased his nostrils, making him want to bury his nose against her flesh.

Nan de Montfort made him feel things he hadn't experienced in years. Things he'd pushed aside when he became the Earl of Leventhorpe and tried to put the shattered pieces of his life back together. He had no remorse for the man he'd become, one far different than the outgoing, adventurous boy he'd been. But with her enthusiasm for life and playful spirit, Lady Nan made Tristan long for those days far in his past.

He mentally locked those thoughts away. He was here to buy horses and, hopefully, find a man for his sister to wed. As head of the Therolde family, it was his obligation to see Gillian settled.

"You don't believe in love?" she asked softly, pity for him reflected in her eyes.

"Nay. Why should I believe in something that cannot be seen and doesn't exist?"

She pursed her lips. "You cannot see the sun at night, my lord, yet I am sure you believe it will rise each morning in the east. Love is the same. 'Tis something that may grow over time or it can come from a place hidden deep within your heart that you never knew existed."

He shrugged. "So you say."

"You have no affection for anything, Lord Tristan? Your land? Your family? Mayhap even your horse or sword? Surely, you feel something for these things," she insisted.

"I have an obligation to my land and its tenants. The same with my sister. I take care of my horse and my weapons so that they function properly. Love plays no role in these responsibilities."

"Merely an obligation to your sister? Is she your only family?"

"She is. And as she's coming of age to be wed, I am obliged to find her a husband. Then she will become his responsibility." He gazed at her a long moment, mesmerized by her deep blue eyes. "Tell me, my lady. Do you believe in love?"

Her features softened. "I do believe in the power of love, my lord. I have had a shining example before me for many years. My parents, though betrothed when young, loved each other from an early age. Their love has only grown stronger over their many years together." She sighed. "I am also fortunate to have seen all my older siblings make love matches, as well, three brothers and a sister."

"And do you already love your betrothed, Lady Nan?"

Her laughter sounded like music to his ears. "I have no betrothed, Lord Tristan, and have no intention of entering a betrothal anytime soon."

He frowned. "Your parents have not done their duty and arranged a marriage for you?"

"Nay. They didn't betroth any of their children. They wanted us to follow our hearts and find love on our own." Her intense gaze caused Tristan's stomach to twist. "If I do find love one day, my lord, I promise you that I will not let it slip through my fingers. I will hold fast to it and cherish the man who brings it to me."

She ran a finger around the rim of her cup. "And what of you? Do you have a wife—or a betrothed?"

"Nay. I suppose someday I must wed. I will need a son to pass along my title and the Leventhorpe lands."

"What if you fell in love with this wife you one day wed?" Nan mused.

Tristan shook his head. "That would not happen. As I told you before, I do not believe in it."

She laughed again, her eyes bright with mischief. "I hope the day comes when a woman wriggles her way into your heart, my lord. I think you might be pleasantly surprised. In the meantime, during your stay at Sandbourne, take note of how happy Elysande and Michael are. They might be able to show you what is missing from your own life when you see the richness love brings to theirs."

Lady Nan rose. "I bid you a good evening, Lord Tristan."

She left the dais shaking her head, as if she could not quite believe the conversation they'd shared. Tristan watched her go, puzzled by the emotions she stirred within him. Nan de Montfort was an enticing minx. Today in the butts, she had shown all the prowess and skill of any archer he had known. Focused and competitive, Tristan believed she could have defeated any challenger. Then tonight, she appeared dressed as the noblewoman she was, alluring and utterly feminine. Her cotehardie fit her curves snuggly. It emphasized her small waist and showed off enough of her bosom to keep his eyes coming back to it repeatedly.

She sought out Toby and Stephen and spoke to them at length. Another soldier joined them, fair and ginger-haired, about Nan's height but heavily muscled through his chest and arms. The foursome laughed often and Tristan found himself longing to be a part of their conversation.

Then she bid his men farewell and left with the soldier, who put his hand on the small of her back as he guided her across the room and through the doors. Jealousy flared suddenly within Tristan, a feeling he had never known. Without thinking, he sprang to his feet and followed the couple from the great hall, waving away Stephen as he passed by him. He searched the space outside the great hall and didn't see them. A hard lump sat unmoving in the pit of his stomach as he supposed the pair had sneaked away in order to be alone. Mayhap this man was a knight. The one Lady Nan might find love with. Tristan burned with rage, thinking of this man putting his hands on her. His lips. Thrusting his cock inside her.

Blind fury drove him outside where he could get fresh air and cool off. He opened the door to the keep and stepped outside.

And saw Nan and the man walking across the bailey.

Without receiving any orders, his feet moved of their own accord, following the two at a distance. The soldier took her hand and led her away from the keep and the light. Tristan increased his stride as he heard her laughter wafting through the cool air. He had no idea what he would do when he caught up with them. Nevertheless, he pushed forward, trying to calm himself as he moved.

"I have no claim to this woman," he muttered to himself. "I shouldn't get involved."

Yet, he continued to track them until they entered the stables. At that moment, his emotions stirred rapidly, a swirl of anger and jealousy and hurt. He had no idea how old Lady Nan was, possibly a score or even less. As skilled as she was with her bow and arrow, it told him she had spent many hours in practice, most likely alone. That meant far less time with other women. Women who might have shared with her the dangers of going willingly to a darkened stall at night with a man.

Nan de Montfort might be adept with a weapon but she did not understand the ways of the world. The man who accompanied her could easily overpower her and bend her to his will—and she had no bow to use against him. This fool of a girl probably went in search of that very thing that she believed in—love. Tristan had warned her it did not exist. A fierce need to protect the dark-haired beauty overtook him. He hurried to the stables and stepped inside.

He spied the pair well in front of him, a lit lantern in the man's hand. Tristan tracked them, turning twice when they did, horses nickering as he passed them. As he rounded a corner, he heard voices and saw the couple had stopped in front of a stall. Tristan came up behind them and paused in the shadows.

"What a beauty!" Nan exclaimed. "Was it a difficult birth, Elysande?"

"Ginger did well for it being her first time. David taking her outside helped soothe her nerves."

"The hardest part was waiting for the placenta," Lord Michael said. "It took nearly five hours for it all to come out, but we got every bit of it." He wrapped an arm about his wife's waist and pulled her close before pressing his lips to her temple.

Tristan saw the smile that lit the countess' face. She rested a palm against her husband's chest and then patted him.

"Michael has learned patience over the years," the noblewoman said. "I cannot think of a better partner to be with me each time a foal is born."

"What am I?" her son complained good-naturedly as he stroked the newborn nursing from its mother's teat.

"You are the best of your mother and me," his father retorted. "You will make an excellent earl and you're already a wonderful horseman." The earl looked back at his wife. "And I hope you find a woman to have by your side that you will adore as much as I do mine." He tenderly kissed Lady Elysande.

Tristan stood there, numb. In the space of a minute, he had witnessed a depth of emotion unlike any he had seen before. And the earl openly kissing his wife in front of others seemed so natural. Their son stood and began to brush the new mother as Lady Nan and her companion stepped into the stall and fussed over the newborn, who had finished its meal.

"Have you a name yet for the little one, my lady?" asked the man Tristan did not know.

"This one is a girl, Drewett, and she began walking faster than any foal I've ever seen. Because of that, I am calling her Argo. Why would I do that?"

"You cannot fool me, Lady Elysande," the man named Drewett replied. "Lord Geoffrey makes sure all his pages and squires are tutored in both Latin and Greek. I remember those lessons all too well. Argo means *swift*."

"Father will be impressed you retained that knowledge, Drew,"

Lady Nan told her companion. She nudged him playfully with her elbow.

Tristan noticed the two no longer held hands and realized the man had probably taken hers in a gentlemanly fashion to guide Nan in the dark since only a few torches lit the bailey. The way she teased him was like that of a sister to her brother. From what these people had revealed, he surmised this Drewett was a squire in service to Nan's father. Tristan wondered why he was here at Sandbourne if he fostered with the de Montforts.

"Is that you, Lord Tristan?" Lady Elysande called out.

He moved from the shadows into the light. "Aye, my lady. I was curious about this horse you spoke of, especially when you did not appear for the evening meal. I decided to come to the stables and see what all the fuss was about." He hesitated. "I hope I am not interrupting."

His hostess smiled. "We have a new foal. This is Argo, my lord." She paused. "I am sure you met Lady Nan this evening. I hope you enjoyed a pleasant meal."

"We did sup together," Nan said, looking at him with curiosity. "I don't think you have met my best friend, however." She indicated her companion. "Lord Tristan Therolde, I would like to introduce you to Drewett Stollars. Drew has fostered with my family for many years and will undergo his Oath of Knighthood Ceremony early next year."

Stollars extended a hand. "A pleasure, my lord. I did meet your two men this evening and enjoyed our time together."

"Aye, Sir Stephen and Sir Toby are most charming," Lady Nan said. "They make conversation so easily." She gave him a wicked smile.

Tristan understood that she teased him for being so silent while they dined.

"Talk comes easily to those two. They are both charming men and capable knights."

"And you, my lord?" Her lashes fluttered at him.

"My skills do not involve the art of conversation. I find it highly overrated. I believe actions speak the loudest and prefer them to do the talking for me."

A loud grumble sounded. Lord Michael said, "Well, my stomach has announced 'tis high time I fill it after all these hours supporting Argo's birth." He clasped his wife's hand and brought it to his lips, kissing it tenderly. "What say you, my love? Shall we go to the solar and dine? Especially since you seemed to gobble up what I brought from the kitchen hours ago."

Lady Elysande blushed prettily. "You know I get nervous during a birth and eating calms me, Husband." She turned to her son. "Stay another hour or so, David. If all is well, you may leave them for the night."

"Aye, Mother."

Tristan followed the others from the stables. Drewett Stollars bid them a good night and headed toward the barracks. Tristan found himself walking beside Lady Nan at a more leisurely pace while the earl and countess left them behind.

"'Tis nice that you have a friend who accompanied you to Sandbourne," he ventured, doing his best to initiate conversation with her.

"Drew and I are as brother and sister," she informed him, "though it did not start that way. I hated him the first year he lived at Kinwick. He always poked and needled me. He belittled me for being a girl. Called me names and pulled pranks on me."

Tristan stopped and turned toward her. "Something tells me that you didn't let him get away with that for long."

She chuckled. "We were at each other's throats for months. Drew resented having to partner with me in training exercises."

"You trained . . . in the yard? With men all around you?" Tristan could actually imagine her being there, a small, thin child, determined to do everything the other boys did.

Lady Nan turned and began walking again. Tristan fell into step with her.

"Aye. I longed to be a page and become a squire and finally a knight. Father convinced me that wouldn't be possible but he willingly opened his world to me. All de Montfort children receive a wooden sword from Raynor Le Roux, my father's cousin and closest friend. I was taught how to use it and other weapons from the time I was six. I knew much more than Drew did when he arrived at Kinwick. We finally became allies instead of enemies and have been close ever since."

"You mentioned your older brothers at dinner."

"Ah, you were actually listening. I wondered about that. All three of them served in the king's royal guard at one point. The middle one, Hal, taught me the most about weapons and strategy. He took me hunting and fishing. Hal is the one who first put a bow in my hands." She paused. "Lest you think I am some heathen, I did learn the womanly arts, as well. I know about gardening and sewing, though I don't really enjoy either activity. I never could sing well but I whistle better than most.

"And not to brag, but I make the best candles for miles around."

"I am impressed with the variety in your skills, my lady. You are the most accomplished noblewoman of my acquaintance."

She eyed him warily. "I have the feeling you don't have a large circle of acquaintances, Lord Tristan. Especially noblewomen."

"You would be correct."

She snorted. "That's what I thought."

"Why are you at Sandbourne?" he asked, stopping again. They had almost reached the keep and he was reluctant to go inside and part from her.

"Sandbourne has been as a second home to me. My family is a close one. Elysande and I are cousins and enjoy one another's company immensely. Though I never fostered anywhere, I did spend the better part of several years here, off and on, learning from her what I could about horses. Michael recently asked me to return and work with his men, especially to teach them what I know about the longbow and the bow and arrow."

"How long will you remain?"

Lady Nan shrugged. "As long as Michael has need of me. Then

Drew and I will return to Kinwick. Father sent Drew with me to help polish his skills in teaching others. And to watch over me, I suppose."

"You don't love this man?"

She looked taken aback. "Of course I love Drew. I told you—he is as a brother to me. I will always love Drew. And his wife. Their children. But no, my lord, I am not in love with him."

Relief poured through Tristan, making him reckless. "What would it take for you to fall in love, my lady?"

She bit that full lower lip, twisting it in thought. The gesture filled him with lust.

Without waiting for her to reply, Tristan's fingers latched on to her shoulders and pulled her toward him.

CHAPTER 4

Nan had no time to consider an answer to Lord Tristan's question because his lips captured hers, brushing languidly against them. A thousand thoughts entered her head and became scrambled, with nothing coherent forming. She grasped his gypon to steady herself as his strong fingers slipped from her shoulders down her back, his hands drawing her against him.

He began to nibble on her bottom lip, sending a surge of awareness through her that she'd never experienced before. She tried to ask him what he was doing but somehow in doing so, she'd issued some unspoken invitation to him. His tongue swept inside her mouth and took its time sampling her. Nan's fingers tightened on his gypon as her heart sped up and then pounded furiously against her ribs.

She responded in kind, not knowing exactly what to do and merely imitating his moves. It must have pleased him for she heard a low groan in the back of his throat. His hands moved to the small of her back and held her firm against him as his tongue continued to wage war with hers. Time became meaningless as the kiss went on and on. A thrumming buzzed inside her, spilling into every limb. She pressed her aching breasts against his solid chest, needing to rub them against him.

Then he broke the kiss and stared down at her. A torch lighting the bailey stood near enough for her to read the look in his eyes. It was one she had seen repeatedly and recently during her time at Kinwick. Hal had looked at Elinor this same way. Sometimes from across the room. Other times when he sat right next to her. He would make their excuses and the couple would be gone in a rush.

But Hal and Elinor loved one another. Nan didn't love this man. She barely knew anything about Tristan Therolde. Why had he kissed her?

And why did his eyes still hold a fiery heat that threatened to send her up in flames?

His thumbs rubbed against her back. "You see, my lady. Men do not need love. They can find pleasure in a woman and keep their heart intact. A man's focus should be on his duty to king, country, and family. Love makes a man weak. It takes his mind off what is important."

Hurt and anger reverberated through Nan. She shoved him violently, breaking the contact between them. The nobleman stumbled back in surprise.

"You insult every man dear to me," she said, her voice low and deadly. "My father. My brothers. My cousins. Their spouses. The de Montfort men are better men for having found love and treating it as the sacred gift that it is. Their lives are richer and more meaningful. You are like most men, Lord Tristan. You do not value what you should. You only care about gold and land and your title. Everything you have accumulated. But none of that is what truly matters. What matters most is who we give our hearts to. Those we love. I would willingly give my life for the people I love."

Nan stepped back a few paces. "I feel sorry for you, my lord. You have no idea what is important in life. You will live and die in loneliness and never realize what you could have had. Oh, you may wed one day and accumulate sons and daughters, but if you do not give your heart to those around you, you are no better than the dust you trod upon and will return to one day."

He looked stunned by what she'd said to him. Nan barely knew this man and should have held her tongue, but his words and actions had offended her beyond measure.

"Forget what I told you about observing the happiness here at Sandbourne. How Michael and Elysande behave toward one another. I understand now that a man like you will only be blind to those very things, no matter how long you watched and studied them. Do what you came to do, my lord. Try and buy your horses and return to your estate. Do your duty to your sister, whom I doubt you love, merely because 'tis something you are obligated to do. I only hope she will find happiness and respect from the man you give her to in marriage for she surely does not have it in her home with you as its head."

Nan looked at this heartbreakingly handsome man, pity now filling her heart. "I will accord you all of the kindness you deserve as a guest at Sandbourne, Lord Tristan. But if you ever try to kiss me again—if you come close to even touching me—you will regret it. I am not some plaything to trifle with. I am a woman who's been trained to think and act as a man. I'd as soon kick you in your balls and then cut them off than have your lips on mine again."

She stormed off, hoping her shaking legs would carry her the short distance from here to the keep. She entered it and quickly made her way upstairs to her chamber, where she slammed the door and flung herself onto the bed. Gradually, her trembling ceased. Nan dug her fingers into the bedclothes.

Her first kiss . . .

It had been everything she'd hoped for and nothing she'd expected. She had no idea a kiss could go on and on like that, melding two souls together. Regret filled her, though. She always assumed her first kiss would be with the man she loved or would fall in love with. The one she would wed and stand beside for all time. A man she would give herself to completely. The one she would share everything with—a home, children, long conversations throughout the years. And couplings. Many, many couplings.

Even now, a banked fire ebbed within her as she remembered Tristan Therolde's touch. Her fingertips came to rest next to her lips, the ones he had kissed so thoroughly until they were now bruised.

But Lord Tristan was like most men. He valued the wrong things. Nan realized that the men in her family were exceptions to that rule in the way they treated their women. De Montforts married for love.

Each couple became not only helpmates but soul mates. They partnered together for life, invincible because they loved one another. It didn't mean they agreed on everything. She had heard some of the arguments over the years between her parents. But even in disagreeing, Nan knew their passion for each other and what they'd created made them stronger together than apart.

That's what she wanted. What she expected for herself.

Instead, she felt tarnished for having allowed a man she did not love, much less admire, to kiss her in such an intimate way. Tristan Therolde was arrogant and selfish. He might physically tempt her but she had no desire to be in his presence more than necessary. Nan pushed away the regret at what had happened tonight. She couldn't change the fact that a kiss had occurred between them but she could make sure that it never happened again.

She rolled to her side and buried her face into the pillow, hot tears of frustration pouring down her cheeks. Though she could not undo what had been done, she would do everything in her power to forget about the kiss. She would ensure they were never alone again during his stay at Sandbourne so no opportunity to repeat the performance might exist.

Weeping softly, Nan fell into a restless sleep.

TRISTAN REMAINED IN the bailey for a long time. He rarely enjoyed being in the company of others and didn't want to run into his hosts. As the spring night grew cooler, he tried to make sense of what had come over him.

Could he have been a bigger arse?

He doubted it.

Leaning against a sturdy wall of the keep, he contemplated the range of emotions that had run rampantly through him tonight. He'd felt desire for the first time in a long time when sitting next to Nan de Montfort at the evening meal. Tristan never was without a woman for long. He made sure his physical needs were met on a regular basis by a variety of women in the two villages near Thorpe Castle.

But the hunger he'd experienced being in Lady Nan's company surpassed physical desire. It was as if he craved her. Needed to possess her.

That had led to the rage and jealousy that had flown through him when he'd observed her with the very handsome Drewett Stollars. Always one to keep his emotions in check, Tristan had barely understood why he barreled after the pair, much less why he felt the need to protect Lady Nan. Then in the stables, watching Lord Michael and Lady Elysande's obvious affection toward one another, a deep yearning overtook him. He wanted what they had.

Whatever it was.

Oh, he knew Lady Nan would say it was love. That's what women chose to call lust. He supposed females could experience it since men certainly did, though the women he coupled with seemed happy enough when he finished the act and rewarded them with a coin for their efforts. Females didn't respond physically as he did, with his manhood swelling and a burning need to spill his seed. A few of them moaned as they stroked his arms but they didn't exhibit the obvious signs a man did when he wished to sate himself.

But Tristan couldn't hide from the truth. Somehow, tonight's kiss had been different from any he'd snatched before. Oh, his blood stirred and his cock began to swell, as usual. That was nothing new. It was something intangible in his kiss with Nan de Montfort that he couldn't explain. A need to know her, body and soul, had overtaken him. He wanted to learn everything about her, from what she enjoyed doing, to every secret curve hidden under her cotehardie. That gown had turned her eyes a deep, mysterious blue. Tristan wanted to explore their depths. He wanted to be inside her. Be one with her. Call her his.

Admitting all this to himself frightened Tristan beyond words.

Lady Nan intrigued him. Challenged him. Made him want to understand her—and himself—better.

Could she be right? Did love between a man and woman truly exist?

His parents had been pleasant but distant toward one another so he had not witnessed anything resembling love between them. They had provided for the physical needs of their six children yet Tristan couldn't remember any expression or gestures of love coming from them. While he had a true affection for his brothers, he had never been close to his sister, who was nine years his junior. Girls served their purposes in the keep but had little to do with his life. While he was considerate to Gillian, who seemed to worship him as the eldest of the pack, in truth, he saw all of his siblings infrequently after he began fostering, only returning home for a few weeks each summer and not at all for a few of those last years. The distance between them grew until they hardly seemed a part of his world.

Moreover, Tristan had never even laid eyes on the babe his mother had birthed—until he arrived home and saw what little was left of the lifeless body.

He pushed aside the ghastly memory. It wouldn't do to think about it. He couldn't go back and change anything that had occurred. The few times he did dwell on it, nightmares occurred. It had been months since the last one. He believed time and distance would make the nightmares eventually fade. He couldn't afford to have them start up again.

Just as he wasn't ready to feel again. That day was the start of pushing all feelings aside. Tristan focused on getting through one day at a time from that moment, fulfilling each duty as it needed handling, until he'd put back the broken pieces of Thorpe Castle as best as he could. Nothing at the castle or on Leventhorpe lands would ever be the same again. The greatest lesson coming from that catastrophe was that he'd learned everything could change in an instant.

It was the reason he guarded his heart so well.

And now Nan de Montfort threatened its well-being.

The door to the keep swung open. Tristan saw Toby and Stephen emerge. Both men caught sight of him and came in his direction.

"Are you retiring for the night?" he asked.

"Aye," Stephen said. "We have a place in the barracks, according to Drewett Stollars."

"And the promise of Lady Nan tutoring us tomorrow in the yard," chimed in Toby. "I tried my best today, my lord. I thought I might be able to defeat Hervey but I doubt I could have performed well against Lady Nan. Her aim is uncanny."

"We're looking forward to what she can teach us," Stephen added. "How did things go for you today? We heard from the soldiers we shared our meal with that Lady Elysande is the most knowledgeable Devereux when it comes to horses."

Tristan nodded. "Though I corresponded with Lord Michael and found he knows quite a bit when it comes to horseflesh, you are right. Lady Elysande runs the stables."

"These are interesting women at Sandbourne," mused Toby. "One an expert regarding horses and another with a bow and arrow."

"I cannot wait to see Lady Nan use her longbow tomorrow," Stephen said. He paused, looking encouragingly at Tristan. "You should come to the yard, too, my lord. Mayhap the lady could even teach you a thing or two."

Tristan thought that's the last place Nan de Montfort would wish him to venture.

CHAPTER 5

TRISTAN AWOKE WITH grainy eyes. He hadn't slept much. In the hours he lay awake, his thoughts had wandered but always seemed to come back to the dark-haired beauty with the heart-shaped face. He would do whatever it took to avoid her today and for the remainder of his visit at Sandbourne. Tristan needed to show Lady Nan that he would prove to be no threat to her. No matter how he longed to visit the butts and see her in action again, he would avoid the area as if it were infested with plague. Let Toby and Stephen get their fill of the maid's knowledge. He would stay with Lady Elysande and hope she found him worthy to purchase a few of her horses.

Coming downstairs, he found the great hall deserted. His grumbling stomach told him it was time to break his fast. Had he already missed the small meal?

Before he could search out a servant to discover why no one appeared, he heard voices of people entering the keep. A great group swelled into the room and efficiently began lifting trestle tables away from the walls and lining them up. He moved out of the way and watched how efficiently they moved. Within a handful of minutes, the people of Sandbourne sat at benches, ready for their meal. He wished the same could be said for those who dined in the great hall at Thorpe Castle. As he had last night, Tristan realized, as a guest, he would need to go to the dais.

Where Nan de Montfort already sat.

Reluctantly, he headed in that direction, wondering how she had slipped past him. As he approached, he saw David Devereux take the seat Tristan had occupied last night and would be sharing a trencher with his cousin. Disappointment swept over him as he started to mount the dais.

"Good morning, Lord Tristan." Michael Devereux slapped Tristan on the back in a friendly greeting as they climbed upon the platform. He held a hand out to his wife and propelled the countess up.

"Come take a seat, my lord," Lady Elysande invited.

Tristan went to the seat she indicated and nodded brusquely before taking his place. Lady Elysande sat on Tristan's left and her husband took the spot on his wife's other side.

Servants appeared with ale and bread. He took both and tore a piece from the small loaf he received.

"We missed you at mass this morning, my lord," the countess said.

So that's where everyone had been. Tristan knew of estates where noblemen required all of their workers and servants to attend mass each morning. He had never been one of those.

Besides having no belief in love, he had no faith in a heartless God.

Still, he thought to make light of the matter, not wanting to reveal his personal beliefs. "Will my attendance at mass be a requirement for purchasing any of your horses, my lady?"

She frowned in disapproval. "At this rate, my lord, I don't know if I will bother showing you anymore of my horses. I only send them to excellent homes."

Incredulity filled him. "You sit in judgment of the kind of home I run based upon my missing mass this morning?"

Lady Elysande's eyebrows shot up, her annoyance with him plainly written on her face. "I prefer to discover as much as I can about the men who seek to buy my horseflesh. What they are like. What their core values are. What they find to be important. A man who gives God His due and honors Him regularly is more likely to treat his family, workers, and livestock well."

Tristan bit back the retort that threatened to fly from his lips. Who did this woman think she was, assessing him in such a manner?

She turned to her ale and raised the cup to her lips, ending their conversation.

Not wishing to admit it, he realized she had made a strong point. The countess treated each horse as a beloved family member and would wish any she sold to go to a place where they would be valued and have a good life. He could understand how she made the connection between keeping the Holy God's commandments and treating others—even animals—well.

"I apologize, my lady." Tristan hoped he sounded as contrite as he felt. "I want you to know that if I am, indeed, fortunate enough to purchase any of your stock, those horses will never be mistreated. I do my best to handle the people on my estate fairly. Mayhap you would care to visit Thorpe Castle for yourself, along with Lord Michael, to see if you approve."

The offer, though made in haste, was one he hoped would not be taken up. Though Tristan took pride in the hard work that he had put into the castle and all the Leventhorpe lands, no one had to tell him that his home and estate fell far short of what he saw at Sandbourne. The Devereux estate ran smoothly and efficiently. The workers he had seen stayed busy. Looking across everyone dining in the great hall, the air buzzed with conversation. This was a happy, thriving place.

Thorpe Castle had not been before the tragedy and wasn't now. Tristan knew it would compare poorly if judged by Sandbourne standards. It had taken visiting the Devereux estate to recognize that.

He'd done the best he could to repair all the damage. He'd taken his time in hiring soldiers who would be steadfast and slowly eased into hiring a few servants and workers for the castle as he brought new tenants on the land. Yet it had been a struggle. The numbers in each of those groups were sorely lacking. Tristan worried it would take many more years to not only return the estate to what it had been before, but to see it became even better.

"Thank you for your kind offer, my lord," Lady Elysande responded politely. "This is too busy a time for me to be away from home, though, with so many foals being born. It was hard enough leaving for a week to attend my cousin's wedding at Kinwick. I don't plan on going anywhere for the next few months."

Curiosity caused him to ask, "Who wed at Kinwick? Lady Nan mentioned to me that all of her older siblings are wed."

"'Twas her middle brother, Hal, who married Lady Elinor Swan recently." She smiled. "Elinor makes a fine addition to the de Montfort family."

"Is she skilled in something unusual?" he asked. "As you and Lady Nan are?"

"Aye," she said enthusiastically. "Lady Elinor is a falconer of some repute."

Tristan's jaw dropped. He'd never heard of a woman as a falconer.

The countess laughed merrily. "Oh, we are full of surprises in this family, my lord." She sipped her ale. "I'm afraid I will be busy today with Argo and Ginger. David, too. I am going to place you in Michael's hands instead. By tomorrow, mayhap you will be back in my good graces and I will deign to show you more of my horses."

Tristan thought she only half-joked with him. He would certainly need to be on his best behavior around this woman.

And Nan.

Lady Elysande rose. "I will see you this evening, Lord Tristan. Why don't you come to the solar for the evening meal? It will give us a chance to know you better in a more intimate setting."

"Of course, my lady."

The earl had also risen and gave his wife's cheek a kiss before he helped her down. He turned to Tristan. "My wife is a true force of nature, Leventhorpe. What say you and I head to the stables? I'll show you our estate from horseback."

Tristan stood. A glance told him that Nan and David had already left the dais. He steeled himself for what lay ahead.

TRISTAN WAITED WHILE Lord Michael drew buckets of water from a well for an elderly woman. He had accompanied the nobleman for several hours. They had ridden the perimeter of the estate and then moved within it, visiting workers who weeded in the fields and various tenants. The earl knew everyone's name and treated each person with polite, friendly respect and freely complimented them. In return, everyone was pleasant and considerate to the nobleman.

As they walked their horses back to the castle, Tristan said, "I am surprised you know everyone's name even though you have such a large estate."

"I was gone from Sandbourne for many years. A falling out with my father when I was a boy. When I returned just prior to his death, I saw few faces that I recognized. Elysande and I wed when I became the earl and we both believed it was important to become familiar with our estate. Part of that responsibility meant getting to know all of our tenants. My wife takes great pleasure in speaking to everyone. She knows about their babes and who has been ill. She takes food and clothing to those in need. And because I want to spend time with her, I am her willing accomplice."

He shook his head, puzzled by such an attitude. "Forgive me, my lord, but you seem openly enamored with your wife. Does she lead you about in everything you do or do you ever make a decision on your own?"

Lord Michael laughed as if Tristan had made a joke and then looked at him quizzically when Tristan remained silent. "You are serious?" he asked.

Tristan nodded. "I don't understand your relationship with the countess at all."

The nobleman halted his horse. "I had the worst example of what a father could be. He treated everyone from my mother to the lowest serf abominably. Sandbourne was a miserable place and I couldn't wait to escape from it."

Tristan frowned. "But you seem so . . . happy. As do those we've spoken with today."

"I learned that happiness is a choice, Lord Tristan. I was a lonely misfit when I went to foster. Made fun of by all the pages who surrounded me until two squires named Geoffrey de Montfort and

Raynor Le Roux took me under their wings. They taught me everything I know about being a man and how to be a great knight. I was fortunate enough to serve in Lord Geoffrey's household before I claimed my title. Kinwick was a cheerful place. Lord Geoffrey was a man everyone admired yet he was open with his affection. His workers knew he truly cared about them. He adored his children, both his sons and daughters, and spent more time with them than most fathers did.

"And he was very much in love with his wife—Nan's mother."

Lord Michael stroked his horse's neck. "I quickly decided I wanted to be the kind of man Geoffrey de Montfort was and when I became the Earl of Sandbourne, I modeled myself after his example. I wed a wife I respect and love beyond words. We have three children who brought us even closer together through the years. We know our strengths and weaknesses. I look upon Elysande as my partner. In life. In our marriage. In running our estate."

Everything this man spoke seemed foreign to Tristan. Lord Michael appeared to be intelligent and capable. Why would he need a woman to help run anything?

"I see the doubt in your eyes, my lord. I realize if I had not witnessed the example Geoffrey and Merryn set—and if I had not found my Elysande—my life would be quite different." He paused. "I only hope you will be fortunate enough to find a woman that can be your equal and bring you as much happiness as I have found."

Tristan thought the nobleman had gone mad. A woman could never be equal to a man. And yet looking at Lord Michael, he appeared the picture of sanity and good health.

"Come, let us return to the training yard, my lord. If I'm away from it too long, I become restless."

The earl urged his horse on. Tristan followed, galloping behind him until they reached the stables and handed off the animals to a stable hand.

He had no excuse to offer Lord Michael so he fell into step beside the man until they reached the training yard. Scanning the area, he did not spy Lady Nan and let out a small sigh of relief.

"My lord?"

Tristan turned and saw Stephen approaching them.

"Aye?"

"I saw you and Lord Michael return. Toby and I are in the butts, working with two knights and some of the pages and squires. Would you care to accompany me there?"

"Go ahead, Lord Tristan," his host urged. "I plan to join Imbert." He headed toward a raised platform where a burly knight watched the exercises with interest.

"This way, my lord," Stephen said, leading him past the soldiers engaged in swordplay and down to the butts, much further from where yesterday's archery contest had occurred. The area was totally flat except for mounds of earth at set points. Seven boys of varying ages held bows in their hands as Toby and two Sandbourne men spoke with them.

All of them sported bare feet—as did Lady Nan. He'd wondered why she shed her boots yesterday and would ask one of his men later about the practice. Tristan also noted each archer and instructor wore a leather bracer on the inside of their forearms. Those, he knew, would prevent the huge, long-lasting bruises from where the bowstring could whack a man as he released his arrow.

The noblewoman addressed the entire group. "An expert marksman can release between ten and twelve arrows a minute," she told them. "We will work first on accuracy and then speed. The targets are set at one hundred yards. Eventually, you will be required to shoot at a destination twice as far."

Tristan noted instead of yesterday's targets, which had five colored rings divided into two bands of equal width, today the targets were merely coiled straw mats sewn into spiral coils and placed against the mounds of earth. Some mounds seemed as small as two meters across, while others stretched to eight meters or more. Each mound stood between one and three meters in height.

The soldiers stepped away from their charges and the boys scattered across the range until each one lined up with a mound directly in front of him, though many yards away.

"When you aim at your target, you will always hear the same commands issued, whether I or someone else directs your practice. Over many years of training and hearing these orders, you will automatically carry them out in case you find yourself in battle."

Tristan could feel the anticipation hanging in the air and caught the excitement.

"Remember, you always lay your body into your bow. You never draw with your arm's strength. Each of you has a bow sized according to your age and power. That will increase as time passes and you grow stronger. Keep your left hand steady and draw the bow with your right. Press all of your weight into the horns."

That had been Tristan's weakness. Doing things with his left hand always seemed natural. He'd had to concentrate for many years to become adept with a sword or any other weapon in his right hand. When he'd taken up a bow and fitted the arrow, it always seemed awkward to him. He practiced enough to be a tolerable shot but had always preferred fighting with a sword, spear, or even mace. He couldn't even remember the last time he'd held a bow and arrow.

"We will commence," Lady Nan said, a calm authority in her voice. "Ready your bows!"

The boys lifted their differing-sized bows.

"Nock!"

Each lad fit an arrow against the bowstring.

"Mark!"

Seven pairs of eyes noted their targets.

"Draw!"

The bowstrings went back in unison.

"Loose!"

Seven arrows flew through the air with a whoosh. Tristan noted which boys were more accurate than others. Lady Nan quickly addressed each lad individually and then relayed the same set of commands. To a boy, each one improved from his first shot to his second. She spoke to each page or squire after the five rounds and then sent them to retrieve their arrows.

When they returned, she explained, "You'll now shoot five arrows one after the other, in under a minute's time. Think on what we spoke about. Do your best."

This time, she issued the five orders at the same pace as before without pausing. Once she cried *loose*, she immediately began the sequence again. After five arrows had sailed from each archer's bow, she again spoke with every boy, who retrieved his arrows after their brief conversation. This pattern continued for the next hour. Tristan thought it would grow old but he found himself fascinated with her patience and drive.

And her curves.

Yesterday, her baggy ensemble looked as if it were two sizes too large for her. But today? The dark pants fit like a well-made glove, showing off her long, lean legs and flare of her hips, while her tan gypon made obvious the roundness of her breasts.

At the end of the session, she called the boys around her. While they returned their boots to their feet, she said, "You all did quite well today because you listened and learned with each round. I am pleased by how precise your aim is. Tomorrow, I'll make sure the targets are back another fifty yards."

"Will we loose our arrows quicker, Lady Nan?"

Tristan saw it was the smallest of the pages who spoke. His eyes were round with excitement.

She grinned. "That, too, William. Speed and accuracy are important skills for an archer to possess."

"I'll be ready," the young boy promised, smiling from ear to ear.

"Sir Martin, Sir Ralph? Have the boys collect all the arrows and targets. We're done for the day." The noblewoman turned to Tristan's men. "Sir Stephen, Sir Toby, thank you for your help. Extra hands make my work much easier."

"We are happy to do so while our lord remains at Sandbourne, Lady Nan," Toby said, a shy smile on his face. He reached over and handed her a pair of leather boots. She slipped a dagger from inside one and held the hilt in her mouth while she placed them on her feet, then slid the blade into place and tucked her pants over it.

Tristan had remained at a distance from her, usually standing to her side and behind a good ways, not wanting to distract her from her task.

Lady Nan now turned and stared at him, a bland expression on her face. "Oh, it's you."

CHAPTER 6

Nan forced her face to remain placid. She'd known the minute Tristan Therolde arrived at the range. He'd hovered in the background the entire time she instructed the group of pages and squires but she had constantly been aware of his presence, knowing he studied—and even judged—her as she tutored her charges.

"You are good at what you do, my lady."

"And what's that?"

"Instructing, to begin with. I observed you for some time. You pace the lessons so there are no gaps in which young minds might become bored. You reinforce what the lads executed well and compliment them enough to make them eager to please you. You address what is lacking in their performance.

"You also model words with actions. They know you are skilled because they have seen you demonstrate what you teach. Actions, I believe, speak the truth." His voice dropped low. "Your truth, Lady Nan, is that you are a superb archer."

His words overwhelmed Nan. The quick retort died on her lips. Instead, she chose to respond as her mother would have wished her to do and merely said, "Thank you, my lord."

Her stomach swirled with nerves so she began to gather her weaponry. Unlike the soldiers and those fostering who had a place in the barracks to store their equipment, Nan knew not to invade that world. She had finally become accepted at Sandbourne. Not as a lady—but an archer. She didn't dare push the men beyond what they were comfortable with so she always took her things back to the keep with her each day after training ended.

Nan slung the quiver's strap over her shoulder and picked up her bow. She watched as Lord Tristan lifted her longbow, which stood at six feet.

"Is this yours?" he asked.

She nodded and reached a hand out for it.

"Are you returning to the keep? If so, I will carry it for you."

He was behaving well so Nan decided to allow him to accompany her. Graciously, she thanked him again, knowing Merryn de Montfort would be pleased once more with her daughter's good manners.

As they walked, he asked, "Why do you practice—and even compete—in bare feet?"

"'Tis something Hal taught me. He said I was a woman taking up a sport dominated by men and that I would need every advantage possible in order to succeed. Freeing my feet allows my toes to grip the earth and my heels to dig in. In turn, it helps to steady both me and my aim. I am passing that along to those I teach."

"I see."

Nan wished she could be barefoot now for she was in great need of steadying. Walking next to Tristan Therolde, she found herself slightly dizzy, with a racing heart and dry mouth that made swallowing almost impossible. She couldn't understand this physical reaction she had to him. Rarely had she felt this way. The only times were when the excitement of a hunt created the same giddy stirring. Spying and then bringing down game, especially if the animal had really challenged her during the chase, always gave her a fluttering feeling inside.

Glancing at the nobleman next to her, she wondered if Lord Tristan challenged her. She thought back to their kiss and, against all odds, she suddenly longed for a repeat performance. Nan shook her head. It was mad to want that, especially when she didn't even like the nobleman. She didn't tolerate arrogance in others—and he was full of it.

Or was he?

Another quick glance at his handsome profile told her somehow his demeanor had changed from the previous day. Mayhap watching her in the butts had provided him with a newfound respect for her, in particular, and women in general.

Nan reminded herself that she came from an unusual family. Females were oftentimes looked down upon by men, only good for breeding and domestic chores. Her parents had given all their children the opportunity to pursue whatever passions they had and taught them to value everyone's contributions. It pleased her to see that her brothers took these lessons to heart. All three had married remarkable women and Nan knew their offspring would be raised the same way.

She had to remember that Lord Tristan was typical of most noblemen and that she shouldn't take exception to his attitude. Besides, by the time he left Sandbourne, Nan was certain the earl would have immense respect for Elysande. Her cousin would teach him more than anyone else could. Lord Tristan seemed intelligent enough take advantage of Elysande's knowledge when it came to horses.

They continued toward the keep without conversing. Nan appreciated the silence after a long day of training. Sometimes, being around others constantly drove her to seek solitude in the woods. She also appreciated that Lord Tristan did not apologize again for yesterday's mistake or fawn over her. Discussing the kiss wasn't something that interested her.

Or so she told herself.

They arrived at the keep and he asked, "May I escort you to your chamber, my lady?"

"Thank you. I accept your kind offer."

Nan led him upstairs to her bedchamber and opened the door. She took the longbow from him.

"I am grateful you carried my longbow for me. It can be a bit unwieldy since it's far taller in length than I am."

"My pleasure." He paused, an uncertain look in his eyes. Then he said, "Thank you for allowing my men to work with you today. I'm sure they learned valuable lessons on how to tutor others."

"Do Sir Stephen and Sir Toby's duties include working with those who foster at Thorpe Castle?"

He shifted uneasily. "No one fosters at Thorpe Castle."

Nan found that to be unusual. "Is it because of your age? Do you feel you can offer more to young men once you are more seasoned?"

"I am already a score and six," he replied. "I am slowly building Leventhorpe into what it should be. Only then would I feel confident to take on others."

She remembered their previous discussion and how it didn't seem he had many acquaintances, much less friends who would send their sons to him. He also may have only recently become the earl and thus not have been involved in boys fostering, especially if he'd been away from his family's estate until he came into the title.

Curious now, she asked, "Why have you come to Sandbourne, my lord? I know you said you wished to buy horses—but *why*? Forgive my saying so, but you don't seem terribly informed about them. What would possess you to want to buy and breed horses?"

He shrugged. "I am beginning to wonder that myself. But I plan to soak up everything I can from Lady Elysande and Lord Michael, both about horses and how they run Sandbourne."

A tremor of awareness rumbled through her. "Ah, you are beginning to understand, my lord."

"Beg pardon?"

"You said how *they* run Sandbourne. You recognize it is something done jointly." She gave him a smile. "Mayhap there is hope for you yet."

With that, Nan stepped into the bedchamber and closed the door.

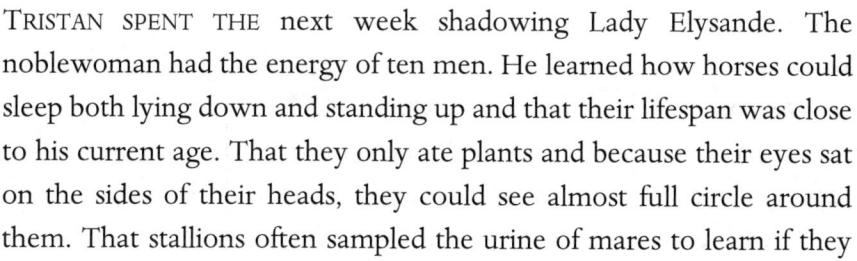

TRISTAN SPENT THE next week shadowing Lady Elysande. The noblewoman had the energy of ten men. He learned how horses could sleep both lying down and standing up and that their lifespan was close to his current age. That they only ate plants and because their eyes sat on the sides of their heads, they could see almost full circle around them. That stallions often sampled the urine of mares to learn if they were in heat. Tristan learned why horses were shod—not only to protect their hooves but to improve traction and help absorb the shock from the earth as they galloped.

Lady Elysande firmly believed horses to be the most intelligent of all animals and claimed they had sharp memories. She told him if he treated a horse kindly and did not see that horse for many years, upon renewing his acquaintance with the beast, the horse would remember him no matter how long they'd been apart. She also warned him that, upon occasion, a bored horse might accidentally learn how to untie himself from a post or open latches or grain bins. If he did, he had to be watched carefully for the horse never would forget what he'd taught himself and might wind up in mischief.

Tristan also stayed for many hours with the noblewoman when two mares gave birth on different days. She quietly instructed him on the various stages of labor and what he could do to make things more comfortable for the mother. Seeing the process unfold and then watching the first few hours of the foal's existence was life changing for him. He constantly asked Lady Elysande questions and gleaned every bit of understanding he could from her.

When he wasn't with the countess, Tristan spent his remaining time with Lord Michael. He grew quite fond of the older man. As his wife did, Lord Michael answered everything Tristan threw at him, from how to improve his crops to what training schedule he placed his soldiers on and how frequently they patrolled the estate and the roads beyond.

During the evening meal, Tristan would do the same with Sir David and Lady Nan, though he much preferred the noblewoman's company. She explained to him the differences in training regarding a crossbow, bow and arrow, and longbow. Tristan learned why bowstrings had been made from flax, silk, and finally hemp, because it was the strongest and least elastic fiber available. She taught him that the string must be soaked in glue to protect against moisture, while the wood could be guarded from the elements with a coating rub of wax, resin, and fine tallow.

After their discussions, Tristan decided he would need to hire an artillator to make all of his men's bows and arrows to these specifications instead of allowing his soldiers to create their own. Lady Nan convinced him an artillator's consistency in the bows and arrows he produced would benefit Leventhorpe's men in the long run and allow them to use their weapons interchangeably.

He ended his conversation tonight with David Devereux, who left him to check on the new foal born that morning. Looking around, Tristan saw Lady Nan had already left the great hall. Lord Michael and Lady Elysande strolled arm in arm around the room, speaking to others. As the evening meal wrapped up, those present shoved the trestle tables against the walls as each table was cleared. Many stayed after the meal, some talking in small circles as their children played at their feet. A few soldiers told stories or threw dice. Occasionally, someone might sing. Tristan had enjoyed the fellowship of others' company in the great hall this past week but he decided to stretch his legs tonight. The sun was setting later and plenty of daylight was left so he thought he might walk in the nearby meadow and possibly visit the horses in their outdoor enclosure.

Tristan stepped outside the keep and walked through the baileys and out the gates of Sandbourne. He ventured across the meadow and decided instead of visiting the horses, he would first spend some time in the forest. He had not been in these woods since his second day at Sandbourne, when he'd accompanied Lord Michael about the estate. He entered and leisurely strolled along, grateful for some time alone.

He'd grown used to his own company the past few years. Once, he'd been gregarious and a young man who loved being around others. Nowadays, he mostly kept to himself. Being here at Sandbourne, he'd probably spoken to more people and held more conversations in a week than he had in the previous seven years. It surprised him how enjoyable the time had been but this felt right, walking in solitude.

Of course, it left him plenty of time with his own thoughts, which wasn't necessarily a good thing.

Because those thoughts turned to Nan de Montfort.

They had actually struck up a friendship as they broke their fast together in the mornings and dined together in the evenings. Tristan had never claimed friendship with a woman and yet it seemed perfectly normal. But what he wanted was more than friendship.

He burned to kiss her again. To undo that jet black braid and run his fingers through her silky locks. His fingers itched to slide down her arms and link their fingers together. Then their bodies.

Tristan wanted her, plain and simple—but there was nothing simple about it.

Nan de Montfort was someone utterly comfortable in her own skin. He knew she was also free to wed—the man *she* chose—not one chosen for her. In a thousand years, he doubted he could ever become the kind of man Nan would want as a husband, for Nan had told him she believed in love. She would never consider speaking vows with a man and binding herself to him for life unless she loved him.

That meant Tristan could never be the man for her because not only would Nan wish to wed someone she loved, she would want to receive that man's love in return.

He didn't have that in him anymore—if he ever did.

Looking up, he'd lost track of where he was. The waning light told him he needed to find his way back to the castle soon before dark fell. Tristan turned and began walking in the direction he hoped was correct. As he continued, he heard a slight rustling. Then it became louder. He halted in his tracks and spun around, trying to locate where it came from.

A flash of yellow caught his eye. He focused on it and saw it was the color Nan had worn tonight. Mayhap she, too, had come to stroll the Sandbourne woods. But the noise became louder, now crashing through the brush. Tristan ran in her direction, a fierce need to protect her possessing him. From the corner of his eye, he spied a wild boar coming from his left.

Straight toward Nan.

Exploding with a speed he'd never known he possessed, he ran to place himself between Nan and the beast. Tristan hurdled through the air in the last seconds when he realized he wouldn't get there in time with his legs alone. And then pain erupted while he was still in mid-air. A long squeal sounded. He fell with a thud to the ground, his left side throbbing and his right thigh burning. The boar had collided with him and then dashed off.

That explained the reason his entire side ached, but why did his thigh pulse in agony?

Tristan looked down and saw that an arrow protruded from it. He became aware that someone hovered over him. Raising his eyes, he saw Nan there, her bow and arrow in hand. She gazed down at him, her face white in distress.

"Not again," she said.

CHAPTER 7

Nan dropped to her knees, a mixture of nausea and despair threatening to overwhelm her. Tristan Therolde lay on the ground—with her arrow protruding from his leg. She swallowed and took a cleansing breath, clearing her mind of everything except helping this man who had sacrificed himself by coming to her aid.

Taking his hand in hers, she calmly told him, "My lord, you have been struck by an arrow. You may not feel the pain yet, but you soon will."

His eyes met hers. "Oh, I definitely feel it, my lady. My thigh is pulsating with a world of hurt. And while we are discussing my injury, we might want to note that the arrow in my leg belongs to you."

Nan cringed. "I am sorry my arrow penetrated your leg, Lord Tristan. 'Twas meant for the boar that charged me. You came from nowhere. I had already released the bowstring when you appeared."

"I caught sight of the yellow you wore tonight as I heard the animal crashing through the woods." He gave her a crooked smile. "Little did I know you would walk these woods with protection in hand. I thought to shield you from the boar's attack. It all happened so suddenly."

"But you threw yourself in the beast's path," Nan said. "It might have killed you."

He shrugged. "I acted on impulse. Who knew deep inside that I was such an honorable man?"

Though he made light of the situation, Nan knew two things. That Lord Tristan had behaved heroically and risked his own life to save hers. And that he must be in a great deal of pain.

Suddenly aware of her hand in his, Nan squeezed it to reassure him. His eyes searched hers for a long moment. In an instant, something passed between them. Something unexplainable, that could not be put into words, but she now found herself bound to this nobleman in a way she'd never been with any other.

Tearing her gaze from his, she withdrew her hand and moved it to his leg.

"I see very little blood. That is a good sign that no artery was struck."

"So I won't bleed to death anytime soon?"

She pursed her lips. "This is not funny, my lord."

He looked at her guilelessly. "Nay, I didn't think it was."

Nan blew out a puff of air. "I am being serious."

"So am I."

But the look in his eyes said otherwise. She saw pain there, but beneath it, humor peeked out—and that surprised her. Tristan Therolde had been self-possessed to the point of arrogance. Distant at times. But the very vulnerable man before her revealed a totally different side to himself.

One that appealed to her immensely.

She leaned back on her heels, her hands resting in her lap. "I must return to the keep for help. It's too far for you to walk without jarring your leg. I'll bring men to—"

"Fetch my horse instead. He can carry me back at a slow pace and then you can seek help carrying me inside to my chamber."

It was a good plan, better than what she had been thinking. Nan started to rise.

"Wait," he said softly. "Stay with me just a bit longer."

She sat on the ground beside him, wanting to protest and explain that the sooner he returned to the keep, the faster his injury could be attended to. Yet Nan understood that somehow he needed her with him a bit longer.

"You will be fine, Lord Tristan. I know how to care for your wound."

He took her hand, his thumb rubbing soft circles along her palm. "What did you mean—before?"

She frowned, pretending she didn't understand when she did. When he remained silent, she decided to speak.

"I have never discussed this with anyone. It happened so long ago that sometimes I think I only imagined it. My arrow has pierced another before you," Nan began. "I accidentally shot one into my brother's thigh when I was first learning how to control my bow. Hal still bears a scar from that arrow wound."

"I know this brother lived because Lady Elysande told me he wed recently. A falconer, she said. One of great repute."

"Aye, he lived. And Elinor will be an excellent wife to him. I lived with the guilt for a long time, but Hal insisted from the beginning that it was an accident and no one was to blame."

His thumb continued swirling, causing her stomach to fill with fluttering butterflies.

"Then I hope you realize tonight's incident was also the same. No one is to blame. You were trying to kill a charging boar that threatened your life. I tried to keep you safe. 'Tis no one's fault."

"Says the man with my arrow stuck in his leg." She shook her head. "You are being kind, Lord Tristan."

His thumb stilled. "I don't know the last time someone told me that. Mayhap never," he said softly. Then he raised her hand and pressed a fervent kiss against the very palm his thumb had massaged.

A tremor ran through Nan. Part of her wanted to yank her hand from his and run away from him as fast as she could. The other half wanted to stay and explore his sensual lips with her own.

Neither half won. He needed help. Now. Nan broke away as she stood.

"I will return soon." She went to where she'd dropped her bow and quiver and brought it to him, bending down to place it by his side. "In case anymore wild animals descend upon you. You will at least have some protection."

Nan rose, her knees shaky and her stomach still aflutter from what she saw in his eyes. "Try not to move about, my lord," she instructed.

"Tristan," he said. "The least you can do for a man you've pierced with your arrow is to drop any formalities."

"Tristan," she echoed.

"Nan."

They inspected one another in a new light. She had no idea what had shifted between them. Only that it had.

"I'll hurry. You won't have to wait alone for long," she promised, forcing herself to step away from him. It took everything in her power not to glance over her shoulder at him as she left the forest and trotted toward the stables. Dusk had fallen.

"Tristan."

She tried the name out on her lips as she reached the stables and slowed down, breathing heavily. Nan liked the way her mouth felt after saying it. She couldn't help herself. She liked *him*. Tristan Therolde was nothing like what he presented to the world. She longed to peel away the layers he surrounded himself with and discover his true essence.

And it had only taken almost killing him to feel this way.

Suppressing a giggle that threatened to erupt, she found a stable hand and had Tristan's horse saddled. The boy never questioned why she asked for him to do so and Nan didn't volunteer why she needed the mount. Quickly, she rode to the gates which were about to be closed for the evening and told the gatekeeper she would return soon and to be watching for her.

Nan galloped across the meadow and slowed the horse as she entered the forest. Being familiar with Sandbourne lands helped her remember where she'd left him, especially as the dark night took over. She climbed from the horse and tethered it to a bush.

"I'm glad you came back for me," Tristan teased and then grimaced.

She hurried to his side. "Push off on your good leg. I'm strong, thanks to my years of archery practice. I will help you rise and keep you steady."

Getting him to his feet proved easier than she'd thought. Nan wrapped her arm around his waist as he draped an arm about her shoulders and limped to where his horse stood. She steadied him as he put his left foot in the stirrups and swung up into the saddle. Tristan sucked in a quick breath, followed by a soft curse. She turned away to retrieve her bow and quiver, slipping the strap onto her shoulder.

"I'll guide your horse back to Sandbourne," she told him, reaching for the reins.

"Nay. Come ride with me."

The thought of this man's arms around her caused her breath to catch.

"I'll be fine, Tristan," she said, surprised her voice sounded normal. "I enjoy walking."

"I would feel guilty riding while you did so." He paused. "Please, Nan."

Her name coming from his mouth nearly did her in. She had to lock her knees to keep from swaying.

"If you insist."

Nan started to place her foot in the stirrup but Tristan reached down and lifted her into the saddle in front of him as if she weighed no more than a blade of grass. He slipped both arms around her and drew her back into his chest.

Oh, my.

The feel of his arms holding her tightly against him caused her to stop breathing. Her heart raced wildly inside her chest. Once again, her mouth went dry. Nan rested her hands upon one of his forearms as he took up the reins and walked his horse from the woods. It took several minutes to reach the road and then the castle walls.

Nan wished they could have ridden together until dawn.

"Head for the keep," she told him. "You don't need to walk all the way from the stables."

Tristan did as she said. When they arrived, she slid reluctantly from the horse's back and motioned for the blacksmith to come from his shed where he stood watching them. Quickly, he brought back help so that Tristan could be taken to his chamber with a minimal effort on his part.

While four men made sure the noblemen arrived there safely, Nan flew up the stairs and knocked on the solar's door. After waiting without acknowledgement, she rapped against the door even harder.

"Elysande! I need your help!"

Finally, the door opened. Michael stood in front of her, bare to the waist, his hair disheveled.

"This better be important, Nan," he cautioned. "My wife and I were having a very interesting . . . discussion."

"I shot an arrow through Tristan Therolde's leg," she blurted out as she felt her cheeks heat, fully knowing what kind of discussion she'd interrupted.

His eyebrows shot up. "I would say that qualifies as important. Come in."

She entered and found Elysande exiting the solar's bedchamber, her cheeks also full of color and her long hair unbraided, spilling down past her waist.

"You *shot* Lord Tristan?" she asked. "No, don't tell me why. Guessing will be an intriguing game to play later."

"I've dealt with this injury before several times. It occurs on the range every now and then. I need a few things if you don't mind gathering them for me."

Nan explained what she required and told Elysande to meet her in Lord Tristan's chamber. She rushed to her own bedchamber to fetch something she always carried and hoped never to use. Locating the small satchel, she went to Tristan's room and found the door open. He'd been placed on the bed. The men had left but a servant hovered nearby. She told the girl to bring boiled water, knowing Elysande would return with the rest of the needed supplies.

Approaching the bed, Nan saw the earl's pain written across his face yet he mustered a smile as she came to stand next to him. She removed a pouch from her satchel and placed some of the crushed mandragora into a cup she found on a side table. Reaching for the wine sitting on the table, she poured a liberal amount and swished it around, mixing the wine with the plant.

Nan handed it to Tristan. "Drink this quickly. It will either dull the pain of what I must do or hopefully send you to sleep so that you won't feel a thing."

He dipped his nose down and inhaled suspiciously. "What is it?"

"Mandragora, a plant in the nightshade family. This has been crushed but it comes from a fleshy, forked root. Both my mother and older sister, Alys, are great healers. This is from Mother's stock. I always keep it with me. Just in case . . ." Her voice trailed off.

"In case you puncture a man with one of your arrows?" he joked, causing her cheeks to heat further. Tristan brought the pewter cup to his lips and downed the contents. He grimaced.

"That's why I told you to swallow quickly. I know it tastes unpleasant." She looked about. "'Tis a very nice bedchamber. Elysande is a marvelous hostess."

Nan began talking about insignificant things while she waited for the herb to take effect. At first, Tristan responded to her questions then slowly his words began to slur. Finally, his eyes closed. She only hoped they would stay that way.

By now, Elysande had arrived, along with the servant and the hot water. Michael also appeared, having dressed again. He shooed the servant from the room and looked from the sleeping earl to her.

"What would you have us do, Nan?"

She tore a piece of cloth Elysande had brought into strips and soaked them in the water. As she did, she said, "I've given him mandragora. He's a large man so he may not be in a deep sleep now. When I begin, he'll probably awaken. The herb will mask some, but not all, of the pain. I may need you to hold him still, Michael, if he begins to thrash about."

Michael went and stood on the other side of the bed. "I'll be ready," he promised. "Even if I have to sit on him."

Nan returned to the case and removed her probe, sometimes

called the Spoon of Diocles, for the Greek physician who created it. The probe would help catch the arrowhead and remove it from Tristan with a minimum of damage since the best arrowheads were glued to their shaft with beeswax. Tristan's body heat would have melted the wax, making it next to impossible to pull the shaft from him without stretching his skin and opening the wound further.

Elysande's eyes went wide as she looked at the instrument.

"Don't worry. I may not have to use these tongs to extract the arrow. They are only here as a precaution. If bone prevents me from pushing the shaft all the way through, then I will extract it using these forceps."

She watched her cousin steel herself against that occurrence.

Nan pulled her blade from her boot and cut away Tristan's pants from his right leg, tossing aside the material. The men had placed the earl on his left side, so she had a good vantage point of seeing how the arrow had entered the front of his leg and then emerged from the back. Using her fingers, she gently explored the area and sighed. She wouldn't need to use the tongs to screw apart the wound and widen it in order to reach the arrowhead.

"I'll be able to forego the tongs," she told the couple, relief pouring through her.

Nan tied a piece of the soaked linen to the end of the shaft. She would push it from the front through Tristan's wound and bring it out the back side. This would be the only way to remove it cleanly.

"Elysande, hold his ankles and keep his feet still. Michael, press down on his shoulders and upper body. When I begin, he may try to fly off the bed."

They situated themselves while Nan washed and dried her hands. Both nodded at her that they were ready and she began to push the shaft deeper into Tristan's leg. He awoke with an unearthly howl. Elysande climbed onto the bed and sank her knees against his ankles and hovered over them as Michael pinned the nobleman to the bed so he couldn't thrash about.

Nan worked quickly and managed to push the arrow in until it disappeared in the front, before she pulled it completely out from the back side of his thigh. Sweat broke out across her brow. She glanced at the still form of Tristan Therolde. After several gasps through gritted teeth, he had either passed out from the pain or the herb had finally overtaken him. Either way, he was quiet now.

Elysande and Michael released him and stepped back.

"You may leave," Nan told them. "The rest is easy and I can manage alone."

"Are you certain?" Michael asked. Elysande was stark white and couldn't speak. Her husband put his arm about her shoulders.

"I am. Go," she urged.

They left the bedchamber and Nan got to work. First, she poured boiled water over the bleeding wound and then washed it with liberal amounts of white wine, drying it carefully. Then she dipped more linen strips in honey and cleaned the wound until the blood flow ceased. After that, she stitched and packed the wound, dressing it with a poultice of barley and honey mixed in turpentine, binding the poultice to Tristan with more layers of clean linen.

Exhausted, she stepped back and assessed her work. She had done what she could to remove the arrow and prevent infection from setting in. It would be important to clean and redress the wound daily for the next week.

She decided to remove his clothing. In case fever set in, it would be easier to bathe him in order to bring the fever down. She removed his boots and placed them on the floor next to the bed. His pants were already ruined so she took her dagger to what was left of them. Soon, his legs were bare, great tree trunks of muscle. Her eyes kept roaming back to his manhood. In all her years, she had never seen a man uncovered below the waist and found him to be fascinating. She shook her head to clear it and worked his gypon from him, folding and placing it on the edge of the bed. Though she had seen many a bare-chested man in the training yard, none had drawn her interest quite as much as Tristan did.

Nan skirted a hand along his huge upper arm and then along his chest, covered in a matting of soft, tawny hair that matched the hair atop his head. The muscles bunched under her fingertips. Touching him thrilled her, seeing so much raw power on display. As she ran her palm from his throat down to his belly, his manhood suddenly leapt to life. Nan pulled back her hand in haste and then paused.

Curiosity got the best of her.

She reached out and touched the growing shaft. The small appendage had increased in size almost instantly. She gripped the shaft in her hand, feeling how firm it was. Then she stroked its head, silky smooth and so different from anything she'd seen or felt before. Guilt washed over her. She should not be taking such liberties with an injured, unconscious man.

Tristan was much too large to move under the covers. She rolled him to his back and folded the bedclothes up on one side and went to the other, doing the same. At least he was covered somewhat now.

Nan pulled the lone chair in the room over to the bed and sat in it. She planned to stay with him through the night in case he needed something and would check at regular intervals to see if fever struck. By the light of the burning candle next to the bed, Tristan looked younger in sleep than he did when awake. Temptation called out to her. She rested her hands against the bed as she leaned over and pressed a kiss upon his brow.

His hand shot out, latching on to her wrist. Nan pulled gently, not wanting to disturb his rest. His fingers held her in a vise. She tried to pry them away and failed miserably. Deciding to let him hang on to her, as if she had a choice in the matter, she sat.

Or tried to sit.

The chair was just out of reach of her bottom.

Frustration filled her. She didn't want to stand all night but she didn't know how to free herself from his iron grip. Giving up, she crawled onto the bed and lay down, facing him, her captured wrist between them.

She closed her eyes. Mayhap he would release her sometime during the night and she could return to her vigil in the chair.

Or not.

Nan drifted off to sleep.

CHAPTER 8

TRISTAN FIRST BECAME aware of the subtle floral fragrance as he drifted awake. He had inhaled it for several nights while seated next to Nan. The intoxicating smell rising from her skin stirred his blood. Then he noticed the warmth against his fingers. Moving his thumb slightly, it caressed soft skin, more silken than a fine garment from the Far East. Last, he listened and heard the light, even breathing near him and felt the puff of warm air against his neck.

Everything rushed back to him at once, crowding out all the sensual pleasures he'd noticed, leaving him conscious of the dull pain in his throbbing thigh. He opened his eyes and turned his head.

Nan lay next to him, her lips slightly parted as she slept. Memories of the night flooded him. The woods. The boar. His daring leap to save her from certain death. And his reward—her arrow launched into his flesh. He glanced down, not at the wound in his thigh but to see his fingers holding fast to her wrist, his thumb moving slowly back and forth. She stirred slightly, a half-smile touching her lips.

His wound didn't hurt as much as the entire left side of his aching body, the victim of his encounter with the boar. He realized how lucky he was not to have been killed by the wild beast or Nan's arrow. He had lived—but for what reason?

It was the second time in life Tristan had asked himself that same question.

After the first instance, he'd received no answer. He wondered if this time would be the same.

Instead of worrying about something beyond his control, he decided to enjoy his unparalleled view. Nan still wore the yellow cotehardie from last night, now wrinkled, but the pale fabric enhanced her dark hair and the long lashes swept against her cheeks. His eyes dropped lower. An expanse of creamy flesh was revealed, thanks to the way her cotehardie bunched as she slept. Tristan enjoyed seeing the curve of her breasts, more of them on display than usual. He longed to run his tongue along the rise of the perfect globes and hear her sigh of pleasure as he did so.

The thought startled him. Somehow, this woman had slipped under his skin and invaded his waking—and dreaming—states. He'd always been a man who took his own pleasure with a woman and never thought about if she gained satisfaction from their coupling. Yet every fiber in his being wanted to please the beauty slumbering next to him. Why this woman and none before her?

What was so different about Nan de Montfort?

Without bothering to ponder an answer to his own question, Tristan instead chose what he longed to do. Easing onto his side, he ignored the silent scream his body made in protest and placed a palm against Nan's porcelain cheek.

So soft...

He tilted his head and pressed his lips against hers, drinking in the wafting floral fragrance. Nan wriggled and made a low noise. Tristan's thumb stroked her cheek as he feathered light kisses from one corner of her mouth to the other.

She awoke.

He knew instantly when it occurred. Her body stiffened. He didn't know if her eyes opened as he continued brushing his lips against hers. She held still for a moment and then two things happened. Her free hand slowly slid up his bare chest, while her tongue darted out and teased the seam of his lips apart.

Hunger for her burst inside him. He cradled her cheek and answered her call, his mouth yielding to hers. Their tongues mated lazily at first, exploring one another without rushing. His ran along the roof of her mouth, bringing a muffled giggle from her. She must be ticklish.

That brought all kinds of wicked ideas to him.

Tristan's hand pushed into her hair, wishing the long locks weren't braided. Knowing that it would take too long to undo the braids, he dragged his hand along her neck to her shoulder, down to the curve of her hip, and then he brought it around to clasp her buttock. Squeezing it, she sighed into his mouth, her hand now clutching his shoulder, the nails digging in.

He kissed her for so long that he lost track of time. All that mattered was the heat between them. Tristan sampled Nan's sweetness over and over, yearning to do more, but he knew her to be a virgin and was aware that she would only give herself to the man she loved.

Those thoughts brought him crashing back to reality. He broke the kiss and opened his eyes to drink in her beauty.

Large, blue eyes stared intently at him as she breathed quickly in and out, her chest heaving, her breasts threatening to spill from her dress. Her already swollen lips would be bruised from their love play, which gave him immense satisfaction. Suddenly, Tristan wished he could wake up to this woman by his side every day.

Even if she had shot him with her arrow.

"Good morn to you," he said.

Her hand went to his forehead. "You have a slight fever," she told him. She sat up and started to pull away but his fingers tightened around her wrist, keeping her captive.

"Should we talk about it?" he asked, wanting to discuss their kiss and what had been unsaid between them.

Confusion filled her eyes. "What? That I shot you? You do remember that, I'm sure."

He kept the smile from his face. "Aye. 'Tis not every day that a beautiful woman tries to kill me."

She sniffed. "I was *trying* to kill a boar. *You* got in my way."

"I am glad," he replied.

Nan looked at him as if he'd gone mad. "You're glad. Glad that I sent an arrow into you."

"Glad that whatever happened led us to be here." Tristan tugged on her again as she tried to move away. When she gave him an exasperated look, he spoke the truth. "I am reluctant to release you."

"Why?" she asked, chewing on that full bottom lip that drove him to distraction.

"Because I want to do this again."

This time, Tristan yanked hard on Nan. Not expecting the sudden move, she fell against him. Only then did he release her wrist in order to cup her face with both of his hands. He kissed her, feeling her lips throb against his as much as his thigh throbbed—though he'd never tell her that. She clung to his shoulders as he deepened the kiss. Wanting, needing, to consume her.

A tap on the door startled them both. Nan scurried off the bed and plopped into the chair nearby. Already, Tristan missed her.

The door swung open and Lady Elysande appeared with a tray in hand. She came to the bed.

"I see you are awake, Lord Tristan."

He pushed himself up and groaned at the effort. Nan jumped to her feet and plumped the pillows behind him, feeling his forehead again.

"Lord Tristan has a slight fever," she announced. "We need to send for cool water to bathe him. Did you bring broth, Elysande?"

"Aye, and plenty of bread. Are you up to eating, my lord?"

His stomach rumbled loudly in response. "I suppose there's your answer."

"You look tired, Nan," Elysande chided. "Did you get any sleep?"

"Some," Nan said, avoiding his glance, which made him chuckle.

Lady Elysande looked his way. "Something I said, my lord?"

Thinking quickly, Tristan said, "If I snored, as my brothers always claimed, then I doubt Lady Nan got much rest at all."

"Why don't you go wash your face and change your clothes, Nan?" Lady Elysande suggested. "I can stay with Lord Tristan while he eats and then we can both bathe him to help keep the fever at bay."

The thought of Nan's hands on him heated Tristan's blood.

"I will freshen up as you suggest," Nan said, "but you may stay with Lord Tristan and see to his needs for now."

"Are you going to the butts instead?" Elysande asked.

"Nay. I need to gather clean linen and the items to make a new poultice for his wound. Do you have any St. John's wort or comfrey?"

"I do. Are you making a different poultice from the one you created last night?"

Nan shook her head. "Nay, that will remain the same. Mother always said barley and honey keeps a wound clean and closes it quickly, especially when mixed with the turpentine. The other herbs are ones I can use in treating the bruises along his side."

Tristan looked at the left part of his body. Deep bruising in purples and blacks adorned him. "I suppose that's what happens when colliding with a charging boar at full speed."

Elysande shuddered. "You are fortunate to be here, my lord." She glanced at her cousin. "And to have someone as knowledgeable as Nan to care for you. You never seemed to care much for herbs, though," she mused.

"Just because I don't live to talk about herbs as Mother and Alys do does not mean I did not learn from them both. I know how to care for many ailments, especially ones that occur in the training yard and on the battlefield."

"You know where I keep the stored herbs," Elysande said. "You'll find everything you need there. Take your time." She gave Nan a sweet smile and watched as she left the bedchamber.

Once the door shut, Lady Elysande turned to him, her smile now gone. In its place, accusations filled her eyes. "Fever or not, Nan's lips were swollen. My guess is from your kiss, Lord Tristan. What do you have to say for yourself?"

Tristan could almost see the waves of anger emanating from the noblewoman and sought to placate her.

"My lady, I must say—"

"Whatever you say is unacceptable to me. Though I did not give birth to her, Nan is like a daughter to me, Lord Tristan. I am as protective of her as I am my other children. If you think to dally with her, you will have a serious problem. There'll be no talk of which horses you might purchase. Horses will be the least of your concern. You will be expelled from Sandbourne and never allowed on our lands again."

"Lady Elysande, I do not wish to toy with Nan."

"Good. She may appear invincible to all who meet her but Nan has a tender heart. I would not see her hurt by anyone. Including you."

Tristan swallowed. "I'll admit that we did kiss. I am attracted to Lady Nan. However, I know of her desire to wed a man who will love her." He paused. "I am not that man."

She eyed him carefully. "Then see to it that you keep your hands—and your lips—to yourself." Setting down the tray, she added, "Eat what you can. I will bring water to bathe you."

With that, the noblewoman left him. Tristan only hoped he could adhere to Lady Elysande's advice.

NAN HURRIED FROM the bedchamber, thankful that Elysande had not walked in on them while they kissed.

They had kissed. Multiple times.

Why had they kissed?

She lived in an orderly world of her own making. Went where she chose. Did what interested her. Depended upon no one but herself. By the Christ, she liked her life the way it was.

Or had been—until the Earl of Leventhorpe had crashed into it and disturbed everything.

Nan admitted to herself that she liked him better than she had when he first arrived at Sandbourne. Else she wouldn't have kissed him. Or let him kiss her.

Why did he keep kissing her?

If she found the answer to that, she could figure out how to keep him from doing so again. Nan didn't like to be bewildered and unsure of herself.

Lord Tristan made her feel both of those things.

She dug through her trunk, trying to decide what to wear and then stopped. She refused to dress in order to please him. Pushing all thoughts of looking feminine for him aside, she stripped off her cotehardie and the smock beneath it. Rolling them up, she tossed them onto the bed. She would don what she felt comfortable in. What she usually wore. What acted like a second skin. Nan yanked on a pair of dark brown pants and a hunter green gypon. She replaced her boots and took a deep breath.

"Better," she told herself. She was no longer dressed like a woman. She wouldn't think like one or act like one. She would be her usual self around Lord Tristan.

And she would stop kissing him. She'd threatened to cut off his balls if he touched her again, yet she'd allowed him to kiss her senseless. No more nonsense.

As she marched to where Elysande stored her herbs, she admitted she was partially to blame. After all, she had curled up next to a naked man in his bed. What else was he supposed to think? She hadn't had the time to explain to him how she was unable to sit in her chair. That wouldn't be a problem in the future. If he grasped her—in sleep or otherwise—and refused to let go?

Nan would bite his fingers. To the bone, if necessary.

She located both the St. John's wort and oil to mix with it. This could be applied to all of his bruised areas. For the most severe bruising, she could gently place a few drops directly onto his skin and allow it to soak in. She also found the comfrey, which her mother used for many different kinds of skin problems. After a day or mayhap two of using the wort, she would need to create poultices from the fresh leaves of the comfrey and employ those to promote healing and reduce any bruising and swelling that remained.

Taking both with her, Nan left the comfrey in her bedchamber. She wanted to make sure she had a good supply of it because of how much of Tristan was bruised.

That was another thing. She now thought of him as Tristan. He had asked her to use his Christian name after whatever passed between them in the forest. She couldn't stop using it without him protesting overly much. Nan decided she would continue to call him by his given name—but not often.

Because she liked the way it sounded on her tongue too much.

She swore under her breath and gripped her bedpost for support. Damn the man! He had a tongue that worked magic on her. It had woven a spell around her, making her want nothing more than to kiss him until her lips bled. And the more they kissed, the more she wanted from him. Nan didn't even know exactly what she wanted. Oh, she understood the physical part. His touch was meant to make her desire him. To ache for his hands to rub against every intimate place on her. For his cock to push inside her.

But what she really wanted was affection. Understanding.

Love.

And that was something she would never receive from Tristan Therolde. He'd already warned her that he didn't believe in love. She must start taking him seriously or else she'd be severely compromised by him. Nan didn't want to continually kiss a man who wouldn't let her—and love—into his life. As a pair, they weren't meant to be.

Men were weak, always giving in to their physical desires. She had to be the strong one between them. The next time Tristan attempted to kiss her, she would calmly warn him not to. If he tried again, she would knock him straight to Hell.

She composed herself and returned to his chamber, balancing the bowl of salve and the makings for the poultice in hand. Knocking once to be polite, she nudged open the door. The tray sat on the floor, so he had finished eating. Elysande gathered up cloths and lifted a bucket of water.

"I am glad you've returned, Nan. Lord Tristan has eaten and been bathed. He doesn't seem feverish to me. I'll return these things to the kitchen." She pointed to the chair. "I've already set out new clothes for him to wear when he feels up to it."

Nan nodded. "I plan to cleanse his wound and apply a new poultice to it. I also brought salve to rub into his bruises. After that, I will go to the range where I am needed. You might have a servant sit with him until he is definitely free of fever."

"Then I will leave him in your capable hands," her cousin said. After a long look, Elysande added, "Call me if you need anything."

"Of course," Nan agreed.

Elysande left and Nan bustled about, ignoring the looks Tristan threw her way. She finally came to the bed, noting he was now under the bedclothes.

"May I remove your dressing?" she asked.

"Do as you wish." His voice sounded husky and low, causing a chill to run along her spine.

Nan pushed back the bedclothes so that she could access his leg. Concentrating, she carefully unwound the linen cloth and then gently lifted the poultice. She inspected both the entry and exit of the arrow, pleased at how both had already begun to heal. Her mother would have been proud of her.

"You looked pleased with yourself," Lord Tristan said.

"I am happy with your progress," she admitted. "And that you seem to have no fever. Infection and fever are always something to worry about. I wouldn't want to be responsible for you losing your limb."

Nan bathed the wound again in white wine and honey and then created a new poultice. She wound clean linen around his leg once more, securing the poultice to his thigh. Now would come the hard part.

Bravely, she looked Tristan in the eye. Having three brothers had taught her to show no sign of weakness and she drew on that strength and experience.

"I'll need to address your bruising now. I should have done so last night but you needed your rest."

"What would you have me do?" he asked, his eyes burning into hers.

"Roll to your side to give me easier access."

He tossed the bedclothes away and did as she instructed. Nan caught herself holding her breath as she gazed on his magnificent form again. His muscled torso and long, strong limbs seemed as if carved from impenetrable stone. She averted her eyes from his manhood and retrieved the bowl that contained the salve that she had blended.

Perching on the bed, she said, "I will be as gentle as I can."

Tristan laughed. "You couldn't do any more damage than the boar did."

Nan bit back a smile. "Oh, really? Then what would you call the holes in your leg?"

He roared with laughter. "I suppose you're right. Have at me, Nan. Do as you will." His gaze held hers a moment before she forced herself to look away.

She focused on her task at hand, dipping her fingers into the bowl and applying the salve to his body. Her fingers gently massaged it into his battered skin. Already, dark purple and black blotches covered from his shoulder and along his side down to the end of his hip. On the worst places, she used drops of the St. John's wort, dousing the bruise and allowing it to seep into his skin before using her fingertips to rub it even more deeply.

His arousal became obvious to them both the longer she touched him but neither of them acknowledged it. Nan watched it grow from the corner of her eye, swallowing when she saw how huge it became. She, too, had become aroused as she touched him, feeling her pulse jumping in her throat and her heart drumming against her ribs. At the apex of where her legs joined, a quivering began. First, it tingled to make her aware of it. Then it began pulsating. She wanted to move her hips but kept them still.

Finally, her task ended. Nan stood and tossed the bedclothes back over him. "I have coated every bruise I can find. I think by tomorrow you will be able to blend the salve into your skin without my help."

"Nan?" Tristan reached for her but she took a step back.

"You need rest, Tristan," she said firmly. "Try and get some. I need to return to the range to work with Michael's pages and squires."

Scooping up her supplies, she hurried to the door.

"Nan?" he called again. She heard the urgency—and tenderness—in his voice.

Ignoring him, she left the bedchamber.

CHAPTER 9

If Tristan could have climbed the walls, he would have. Keeping to his bed with nothing to do might be the end of him.

Especially because with all the long hours spent on his own, all he could think about was Nan de Montfort. Her smile. How soft her skin felt beneath his fingertips. The way she laughed. How the pants she wore emphasized her rounded bottom and the curve of her hips.

She came twice a day to examine his wound and change his dressing, every morning after mass and at night before the castle's occupants bedded down for the night. She reported to him on his progress and guaranteed him that within a week he could leave his bed and begin to walk with a cane. Nan had already brought the cane and allowed him to move about his bedchamber some. That was the only contact they had. Nan still called him Tristan on occasion but she had erected an invisible wall between them. She was polite but never stayed to converse with him as he longed for her to do.

Tristan did have visitors every night after the evening meal during the long week of inactivity. Stephen and Toby always came by to share with him how they'd spent their day at Sandbourne. Lady Elysande and Lord Michael were regular visitors, as well, entertaining him with stories about their extended family. He continued to quiz each of them about various tasks at their estate and how they managed their affairs. Lord Michael had brought his steward along on two occasions for Tristan to question and learn from.

David Devereux came thrice and eagerly discussed horses with him. The more time he spent around this young man, the more

Tristan believed David would be an ideal match for Gillian. He'd thought previously to approach Lord Petyr, the nobleman who lived two estates away to the north of Leventhorpe, but the baron was close to two score. A widower, he already had his heir and three other boys, so any male children Gillian produced from the marriage would not have many advantages. Sir David was much closer to his sister's age and would one day inherit his father's title and lands. Tristan would rather see Gillian taken care of by this caring family once she left home.

He'd grown fond of all the Devereuxs, even after Lady Elysande castigated him for kissing Nan. He accepted her rebuke and told her it had been a momentary lapse, promising his hostess he would be on his best behavior during his remaining time as their guest. Of course, Tristan had also given Nan the same pledge once—and he had quickly broken his word to her. She had done the same, though, her threats against him touching her proving empty. At least for that short lapse. If he tried to capture even her fingers for a brief kiss now, he wasn't sure his hand would come back to him whole.

Surprisingly, he'd grown fond of young Drewett Stollars. Drew had visited him faithfully every night. He enjoyed the squire's company and thought he would make an excellent knight. Once Drew earned his spurs, Tristan hoped he could lure him away from Nan's father. Tristan needed knights such as Drew Stollars, to protect Leventhorpe lands and its people.

A servant brought him his meal on a tray. He thanked her and ate quickly, eager to see who might stop by his bedchamber this evening. The earl and countess appeared shortly after he finished. Tristan decided the time had come to broach the idea of a betrothal between their families.

"Nan tells me she will allow you out of bed for good in the morn, my lord," Lady Elysande told him.

"Ah, she has not informed me of this," he replied. "'Tis good to know. I hope we can continue discussing the possibility of my purchasing horses from you once I'm up and about."

She studied him thoughtfully. "You had made good progress before your accident. David is also impressed with how quickly you've learned during your conversations together. I believe we can start small for now and allow you to add to your stock slowly over the next half a dozen years if that is agreeable with you."

"Knowing how valuable your horses are, my lady, I will buy whatever you allow me and return each year to conduct a new transaction." Tristan paused. "Since that's the case, I'd like to speak with you about a few other matters."

Lord Michael sat up, now interested that the talk had turned from horses. "What is on your mind, my lord?"

"I would ask that your son accompany me back to Thorpe Castle for a few weeks. He could help see the horses settled in and teach my stable hands what they need to know about the training and care required."

The earl looked to his wife. "I don't see that as a problem. Do you, my love?"

"It would be good experience for David and helpful to Lord Tristan. We are drawing near the end of foaling season. That frees David up, except for retrieving Tucker from Ashcroft."

Tristan had learned that Tucker was their youngest child, currently a squire fostering with Lord Raynor Le Roux. The couple had mentioned the boy several times over the last few weeks.

"I will be fetching my sister, Gillian, as well, when we return to Leventhorpe. She is fostering at Shercastle. I would like to discuss with you the possibility of a betrothal between her and Sir David."

Lady Elysande's brows arched. "Oh, really?"

"Aye. I have been favorably impressed with your son, my lady. 'Tis time to find Gillian a husband since she is ten and seven, soon to be ten and eight. Is Sir David betrothed to another or free to enter an arrangement?"

"David is his own man, Lord Tristan," the earl said firmly. "We will not arrange anything on his behalf. I will allow him to journey to your estate. Let the two of them spend time with one another. If they believe they would be a good match, then Elysande and I will give our blessing to their union."

Once again, Tristan thought how odd this family was, turning time-honored traditions on end. Still, it couldn't hurt to let the two meet. If David Devereux did not seem inclined to wed his sister, Tristan could always return to his original plan and approach Lord Petyr.

"I agree," he said. "Last, I have also been most impressed with Lady Nan's skills and way of teaching. I wonder if she would be able to accompany Sir David to Thorpe Castle and work with my men for a week or two."

Lady Elysande's eyes narrowed. "That is not our decision to make. 'Twould be up to Nan."

"What decision?" Nan entered and crossed the room, curiosity written on her face.

Before he could speak, Lord Michael said, "Elysande has agreed to part with a few of her horses. David is to accompany the earl and his men back to Thorpe Castle and work with the stable hands on their care for a week or two. Lord Tristan has also thought to invite you to come, as well, and work with his men regarding archery. The choice is yours, of course."

Tristan held his breath. Nan had been distant with him. He didn't know how she would react to this sudden invitation.

"I received a missive from Ancel this morning. He and Margery wish for me to come to Bexley for a visit. Ancel implied Margery might be with child again, so she will need some help with Cyrus and Miranda. He also wanted me to work with the boys fostering with him on their crossbow and longbow skills."

Nan placed her basket on the table. It held the supplies to redress Tristan's wound. He saw from the look on her face that she struggled to come up with an answer.

And more than anything, Tristan wanted her to come with him. Nan de Montfort intrigued him. Frustrated him. Challenged him. He wasn't ready to part from her yet.

Knowing how competitive she was, he said, "My men are sorely lacking in their archery skills. I had thought you would be an answered prayer if you came to Leventhorpe while Sir David was there. He could even escort you to your brother's estate afterward." Tristan shrugged. "Though I suppose Sir David could also help with the training in the butts if you cannot."

As he suspected, Nan's demeanor changed with his new suggestion.

"David is an adequate archer, my lord, but it would be wrong to draw him away from working with your horses. From what you've said, you live within two days' ride from Ancel's estate." She paused. "I suppose I could go to Thorpe Castle first and then on to Bexley in Kent and would appreciate David's escort there. It would be convenient." She looked to Lord Michael. "That is, if you think my work here is done."

The earl wrapped her in a bear hug. "You have been at Sandbourne long enough, Nan. If my men and those fostering here haven't learned your lessons by now, they never will." He kissed her forehead. "You know you are always welcomed to visit anytime."

"I do, Michael." She smiled up at him and looked to Tristan. "Of course, Drew must come with me. He will insist. So would Father. In fact, I will write to Father now and tell him of the opportunity to spend a short while at Thorpe Castle before we go to my brother's estate. I'll write to Ancel, as well, and tell him what my plans are."

"I'll send a rider out in the morning to deliver both messages," Elysande told Nan.

"Then it's settled," Tristan said, pleased at the outcome of the conversation. He would be able to begin breeding horses and hopefully see his sister wed to David Devereux. More importantly, he would be able to spend a little more time with Nan. She had become a part of his life that he wasn't ready to relinquish yet.

"Can Lord Tristan leave his bed tomorrow?" Elysande asked.

"Aye. I brought him a cane a few days ago. He's used it to walk about his chamber and will need it for longer stretches for a bit."

"Then we will meet in the stables after we break our fast, Lord Tristan," Lady Elysande said. "David and I will select the horses you will be taking to Thorpe Castle." She looked to her cousin. "When can the earl ride again?"

"By the end of the week," Nan said. "If not sooner."

"Good. That will give plenty of time for your parents to receive word of your plans. David can ride out and bring Tucker home for his summer break and be back in time to join you on the journey to Essex." Elysande looked to Tristan. "If that is satisfactory, my lord."

"I would agree to anything in order to leave this chamber, my lady. I look forward to seeing which horses you choose for me and to welcoming Sir David and Lady Nan into my home."

"And Drew," Nan prompted.

"Oh, I won't forget about young Drewett," Tristan said. He looked to the Devereuxs. "Will you tell your son about my sister?"

"Nay," Lord Michael replied. "If he becomes interested in her on his own, he will let you know." He looked to the countess and tucked her hand into the crook of his arm. "Shall we go discuss things with David now?"

The noble pair left the room. Nan collected her basket and treated Tristan's wound.

"It is healing exactly as it should," she told him. "Clear of any infection and closing nicely."

"Thank you for agreeing to come to Thorpe Castle."

Nan looked into his eyes, the first time she'd directly gazed into them in over a week. "I am happy to help your men, Tristan. I'll also be closer to Ancel and Margery. That will be most convenient. If you'll excuse me, I have to write to my parents and Ancel now."

Tristan enjoyed the view of her retreating form, his hands aching to cup her buttocks again.

"Have a pleasant evening, Nan," he called out.

She paused at the door. "You, too, my lord," she said and shut the door behind her.

TRISTAN HAD SPENT three days traipsing behind Lady Elysande, watching her decide which horses she would part with. The first day, she had discussed her choices with David, listening to his recommendations before he left for Ashcroft. The second day, Lord Michael had been called in for his opinion. He gave it readily and returned to the training yard, giving Tristan a huge grin as he passed.

Now that the third day had dawned, Lady Elysande had to finalize her choices since Tristan planned to leave for Leventhorpe in the morning. Because of that, she had called in Nan for her advice. Tristan had learned from Drew Stollars that while Nan had never fostered anywhere, she had spent several months at a time at Sandbourne with her cousin over a smattering of years, in order to glean knowledge about horses. Because of that, Nan's opinion was one Lady Elysande valued.

He trailed the two women at a distance, Drew by his side. Today, Tristan had finally given up the cane since his leg felt strong. Depending upon the crutch had grown tiresome.

"That is the only one I disagree with, Elysande," he overheard Nan say and she explained to her cousin why the mare was a poor choice to send to Leventhorpe.

"I understand your reasoning. I can't believe I didn't think of that myself. Come, we need to find a replacement. I've promised Lord Tristan five horses and five horses he shall have."

They left the stall they stood in front of and turned the corner. Tristan looked at Drew, who shrugged.

"Nan knows more about horses than you can imagine," the squire said. "Lord Geoffrey always counts on her advice. She learned much from the countess over the years."

"How is it to foster with Lord Geoffrey? I ask because Lady Nan is such an unusual woman."

Drew smiled broadly. "No one is finer than Lord Geoffrey de Montfort. And Lady Merryn," he added. "I feel blessed to have been with them for all of these years. My father died weeks before I left to foster at Kinwick. I'm a good bit younger than my two brothers. I fear

I turned somewhat surly and craved attention. Lord Geoffrey set me straight and on the right path to becoming a good knight and a better man."

"You and Lady Nan have grown up together then," Tristan noted.

"Aye, my lord. We couldn't stand the sight of each other for months after I arrived. I was always teasing her and causing mischief, hoping she'd be blamed for it. But we came through that and are as close as a brother and sister could be. Probably closer, now that I think about it. A sister wouldn't have spent nearly as much time with me. Nan and I learned weaponry together. Served as sparring partners. We rode and hunted and fished, along with Hal and Edward. Those are her brothers. Oftentimes, I didn't go home for the summer break. My oldest brother assumed the title upon my father's death. He found it easier to leave me at Kinwick. The earl and countess have always treated me as family. I can't say enough good about them."

"Didn't you find it unusual that their daughter spent all her time pursuing activities meant for boys?"

Drew nodded. "At first, I did. But Nan's parents are supportive of their children. They allowed Nan to follow her heart." He chuckled. "And her heart liked to swing a sword and fire arrows." His face grew serious. "I would trust Nan with my life, my lord. More than I would any man."

"I am pleased that you will accompany her to Thorpe Castle and then to her brother's estate."

"Lord Geoffrey charged me with keeping his daughter safe. I plan to do that," Drew swore.

They came in sight of the women, chattering animatedly in front of a stall.

"They'll still be at it for some time," the squire said. "I think I'll head back to the training yard." He bowed and left Tristan.

Tristan decided it was time to visit his horse since he carried a treat for him. The poor animal hadn't even had a name when they'd arrived at Sandbourne. Tristan hadn't cared enough to give him one before. It was one of the ways he had changed since he'd been here. He'd learned to care about those around him, including his mount.

He greeted the black. "How are you today, Skybourne?" Pulling an apple from his pocket, he held it up to the horse, who leaned over and snatched it from his palm.

Tristan laughed, something that hadn't come easily to him but which seemed natural here at Sandbourne. He worried about returning to Thorpe Castle, wondering what Nan would think of it and those who resided within its walls. Would he revert back to the man he'd become after tragedy struck—or try to be more like the one emerging now?

Continuing on, he came to Nightfoot's stall and gave that horse a pat. Nan had told him she named the horse thanks to the one black foot the animal possessed.

"I hope you will enjoy our trip to Leventhorpe," he said aloud, marveling that he conversed with a horse. At times, he barely recognized himself.

Voices drifted his way. Tristan saw the two women coming toward him.

"Have you made your final decision, Lady Elysande?" he asked when the pair reached where he stood.

"I have. I hope you will be pleased, my lord," she replied.

Tristan followed them from the stables as they headed toward the keep. As they reached it, a loud noise sounded. He knew a group of horses approached. Within moments, riders arrived inside the inner bailey. Nan squealed with delight and ran toward them.

An imposing man, his dark hair tinged with gray at his temples, leapt from his horse and swept her into his arms, swinging her around. He put her down and kissed her soundly.

"What are you doing here, Father?"

He gave her an incredulous look. "You don't think I would let you ride off to an estate of a man I have never met, did you?" Geoffrey de Montfort roared. He glanced around, his eyes settling on Tristan's form.

Releasing the hold on his daughter, he strode to Tristan and thrust out a hand. "I am Geoffrey de Montfort, Earl of Kinwick."

Tristan took the offered hand. Before he could speak, Lord Geoffrey said so softly that no one else could hear, "I better get the right answers from you, Lord Tristan, else you won't be going anywhere—with or without my daughter."

He replied smoothly, "Lady Nan is certainly your daughter, my lord. She threatened to cut off my balls if I ever touched her."

As Geoffrey de Montfort shook Tristan's hand, a satisfied smile crossed the nobleman's lips. "That's my girl," he said, his pride obvious.

CHAPTER 10

LADY ELYSANDE ESCORTED them to the solar and poured wine. "I will leave you so that you may get to know one another." She smiled brightly and closed the door behind her.

Geoffrey de Montfort turned to his daughter. "Nan, why don't you find Drewett and have him join us?"

"Of course, Father." She excused herself and left the room.

Tristan now faced Lord Geoffrey, knowing the nobleman had made sure they were alone.

"What would you like to know about me, my lord?" he asked.

"Everything. Where your estate lies. Why you are here. Why you wish Nan to accompany you to your home." He leaned back in the chair and crossed his arms.

Tristan explained to him where the Leventhorpe lands stood in Essex and of his interest in adding to his stables, thinking to breed horses.

"You certainly came to the right place. Elysande and Michael have spent years building their stock. You can't find a better horse than those born at Sandbourne. But what of your lands, Lord Tristan? Your people? I know the peasants' rebellion severely affected that area several years ago. My eldest son, Ancel, helped put down the revolt."

Tristan steeled himself but decided to answer honestly.

"Aye, my lord, many estates were touched by the uprising. Because of that, I am slowly rebuilding at Thorpe Castle. Parts of the keep were damaged. Our stables were lit on fire and all the horses lost. Many Leventhorpe tenants abandoned the land and marched upon

London. It is a slow process, not only the physical reconstruction but restoring confidence. Seeking the right men as soldiers and finding tenants that can be trusted. Now that I am the earl, I haven't wanted to rush into anything."

The nobleman appraised him. "Good for you. 'Tis smart to take your time and build something to last. That includes your people. How are you fixed for soldiers?"

"I have a small group that I have handpicked. I need a good deal more." Tristan paused. "That leads me to address something with you that I have given considerable thought to."

Lord Geoffrey nodded encouragingly for him to continue.

"I know that Lord Michael served under you at Kinwick. I have asked him a thousand and one questions about how he runs Sandbourne. He tells me everything he knows, he learned at your feet. I have also been most impressed with Drewett Stollars. He is the kind of man I need to bolster Leventhorpe. If you do not offer him a position in your garrison once he becomes a knight, I would be eager to take him on as one of my knights, knowing the training he's received under you."

"Hmm." Lord Geoffrey steepled his fingers as he thought a moment. "I had assumed Drew would stay at Kinwick, but the opportunity you could afford him at Thorpe Castle would speed his growth as a knight and put his leadership skills to better use. Unless, of course, his brother wants him to return home. Family must always come first." He paused. "Somehow I doubt Drew's brother will request him to come home, though."

The earl lowered his hands. "I will notify you when the time comes for Drew's Oath of Knighthood Ceremony. You are most welcome to attend. At that point, you may extend an offer for Drew to join your garrison. I can advise him on the opportunities afforded him there but I will also let him know he is welcome to remain in service at Kinwick."

"Fair enough," Tristan agreed.

The door opened and Nan and Drewett entered, followed by Lord

Michael, who looked happier than Tristan had ever seen him. The two noblemen greeted one another heartily. Tristan could see the affection and respect between them.

"You only brought yourself?" Lord Michael asked. "What good is a visit from you without including Merryn? She is your better half, you know." The earl chuckled.

"My fair Merryn had other things to do," Lord Geoffrey said. He looked to Nan. "But she sends you her love."

"Mother would have been quite proud of me," Nan said and then frowned. "Unfortunately, one of my arrows pierced Lord Tristan's leg." She brightened. "But I used all the skills I learned from her in order to nurse him back to good health. He ran only a slight fever the first day and no sign of infection has appeared."

Lord Geoffrey's brows shot up. "Was your aim off so much? 'Tis very unlike you."

"Nay," Tristan said before Nan continued. "It was my fault. I am the one who got in Lady Nan's way—while she was trying to kill a wild boar. The boar received the better end of the deal," he added.

"And you still wish for Nan to accompany you to Thorpe Castle?"

"Aye, my lord. Lady Nan is a gifted archer and instructor, something my men could use. She also knows quite a bit about horses and can help Sir David with the ones I purchase, as well."

The door swung open and Lady Elysande entered, her arm about a handsome young man.

"Tucker!" Nan cried and embraced her cousin as David Devereux also stepped into the solar.

Tristan introduced himself to the boy and the group talked for several minutes until it came out that David and Nan would be leaving in the morning for Leventhorpe.

"I want to go along," Tucker said eagerly. "It sounds like a grand adventure."

"You just got home, Tucker," Lady Elysande chided. "Besides, with David gone, I can use your help in the stables."

Tristan saw the noblewoman's word was final, as Tucker did not appeal for a different decision from his father. He marveled again at the men in this family and how they treated women as their equals. He glanced to Nan, deep in conversation with David.

Did Tristan look upon Nan as an equal? In many ways, she had proved to be his superior. He wondered what it would be like to be wed to such a remarkable woman then pushed the thought aside. Nan de Montfort deserved a man who would love her. Tristan had no love in his heart.

But desire? He had that in abundance for the raven-haired beauty.

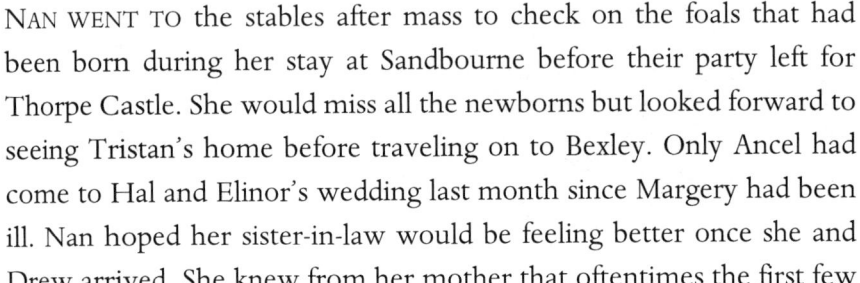

NAN WENT TO the stables after mass to check on the foals that had been born during her stay at Sandbourne before their party left for Thorpe Castle. She would miss all the newborns but looked forward to seeing Tristan's home before traveling on to Bexley. Only Ancel had come to Hal and Elinor's wedding last month since Margery had been ill. Nan hoped her sister-in-law would be feeling better once she and Drew arrived. She knew from her mother that oftentimes the first few months after conceiving a babe made a woman sick and sluggish.

She greeted a passing stable boy who said, "If you're looking for Lord Tristan, my lady, he's down there," and pointed.

Curiosity filled her. They would ride out soon and she wondered if everything was all right with his horse. She passed Skybourne's stall and saw the horse inside it—but no Tristan. Continuing on, she found him leaning into Ginger's stall, his voice low as he spoke to the mare. Nan suppressed a smile.

Who would have thought Tristan Therolde would be telling a pair of horses goodbye?

Yet he did so now, speaking to both Ginger and Argo, her budding foal. A wistful feeling ran through her. Nan had tamped down the attraction she felt for the nobleman, knowing he was not meant for her. Tugging at her heartstrings in this way only made it harder for her to continue to push aside her growing fondness for him.

He looked up, a sheepish grin on his face.

"I see you have caught me in the act," he said. "I am saying my farewells to all the mares and their offspring, especially the ones that I helped in foaling."

"I think it's nice of you to do so, my lord. I'm here for the very same reason." She paused. "Would you like company?"

"Aye."

They strolled through the stables, seeing the designated horses before returning to the keep. Nan had already packed the little she would bring on the journey, just an extra pair of pants and a different gypon and one cotehardie and smock. She'd rolled them up and stuffed them in her satchel, which she would attach to her saddle horn. Elysande had promised to send her trunk directly to Bexley since her stay there would prove much longer.

Reaching the great hall, she said, "I'm going to eat something quickly. I will meet you outside soon. I know David and Drew will be gathering up the horses we are taking with us."

"I've told Toby and Stephen to help with that," Tristan said.

They parted ways and she ate some bread and sipped ale while Elysande gave her last minute instructions over the care of the horses that would accompany them to Essex.

"You know, Elysande, all these horses will be perfectly fine. David will be there. Drew and I can assist him. Both Sir Stephen and Sir Toby are most capable knights." She squeezed her cousin's hand. "You worry too much."

"And you don't worry enough," Elysande quickly retorted.

Nan rose, wondering for the first time if Elysande had an inkling of what had passed between her and Tristan. "It's time." She glanced to where her father and Michael sat on Elysande's other side. Both men stood in unison. Her father embraced her, dropping a soft kiss on the top of her head.

"Write to us when you arrive at Thorpe Castle and again before you leave," he told her. "If not, your mother will be frantic."

"And also when I arrive at Bexley," she said. "I believe Margery may be with child again. You know how she gets very ill early on and can't stop retching."

Geoffrey shook his head. "Let's keep that from Merryn for now or she'll be off to Bexley to care for her." He grinned. "I need a little time alone with my wife now that Edward and Rosalyne have left Kinwick and Hal and Elinor are settling in after their wedding, but we will both come for you in a few months. By then, I hope Margery will be able to keep her meals down."

Geoffrey kissed her again. "Be safe, Nan. Stick by Drew. Do your best for Lord Tristan's men and enjoy your time with Ancel and Margery."

They walked to the stables together. David and Drew had the selected horses ready.

"Are you sure you don't wish for any of my men to accompany you, Lord Tristan?" asked Michael. "I can easily summon Sir Martin and Sir Ralph and they could be ready to ride with you. Just say the word."

"Nay," Tristan said. "Six of us should be able to watch out for five horses. We're only two days away from retrieving my sister and less than two after that to Leventhorpe lands."

Elysande pressed sacks of food upon each rider. "Cook has made some things for you to eat while on the road."

Nan allowed Drew to help her onto Nightfoot before he mounted his own horse. She waved to Elysande, Michael, and Tucker and blew a kiss to her father, then they spurred their horses on and rode away from Sandbourne.

The countryside they passed had turned a deep green as June bloomed throughout the landscape. Nightfoot enjoyed the long ride that first day and was still frisky the next morning. Fortunately, she knew her horse well and could control his high spirits.

They stopped mid-afternoon in order to water and rest the horses and drew from the food the Sandbourne cook had sent.

As they sat facing each other in a circle, Nan asked Tristan, "How long until we reach where your sister fosters?"

He used his baselard to cut a slice of cheese. "We should be at

Shercastle in another three hours or so."

"What is your sister's name?" David asked, tearing a piece of crust from some bread.

"Gillian," replied Tristan. "She has fostered with the baron and baroness for many years. Lady Magdalen is quite fond of Gillian and has threatened not to give her back to me."

"Would it possible for her to remain at Shercastle?" Nan asked. "Do they have a son she might wed?"

"They have two sons but both are spoken for. One is already wed and one is supposed to marry this summer."

"Is your sister betrothed?" Nan was curious since she knew Tristan himself wasn't and remembered he had spoken of his obligation to see his sister wed.

"Nay. In fact, I hope to find her a husband in the near future."

Nan noticed he glanced David's way when he said this. Her cousin was too busy eating a fruit tart to have noticed. She wondered if Tristan might be considering David as his future brother-in-law.

Once Drew and Sir Stephen brought the horses back from the nearby stream, everyone remounted and continued toward Shercastle. Hours later, they were granted permission to enter the gates of the castle.

"More than likely, Lord Wymun will ask us to stay the night. Let's ride to the keep first," Tristan told the others. "If the invitation is extended, we'll need to get all the horses settled in their stables."

Their party rode through both baileys. Nan saw a couple awaiting them, standing arm in arm. A young woman stood slightly apart from them. As they drew near, she knew beyond a doubt that this was Tristan's sister. She was very petite and possessed the same tawny hair her brother had. As Nan dismounted, she noticed Gillian's eyes weren't the brown rimmed in gold of her brother's but the light blue color of a summer sky instead.

The baron and baroness greeted them and, as Tristan predicted, asked them to remain overnight in order to start their journey to Thorpe Castle afresh in the morning. He agreed. Only then did Tristan turn to address his sister.

"How do you fare, Gillian?" he asked formally, making no move to embrace her.

"I am well, Tristan. Thank you for coming to retrieve me."

Nan was stunned. She assumed that it had been months since the pair had seen one another yet neither seemed inclined to touch the other or show any outward sign of affection. If she had been separated from any of her siblings for that long, Nan would have clung to them, laughing and crying at the same time, happy to be in their presence again.

Instead, Lady Gillian turned abruptly without a further word and followed Lord Wymun and Lady Magdalen.

Drew edged next to her. "Do you find that a bit odd?" he whispered.

"I most certainly do."

Tristan instructed his men to move all of the horses to the stables, both the ones they'd ridden and those he'd purchased from Lady Elysande.

"I'll help you," Drew offered.

It was only then that Nan glimpsed the look on her cousin's face. David's eyes followed Lady Gillian's progress as she made her way up the stairs to the keep. Wordlessly, he began to follow.

Nan chuckled to herself. It seemed David might be smitten with Gillian Therolde.

CHAPTER 11

TRISTAN QUICKLY FIGURED out that David Devereux was interested in his sister. The knight had sat next to Gillian and shared a trencher at the evening meal with her, their heads close together as they spoke in quiet tones. Tristan watched the pair as they retreated to a corner of Shercastle's great hall after they finished eating and continued their conversation until Tristan finally interrupted them, telling Gillian it was time to retire since they would rise early and leave at first light the next morning.

Since Gillian had no horse and had never learned to ride, David immediately volunteered the next day to be responsible for her, taking her up into his saddle. Twice when they stopped to rest their horses, the two strolled the nearby woods, side-by-side. No one said anything but it was obvious to all present that the couple was taken with one another.

Tristan now stood across from the young knight as they finished up their watch guarding the camp's inhabitants and horses. Soon, Toby and Stephen would come to relieve them so they could get a few hours of sleep before they broke camp. Tristan noted how seriously David took his sentry duty. He had not uttered a word since it began. The knight's eyes swept across the dark at intervals, ready to fight at a moment's notice.

This was a good man and soldier. David came from a respected family. He would make a fine husband for Gillian, while Lord Michael and Lady Elysande would be kind to her. Tristan believed when it came time for David Devereux to return to Sandbourne, he would speak to Tristan about wedding Gillian. For now, he would take Lord Michael's attitude and say nothing to either of them.

A brushing sound captured his attention and he knew his men reported for duty. He told them all was well and left them to return to their camp. The fire's embers burned lowed but he could make out the shapes of his remaining companions. Gillian slept on her side, her hands curled under her chin as if she were in prayer. Nan and Drew both slept on their backs, Drew's sword next to his right hand and Nan's bow and quiver resting on each side of her. David went and lay several feet from Gillian, unsheathing his sword and placing it within reach.

Tristan eased to the ground, his eyelids heavy and his body tired from long days in the saddle. His healing thigh had held up well and hadn't troubled him during their travels. He closed his eyes and drifted off to sleep.

Until something woke him. A hissing. He opened his eyes and looked around without sitting up. In the shadows, Tristan saw Nan and Drew slinking off. For a moment, jealousy flared within him. He knew the two were friendly and that this was no romantic tryst they sneaked off to. But where were they going in the dead of night?

He grasped the hilt of his sword and quickly touched David's shoulder. The knight shot up, his sword in hand.

"There's trouble," he whispered. "Stay with Gillian."

Determination filled the young man's eyes. "I will keep her safe, my lord."

Tristan nodded and then followed Nan and Drew. As he did, he heard faint sounds coming from the area where they had hobbled the horses.

Someone was there. Someone who didn't belong.

Why hadn't Stephen or Toby called out a warning?

In the quiet of the cool night, the whiz of an arrow broke the stillness, followed by a loud grunt. Then a cry of pain and astonishment. Tristan began running, knowing Nan and Drew did the same. The clang of two swords striking together sounded three times, then someone uttered a loud groan.

As Tristan reached the horses, he saw men scrambling onto mounts and taking off. Nan and Drew slice through the loose rope around their horses' legs and jumped onto their backs to follow. He glanced around and saw two strangers lying on the ground. An arrow protruded from the chest of one. The other lay still in a pool of blood spilling from him. Tristan turned and froze.

Toby and Stephen lay sprawled on the ground, their eyes staring vacantly up at the night sky.

"No," he moaned hoarsely. "No."

The three had fostered together and been the closest of friends. He had known them over a score, from childhood to becoming men. Tristan trusted only a handful of people. These two were the ones he had turned to in his darkest of days. They had stood by him and supported him and come to live at Leventhorpe when he became its earl.

And now these treasured friends lay dead.

Rage surged through him as he freed Skybourne. Sheathing his sword, Tristan leapt onto the animal. He drove the beast hard, miraculously catching up to Nan and Drew and the men they chased. As he came close, he watched Nan pull an arrow from the quiver slung over her shoulder. She tossed her reins to Drew, who caught them and held them steady as Nan fixed the arrow and drew back her bowstring. The arrow sailed through the air, striking the first of three riders in the back of his neck. The man fell from his saddle.

Again, Nan released an arrow and struck another man in the same place. His hands dropped the reins and flew to his neck before he rolled lifelessly to the ground.

Their three horses galloped past both of the fallen men. Tristan pulled abreast of Nan and Drew as she yanked a third arrow from her quiver. How she could ride at breakneck speed and fire with such accuracy amazed Tristan, much less that Drew could keep her horse on course as he did. The two moved as one, needing no words between them. He realized their years of training together bonded them in a way he might never understand.

Nan's arrow flew through the air again. This time, her aim was off. The arrow alighted in the fleeing man's left shoulder. He glanced over his shoulder at them but continued to race down the road without altering his pace.

She drew another arrow and quickly sent it on its way. Again, she missed bringing down her target. The arrow hit the man's right shoulder. The second injury was enough to cause him to slow his horse and bring it around to face them. He released the reins and held his hands up to show he was no longer a threat to them, grimacing as he did so.

Drew flipped the reins back to Nan and the trio brought their horses to a halt. The squire leapt from his horse and stormed over to the man. He yanked him from the saddle and slammed his fist into the stranger's nose.

As Tristan and Nan dismounted, he said to her, "Your first two shots amazed me, my lady. To ride as you did and shoot so precisely takes great skill. I'm almost disappointed that you didn't kill all three."

"I wasn't trying to *kill* him, my lord," Nan said in exasperation. "We need to question him and find out why he killed Toby and Stephen. Why he and the others wished to steal your horses." She gave him a hard look. "Dead men cannot give the answers we seek."

His awe grew. Tristan realized her arrows had gone exactly where she directed them, while a cool head prevailed, knowing it was important to keep at least one of the thieves alive to interrogate him.

The man had crumpled to the ground. Drew latched on to his tunic and jerked the robber to his feet. Blood gushed from his mangled nose.

"Look at me," Nan commanded, her voice strong and firm.

Slowly, the man's head rose. He gave her a withering look as he glanced at the bow in her hand.

"*You're* the one firing the arrows at me? God's Bones! Brought down by a woman." He spat on the ground in disgust.

"Aye. I killed your friends. Just as you killed two valiant knights."

The man shrugged, causing him to wince in pain. "What of it?"

"Answer my questions and I may allow you to live."

He smirked at her.

Nan kicked him in the balls.

The man howled and fell to the ground. She stepped toward him and placed her boot atop one of the arrows still protruding from him.

"Were you and your men trying to steal our horses?"

He glared at her. Nan stomped on the arrow, driving it deeper into him until it almost disappeared.

"Aye!" he roared.

"Did you take them for yourself or did someone else instruct you to steal them?"

The thief took a moment and then said, "We was going to sell them. Me and the others sell what we can get our hands on but sometimes we know places to go. Where we sold to before."

"Name who you would have taken them to first," she demanded.

When he didn't answer immediately, Nan wrapped her hands around the arrow jutting from his left shoulder.

Seeing that she would rip it from him, the man cried out, "The baron! He'll always buy good horseflesh, especially at a bargain price."

"What baron?" Tristan asked, a chill invading his soul.

"Wycliffe," the thief said, breathing hard. "The Baron . . . of Wycliffe."

Petyr Medford, Baron of Wycliffe, was the widower two estates from Leventhorpe that he had considered as a husband for Gillian. The nobleman wielded a strong influence in Essex, which is why Tristan thought it might be a suitable match, despite the disparity in their ages. Disappointment filled him, knowing the nobleman showed one face to the world and was a much different man than the one he portrayed. It only reinforced to Tristan how no one could be trusted. Thank the Living Christ he had not betrothed Gillian to the baron.

Nan turned to him. "Do you know this man, Tristan?"

He nodded. "He is an acquaintance of mine." Looking back at the robber, he asked, "How many times have you sold stolen goods to

Wycliffe?"

"What's it to you?" the highwayman snarled. "You still have all of your horses. We didn't get a single one. And neither will the baron."

Something in Tristan snapped. Moving swiftly, he unsheathed his sword and ran it through the man, pinning him to the ground. Blood bubbled up from his mouth, spilling down his chest. He trembled violently then stilled. Tristan jerked the sword from him.

"That's for Toby. For Stephen. My friends."

Tristan wiped his sword clean and returned it to his side. Wordlessly, he walked away and mounted Skybourne. He returned to their camp, while Nan and Drew gathered the three highwaymen's horses.

David and Gillian met him. Tristan saw the anguish in her face and knew she had seen the bodies of the two dead knights, men she had known since she was a child.

"I am sorry, Tristan," Gillian said quietly.

He nodded in acknowledgement. Though he wanted to take his sister in his arms and comfort her, she turned away. It was David Devereux who followed her and put an arm about her as she sobbed.

Tristan waited until Nan and Drew returned and told them, "We can reach Thorpe Castle by the end of the day. I cannot bury them here. I must take them home." He swore to himself that he would visit their graves every day and never forget the friendship these two men had offered him and the loyalty they had given him.

"I'll stay with Gillian," Nan said, looking to Drew. "Help Lord Tristan prepare the bodies for travel."

She went to his grieving sister and sent David Devereux over. The three men secured the bodies to their horses. Drew draped a blanket over each man.

They started out for Leventhorpe immediately afterward. No one mentioned eating. Tristan doubted he could have swallowed a single breadcrumb. The group rode in silence the entire day until they arrived at Thorpe Castle.

It was the second darkest day of Tristan's life.

CHAPTER 12

Nan brought Nightfoot to a halt as their group approached the stables. Though not nearly as large as that at Sandbourne, the structure appeared to be fairly new. Everyone dismounted and while Gillian stayed back, the rest of them brought all of the horses into the building, from their own to the ones which had belonged to the dead highwaymen, as well as the group Tristan had purchased from Sandbourne. It surprised her how many open stalls stood available and she wondered if a bulk of the Leventhorpe horses were held in a pasture nearby during good weather.

David and Drew removed the bodies of the two dead knights. Tristan had Stephen and Toby placed in an empty stall and covered with blankets. She wondered why they had not taken the bodies directly to the chapel but didn't question Tristan. His eyes, usually so warm and vital, had taken on a wintry look ever since the death of his friends.

Together, they walked to the keep. She brought her satchel, not wanting to leave it in the stables, but left her other weaponry in a corner of Nightfoot's stall. Nan saw no activity present in the bailey and decided everyone must be at the evening meal. Entering, they came to stand at the doors to the great hall.

Suddenly, a broad-shouldered man with a head of white hair appeared in the doorway. He wore a black eyepatch over his left eye and she wondered how he had lost it. One lone, pale blue eye sparked with joy as he recognized Tristan and Gillian. Then he took a few more steps toward their party. It struck her that something was off about his gait. Nan noticed one leg of his pants seemed almost empty compared to the other one, its muscles straining against the material. She realized besides the eye, the man also was missing a leg.

"Lord Tristan, Lady Gillian, 'tis very good to see the two of you again," he said.

"Hello, Sir Dawkin," Gillian said politely. "I am happy to see you, as well."

Tristan nodded curtly in acknowledgement of the older man. Then he indicated his companions. "This is Sir Dawkin. He is my captain of the guard and has been at Thorpe Castle most of his life. You will not find a more loyal man on Leventhorpe lands."

The nobleman turned back to his captain. Without preface, he said, "Toby and Stephen were killed early this morning while on sentry duty. We have brought them home for burial."

Tears welled in the knight's good eye. "I am most sorry to hear this, my lord. I will send to North Colnbourne for a priest to say their burial mass."

Send for a priest? Nan couldn't imagine why a priest needed to be summoned when there should be one in residence at Thorpe Castle. She bit her tongue to keep from asking why.

"Thank you," Tristan said. "If you will assign chambers to my guests, I would appreciate it." Without introducing them, he turned away and mounted the stone stairs leading to the upper floor, a heavy air of sadness enfolding him.

Once again, questions filled Nan. Why would a knight in charge of the castle's soldiers be involved in deciding where guests would stay? With Tristan being unmarried, who was in charge of the domestic affairs of the keep? Did he even employ a steward?

David shot a questioning glance in her direction and then said, "I am Sir David Devereux of Sandbourne. This is Drewett Stollars, a squire fostering with Lord Geoffrey de Montfort of Kinwick. We would be happy to stay in the barracks with your men, Sir Dawkin." He indicated Nan. "And this is my cousin, Lady Nan de Montfort."

The knight wiped his eye with his sleeve. "Ah, I am pleased to meet you all. We have plenty of room in the barracks, Sir David, and would be happy for you both to join us there." He turned to Gillian. "We knew you would arrive soon, my lady, since your trunk came this morning. Your bedchamber has been made ready for you. Should we have Lady Nan stay in the solar?"

"With Lord Tristan?" Nan blurted out, then felt her cheeks flame.

"Nay," Gillian reassured her. "Tristan never sleeps there. He has kept to the bedchamber he shared with my brothers growing up."

"Even though he is the Earl of Leventhorpe?" she asked, finding it peculiar that the solar stood empty.

"Aye," Gillian confirmed. "He . . . prefers it. I think he feels closer to our brothers by doing so."

Since Tristan had never mentioned any siblings beyond Gillian, Nan had no idea how many Therolde brothers there were or where they had gone. They didn't seem to be present at Thorpe Castle.

Sir Dawkin frowned. "Mayhap Lady Nan might stay with you tonight, my lady," he suggested to Gillian. "That would give time to prepare the solar for her." The soldier told Nan, "It has not been used for several years. I'm afraid you would be covered in dust if you ventured inside it, my lady."

"Do you mind sharing with me, Nan?" Gillian asked.

"Of course not."

Sir Dawkin extended a hand. "If you would like to come partake in the evening meal, we had only begun when you arrived."

They followed him into the great hall. The dais was empty.

"I think it best that we join the other soldiers," David said, and he led Drew to where they sat at a few tables.

Nan caught the disappointment on Gillian's face as they moved to the dais. Once they were seated, a servant brought a trencher for them to share and poured ale. Nan looked around the large room, surprised that it was only about half-filled.

"Where are all of your workers and tenants?" she asked.

Gillian shrugged. "I suppose they are all here. I have no idea how many reside on the estate. I never thought to ask."

A thousand questions whirled through her brain. Nan voiced the first that came to mind. "How large is Leventhorpe?"

"I would venture about the size of Shercastle and its lands." Gillian took a sip of her ale.

Nan knew if that were the case, many more people should be present in the great hall. Between the empty space here and the numerous vacant stalls they'd seen, she gathered the castle had only a handful of servants and that much of the land wasn't occupied by tenants.

But why?

Her mother hadn't tried to curb Nan's curious nature but she had taught her daughter good manners. As much as Nan wanted to pepper Gillian with questions, she wouldn't.

At least for now.

She turned to her meal. Everything tasted bland and the meat was so tough, she chewed endlessly before being able to swallow it. If this was what their cook produced on a regular basis, Nan might have to go into the kitchens and give the woman a lesson or two in how to prepare food.

They ate in silence. Nan could see Gillian was weary from not only the long day, but also from the emotional toll the deaths of Sir Stephen and Sir Toby had brought.

When the girl finished eating she excused herself, urging Nan to stay in the great hall and visit with Sir Dawkin while she made sure her bedchamber was suitably prepared and that the solar would be the first priority in the morning.

Nan found herself standing with Sir Dawkin near the fireplace and decided to explain why she was at Thorpe Castle since Tristan had abandoned them.

"I'm sure you knew that Lord Tristan journeyed to Sandbourne to purchase horses," she began.

"Aye, my lady. We have plenty of empty acreage that can be used as pastureland for horses. The earl discussed with me about buying and breeding horses."

"My cousin, David, is the heir to Sandbourne. He knows a great deal about horseflesh and their care, which is why Lord Tristan asked him to come to Thorpe Castle for a few weeks and impart his knowledge to your stable hands."

"A good decision," agreed Sir Dawkin. "The workers could use Sir David's help in establishing the stables." He paused. "We lost a good many horses several years ago. When the peasants revolted."

It hit Nan that Essex had been the center of the rebellion, which had spread to London and beyond. Many serfs in Essex had abandoned their cottages and marched on London, burning large parts of the city and murdering hundreds. Ancel had seen the fires and dead bodies firsthand and had helped quell the rebellion as part of the army King Richard sent out. He had only shared a few stories of those days with Nan but his words remained vivid in her mind.

She now understood why Leventhorpe was in such poor shape. Many servants and tenants must have left the estate and never returned. Because of the revolt and the thousands lost to the Black Death in the years before that, some estates found it difficult to find enough workers to farm the land. Some had turned toward raising sheep. Will all the acreage standing idle at Leventhorpe, no wonder Tristan had thought to raise horses on the property.

Sadness filtered through her. She had no idea how long he'd been the earl, much less how his father had dealt with the results of the rebellion and the damage caused. Obviously, the stables had been burned and that was why they looked so new.

She pushed aside those thoughts and continued her conversation with the captain of the guard. "Lord Tristan also asked that I accompany him home to work with his soldiers."

Sir Dawkin's thick, white brows shot up. "Doing what, my lady? Teaching them to dance?"

Nan swept a hand down. "I'm sure you noticed my attire, my lord. Though I usually don a cotehardie to dine in, I am most comfortable in men's clothes. Though I have learned a great deal about horses over the years from the Countess of Sandbourne, my cousin, my true skills lie in the area of archery."

"Indeed." The knight looked doubtful.

"When Lord Tristan arrived at Sandbourne, I was already present working with the earl's soldiers and those boys fostering with him. I am an expert with a crossbow, bow and arrow, and the longbow."

The older man snorted, shaking his head in disbelief. "I don't see how, my lady. Forgive me."

Nan gave him a gracious smile. "Everywhere I go, I understand that I must win men over. Still, your liege lord invited me to his home and I will be working with your men in the training yard and the butts. I thought you should know before I showed up tomorrow morning."

His one eye made him appear more perplexed by her words. "I will give you the opportunity to prove yourself to our soldiers, my lady. 'Tis the best I can do." Giving her a last look, he said, "Will you excuse me?"

"Of course."

She watched the knight leave, noting how he compensated for his missing limb as he walked. Somehow, he must have fashioned and attached some type of wooden leg to himself so that he could walk. How odd. Tristan had very few soldiers for such a large estate and his captain of the guard was someone who had been severely injured at some point—but was still in charge of the soldiers at Leventhorpe.

Nan told herself that she would bide her time for now but before she left, she would find the answers to her many questions.

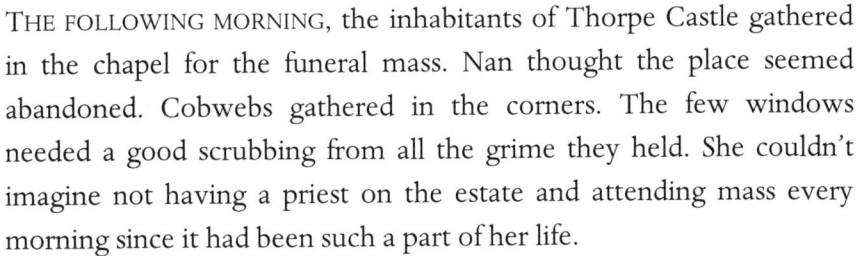

THE FOLLOWING MORNING, the inhabitants of Thorpe Castle gathered in the chapel for the funeral mass. Nan thought the place seemed abandoned. Cobwebs gathered in the corners. The few windows needed a good scrubbing from all the grime they held. She couldn't imagine not having a priest on the estate and attending mass every morning since it had been such a part of her life.

As the priest droned on in Latin, she kept her eyes focused on Tristan and Gillian. They were next to one another but never touched the other. No arm of support around her shoulders or taking hands and drawing comfort. In a way, they appeared to be strangers instead of family members. Nan thought back to the joyous reunions over the years whenever she and her siblings reunited and found it hard to understand these two Theroldes.

She thought to say a prayer to the Virgin Mary asking for strength and patience as she would begin anew with a group of men who would not respect her. Some might even refuse to listen to her instruction. It would take time and demonstrating her skills to convince the Leventhorpe soldiers of her worth. Nan begged the Virgin to be with her and guide her as she sought to prove herself to strangers.

Mass ended and people began filing from the chapel. She noted that no one, not even the soldiers present, offered any words of comfort to Tristan. From what she gathered, he had known the two knights for many years. She couldn't imagine his suffering for she was fortunate enough not to have endured such a heavy loss.

Returning to the great hall, those gathered broke their fast. Once again, she shared her trencher with Gillian while Tristan had one to himself. Gillian told Nan that she would make sure the solar would be readied for her.

"Are you certain I should stay in it?"

"Aye. 'Tis the nicest chamber in all of Thorpe Castle." Gillian smiled wistfully. "I only wish you could remain in it permanently—as Tristan's bride."

Nan almost choked on the bread she had just swallowed. Gaining her breath and composure, she asked, "Why would you say such a thing?"

Gillian shrugged. "Because I like you. And I know Tristan does, too."

"Did he tell you that?" Nan demanded.

"Nay. Tristan never tells me much of anything." Gillian glanced over at her brother. "He keeps his thoughts and feelings to himself but I still know him. He laughs more readily around you. Knowing you has been good for him—and me. I have longed so many times for a sister."

Gillian paused. "Forgive me, Nan. I grow maudlin. I am like Tristan and rarely express my feelings." She sighed. "I love my brother. Truly, I do. But I can't seem to express that to him. If I did, I fear he would push me away or punish me."

Nan took the girl's hand. "I have noticed how formal you and Tristan are toward one another. You never embrace. You must have been separated for months before we arrived at Shercastle and yet neither of you showed any emotion when you reunited."

"It has been like that since I can remember," Gillian said softly. "Even more so since my parents died." Her lips trembled.

For a moment, Nan thought the girl might share a confidence with her. Instead, Gillian sprang to her feet, insisting she needed to speak with the cook and supervise the work in the solar. She fled the great hall.

Tristan rose. "Are you ready to go to the training yard?"

Nan stood. "I need to stop by the stables first to retrieve my bows."

"Then I will see you in the yard."

He stepped from the dais and helped hand her down before walking over to Sir Dawkin. Nan returned to the stables to fetch her gear. Part of her dreaded the opposition she would face from Tristan's men yet excitement filled her, knowing how the confrontation would end. She was here to help Tristan in any way she could before she left for Ancel's estate. Hopefully, she could make a difference as he tried to rebuild Leventhorpe.

David fell into step with her and accompanied her to the stables.

"How strong are your feelings for Lady Gillian?" she asked him.

Her cousin laughed heartily. "You never have minced words, Nan. 'Tis one of the things I like most about you." He grew serious. "I already care for Lady Gillian a great deal. She is a sweet girl and it seems as if we have known one another forever."

"What is it you like about her, David?" Nan asked as much for him as for her, thinking how she also had strong feelings for Tristan Therolde, which she doubted she could put into words.

"'Tis not merely her beauty that turns my head, although I'll admit that she is most pleasant to gaze upon," her cousin began. "That beauty goes deep within her. She is kind to everyone, be they servant, soldier, or a member of the nobility. She seems girlish and yet wise beyond her years. When she speaks to you, she isn't thinking other thoughts in her head. You can see she's truly engaged in the conversation, from the way she looks at you to the questions she asks. She has a great thirst for knowledge and is eager to learn any new task."

He paused, shaking his head. "I don't claim to understand her relationship with her brother but I believe she has much love in her heart."

"And you would like to win her heart and show her how to love."

"Aye," he responded, a smile crossing his lips.

"Has she indicated she is interested in you?" Nan already knew the answer to her question but wanted to see how David responded.

"Though she is not good with words, I am certain my feelings are returned."

"Will you speak with Tristan soon?"

David nodded. "I plan to before I return to Sandbourne. I would make a good husband, Nan, I know I would. I have had the best example in the world, growing up and watching how Mother and Father love one another."

Nan gripped his arm. "You will be a wonderful husband, David. I hope to find a man half your equal, for that would make me very lucky indeed." She pressed a kiss against his cheek.

As she turned to go, he caught her elbow. "And what of Tristan?"

She frowned. "What of him?"

"There is something between the two of you. I see how he looks at you." Concern filled his face. "Do you have feelings for him, Cousin?"

Nan refused to admit aloud the depth of her feelings for a man she could never wed.

"Tristan Therolde is not for me, David," she said, her voice thick with emotion. "What I want—what I need—and what Tristan can provide are worlds apart."

She pulled away from him and hurried away. David caught up to her, keeping silent, which Nan was grateful for. They arrived at the stables and Nan collected her weapons. Waving farewell to David, she hurried to the training yard. As she drew near, she quickly counted the number of men she saw. Tristan needed many more knights to secure a strong defense for his home. The ones present were either very young—which meant inexperienced—or very old. With no pages or squires in training, she worried about the survival of his estate.

Tristan stood on the raised platform addressing his men. Nan realized he spoke of her and the contributions she would make to their training. An air of restlessness blanketed the soldiers.

"I ask that you give Lady Nan your full attention when she works with you in small groups or even one-on-one," he said. "You will be surprised how she will help us."

A grumbling permeated the yard. Nan knew she had her work cut out for her.

"Ah, here she is."

Tristan waved her over. He extended a hand. She left her quiver tossed over her shoulder but rested her set of bows on the edge of the platform and allowed him to hoist her up.

Looking out over the crowd, she didn't spy any friendly faces. Nan braced herself. She had faced worse. She believed in her talent and knew, if given a chance, she would prove her worth to this crowd.

"I know it seems odd to find a woman in your training yard," she said, her voice loud enough to carry so that each man could hear her clearly. "I will do my best to pass along the skills I have learned to help the soldiers of Leventhorpe. Lord Tristan has great faith in you and I look forward to our time together."

"How about rutting together?" a voice called out from the far left. "I could show off my skills to you."

Laughter filled the yard. The speaker grinned cheekily.

In one swift movement, Nan claimed her bow and nocked an

arrow, sending it sailing in the soldier's direction. It whizzed by his ear and he cried out. He lifted a hand and clapped it over the ear. Pulling it away, blood stained his fingers. His jaw fell open.

"You nicked me!" he cried, surprise evident in his voice.

Nan shot a series of six arrows in quick succession. They landed and formed a semicircle around his boots.

The soldier looked down at the arrows a hair's breadth from his feet and back up at her in astonishment.

"Any more questions?" she called out.

Silence reigned as king.

"Good." Nan glanced at Tristan. "I think we are ready to start, my lord."

CHAPTER 13

NAN SURVEYED THE archers as the group who had just fired at the earthen targets collected their arrows and the next set of men readied themselves for their turns. A week had passed since she had come to Thorpe Castle and the progress Tristan's troops had made pleased her. After the incident that first day with the jeering soldier, the men had been very respectful toward her, even keen to learn what she had to teach them.

She hadn't spent much time around Tristan since usually she worked in the butts while he remained in the training yard when he wasn't working on the estate's affairs. Nan had learned Tristan also served as the Leventhorpe's steward. She found it hard to believe he carried such a heavy load of responsibility and believed it was because he found it difficult to have confidence in anyone. Her curiosity burned, wondering why he found it hard to trust. To love. To open up to others. His own sister seemed starved for his affection but he held her at arm's length, only politely inquiring about her day at the evening meal. Nan doubted he truly listened to Gillian's response, which only made the girl even more desperate for her brother's attention. At least Gillian now had David in her life, hopefully for good. Nan believed them well suited for one another and didn't foresee Tristan having any complaints against a union between the two. If he wanted his sister wed, he could find no better man than David Devereux to be her husband.

Seeing the first group of archers was now out of the way, she gave the orders in quick succession, telling the second set to ready themselves, nock, mark, draw, and finally loosen their arrows. She repeated the instructions until five arrows had been fired and inspected the targets to see where the arrows had landed and how accurate the archers had been.

"Diggin, you have done the best work today of those present. I commend you."

The soldier grinned broadly and accepted a few slaps on the back from his comrades. He had been the one who mocked her that first day. Now, Diggin was her biggest supporter on the range, eager to listen to her advice and even helping others as he proved to be more competent than his fellow soldiers. Nan would make sure Tristan knew this. Hopefully, Diggin could be given more responsibility to reward his efforts.

"Collect your arrows," she told the men. "That will be it for the day." Pausing, she added, "I think we should hold an archery contest tomorrow, both with crossbows and bow and arrows. It's time to see you put into practice what we've worked hard on this past week."

The soldiers gathered up their equipment and left the butts, excitedly discussing tomorrow's competition and ready to spread the word to the others. Seeing them leave, Nan wished again that Tristan could take on more men and wondered if lack of coin to pay them was an issue.

She returned to the keep and removed her clothes, washing with the water from a jug and placing her smock and cotehardie over her head. Smoothing them into place, she headed down to the great hall for the final meal of the day. Gillian already sat upon the dais and Nan joined her. She'd gotten to know the girl fairly well during their shared meals. Gillian proved to be kind and friendly and not nearly as shy as she had been when they'd first met at Shercastle. Nan hoped her influence was bringing the girl out of her shell.

Gillian greeted her warmly. "How did your training go today, Nan?"

"Exceedingly well. In fact, we're holding an archery contest tomorrow morning. Mayhap you would enjoy attending it to see the men's progress."

"Will Sir David be there?" she asked eagerly.

"He could be," Nan said, not bothering to hide her smile. "Would that please you?"

Gillian took her hand. That gesture alone touched Nan's heart, knowing how withdrawn and undemonstrative the young noblewoman had been such a short time ago.

"Nan, I must tell you something. I have to tell someone and you are my closest friend." Her eyes darted to the area where the soldiers sat and a smile lit her face. Nan assumed she had spied David.

"I hope to wed your cousin," Gillian revealed. "I think . . . I believe . . . oh, I *know* that I am in love with him."

Nan squeezed her hand. "That's marvelous news, Gillian. Have you spoken to your brother about your feelings?"

Tristan had yet to arrive in the great hall, which led Nan to believe this was why Gillian spoke so openly about her feelings for David.

"Not yet. David urged me to wait until he has met with Tristan." She sighed. "I cannot believe this has happened to me. I never thought it could. I didn't know . . . I didn't think . . . that love really existed. My parents . . . well, they were courteous toward one another, but I never saw any true affection expressed between them."

"Most arranged marriages are that way," Nan said. "But I will tell you now that you are marrying into a most romantic family, Gillian. Love matches abound." She thought a moment. "This means you will come to live at Sandbourne. Oh, you will adore Elysande and Michael. They will love you like a daughter of their own. I'm so happy for you and David."

"I only hope Tristan agrees to the match," Gillian said. "I am nervous about that."

"You are of an age to wed and, as your guardian, 'tis his responsibility to see you settled," Nan assured her. "I am sure he will respond favorably to David's petition."

"Tristan told me the last time I left for Shercastle that it would be the end of my fostering days and that I would not be returning to Lady

Magdalen's care. He hinted that he would begin to look for a husband for me. Oh, Nan, it must be David. It must!"

Nan reflected on the day they departed from Shercastle. If Gillian had fostered with Lord Wymun and Lady Magdalen for years, she wondered why the girl had not been more emotional when she left the couple's care. Quickly, Nan uttered a prayer of thanks to the Virgin for how very different her upbringing had been from the Theroldes. That made her think of where Tristan slept and she decided to work this into their conversation.

"You had mentioned your brothers on a previous occasion but not where they are. Have they become knights and serve on different estates? Will they be able to attend your nuptial mass?"

Tristan entered the great hall and came to the dais, inclining his head to them both. He took a seat and reached for the pewter cup before him.

Gillian turned her head away from him and faced Nan. The stricken look on her face and the tears welling in her eyes caused Nan's throat to thicken with emotion, seeing her new friend's distress.

"They are no longer with us," she said, her voice quivering.

"They have all passed on?" Nan gently inquired.

"Aye."

Gillian took in a deep breath. "Will you excuse me? I am not feeling hungry tonight." With that, Gillian hurried from the great hall.

Guilt oozed through Nan for upsetting the girl. She looked up as a servant began to set a trencher down in front of her. The girl seemed confused with Gillian having left.

Nan glanced to her right and saw Tristan, silent as always.

"Lord Tristan and I will share a trencher this evening," she told the servant and then slipped into the seat beside him.

He nodded at her again and asked, "How do you think the training is going with my men?"

"I think very well," she told him and decided to broach what had been on her mind. "Have you ever thought of adding more men to your barracks? With such a large estate, I'm sure you can be stretched thin at times when men are patrolling the roads and on duty at the wall walk."

"If I could find more qualified soldiers, I would be more than happy to add them," he confided. "But 'tis not always easy to find men who possess the necessary skills—and the loyalty required."

"Mayhap my father could help," Nan suggested. "Or Michael. Even my brothers. Ancel is Earl of Mauntell and Edward is Baron of Shallowheart. If each of them could spare a man—or even two—then that would give you a strong foundation to build upon. I promise you all of them would be well trained."

Tristan looked stunned by her proposal. "I would never ask that of anyone, much less your family." Color rose in his cheeks.

"But I can," she said quickly. "Especially with Sir Stephen and Sir Toby gone, you have a great need to supplement the soldiers already in place."

A stricken look flickered across his face before Tristan masked his features again.

"You knew both of them well, didn't you?"

"Aye," he said. "The three of us fostered together. We were as close as brothers. Stephen was a third son and Toby a fourth. They could have returned to their families but instead they came to Leventhorpe when I needed them most. In doing so, they earned my gratitude and appreciation for all they did. They were men I had faith in."

"As you do Sir Dawkin?"

Tristan nodded. "He fostered here as a boy under my grandfather. Came when he was seven and has remained all these years. Dawkin is the only man at Leventhorpe who has my full confidence now."

Sadness flooded Nan. "You're so alone," she said softly, her heart aching for him. She longed to reach out and take his hand to offer him comfort.

He sighed. "Sometimes, I feel the weight of the world crushing me." Tristan excused himself and left the great hall, his meal untouched.

Nan wished she could find a way to help him. He seemed adrift, heading out to sea with no anchor—and no hope of ever finding one.

She finished her meal and watched as the handful of servants collected the remains and others pushed the trestle tables back against the walls. Strolling over to David, the two of them spoke of how quickly the week at Thorpe Castle had passed and that this time next week they would be leaving for Bexley. Nan also told him about tomorrow's archery contest, which he had already heard about several times.

"The men are looking forward to it, Nan. I'll make sure I'm there to assist. Drew, too."

"That will make Gillian happy. She spoke to me tonight about wedding you," she confided to her cousin.

"Aye, we know it's what we want to do," he confirmed. "I plan to speak to Lord Tristan soon and then I will take you to Ancel and Margery. I'll return home and let Mother and Father know of our plans. Oddly enough, Gillian wishes to marry at Sandbourne. She says since it's to be her home, she would like her new beginning with me to start there."

"I can understand why," Nan said. "She has few ties to this place. Did you know she had brothers other than Tristan and that they've all passed away?"

Surprised showed on David's face. "Nay, she has never spoken of them. How many? Why? Was it illness that struck?"

"I don't know. Speaking of them greatly upset her. I would not bring it up unless she does, David. She seemed very fragile."

"I saw her leave the meal early. Is that why?"

"Aye."

"I will go find her now. When she's upset, she likes to walk. I will see you later, Nan. Thank you for telling me."

Once David left, Drew motioned her over. Her friend had split his time at Leventhorpe between helping her in the butts and David in the stables and pasture.

"How about a game of chess? We haven't played in a good while."

"You miss losing, Drew?" Nan teased.

"We'll see about that."

They played two games, each winning one.

Drew yawned. "It's getting late and I grow weary. That's always when you take advantage of me," he said. "Promise me we'll play again tomorrow night."

"Prepare to lose."

"Oh, you will be challenged beyond your wildest dreams," Drew promised.

Nan left the great hall and returned to the solar. It still seemed odd to be sleeping in it. She believed Gillian had done most of the cleaning herself since so few servants were visible. Nan had made a point of thanking Gillian and Tristan for her accommodations.

Looking around, she thought that someday Tristan would move into these rooms. Here, he would be surrounded by family and hopefully a wife who would finally make him happy.

Nan wished she could be that woman.

She had fought against her attraction to him. It had helped that they hadn't spent much time around each other since her arrival at Leventhorpe. But sitting next to him tonight? All the strong feelings had returned in abundance. She realized she needed to leave Thorpe Castle soon before she couldn't hide it anymore from him—or others.

Unplaiting her hair, she combed through it and left it loose as she did every night. Most women chose not to but Nan loved the feel of the silken locks surrounding her. She removed her cotehardie and left her smock on to sleep in. Drawing back the curtains from the bed, she slipped under the bedclothes.

Sleep failed to come.

Restlessly, she tossed and turned. Mayhap it was the upcoming contest that had her on edge. Or the idea of soon being with Ancel and Margery and their children. Then she finally admitted to herself that it was Earl of Leventhorpe that had her tied into knots. Why she was drawn to a man who was nothing like what she wanted bothered her. Nan hoped to find love, just as her parents and siblings had. She wished to wed a man who loved her as much as she loved him. One who was happy and open with his feelings.

The opposite of Tristan Therolde.

Throwing back the bedclothes in frustration, she decided to go to the kitchen and find something to eat. She had picked at her dinner after Tristan left. Once her empty belly was filled, she might be able to fall asleep.

Nan went to the door and opened it. She hesitated, wondering if she should put on her gypon and pants, and then decided at this late hour no one would be up. Besides, her smock covered her to her ankles. Only her bare feet showed and everyone at Thorpe Castle had seen them by now since she usually had her boots off the entire time she trained with the men.

A few flickering torches in the corridor lighted her way as she stealthily moved along. Then she stopped.

What was that?

A low moan from faraway sounded. Immediately, she thought someone was in pain and needed help. Though she was no healer like her mother or Alys, Nan knew enough to help someone who was sick. She listened again and determined where the groans came from and pushed open the door.

A lone candle burned near the bed in the small chamber. Nan hurried over and realized it was Tristan making the harsh noise. His body moved restlessly as he murmured something she couldn't understand. Then he began flailing, his arms fighting the bedclothes as he continued to speak nonsense. She perched on the bed next to him and grabbed his wrists, easing his arms down next to his head as she leaned over him, her hair spilling around him.

He awoke, wild-eyed, his hair damp, sweat glistening on his bare chest. She swallowed hard, seeing the magnificent expanse of muscle and fine dusting of tawny hair against it. She released his wrists and sat back up.

"You were having a nightmare," Nan said. "I heard you from the hallway."

He must have suffered something terrible in his past for it to haunt his dreams so. Her hand went to his shoulder and squeezed it encouragingly.

"It was nothing," he said, his voice rough. "Go to bed."

Nan hated to leave him. He might deny what had occurred while he slept but she knew he was a very troubled soul. Gently, her thumb rubbed his shoulder, wanting to reassure him that he would be all right.

"Please, Tristan, tell me what you dreamed of that upset you so."

"I would never burden you with something so vile," he declared. "Some things are best left unsaid."

"I disagree. If you are troubled, I wish to help you. Speaking of it might—"

"No," he said harshly. "It's too gruesome to talk about. Talking of it would change nothing and only give it power over me. I refuse to be a slave to my past. It's done, Nan. Buried. Leave me be."

He looked so vulnerable in that moment, as the hurt and pain from whatever had occurred enveloped him. She wanted to help him. Comfort him. And then, from out of nowhere, Nan wished he would touch her. Kiss her again.

As if he read her mind, Tristan's hand cupped her cheek, his palm hot against her face. His thumb brushed languidly against her bottom lip, sending a rush of desire racing through her. His other hand pushed into her hair and wound a lock around his fingers.

"Do you know how beautiful you are?" he asked softly.

Nan shook her head. "No one ever told me that."

"Everyone should. Because you are."

Their eyes locked. Nan couldn't have looked away if she tried. Her tongue darted out to moisten her lips and made contact with his thumb. Tristan sucked in a quick breath, his eyes now smoldering with heat. He pulled his hands away.

"Go, Nan. Now," he commanded hoarsely as his eyes darkened in desire.

Her heart pounded rapidly as she continued to stare at him. The air between them crackled with want and need. Nan was afraid what might happen between them would go beyond a kiss if she stayed. She jumped from the bed as if scalded and hurried away back to the solar. Climbing into the now cooled bed, her body burned.

Why couldn't he love her? Why couldn't Tristan be the one for her?

Nan pounded her hands into the pillow as hot tears fell.

CHAPTER 14

THE CONTEST WAS slated to begin an hour after the soldiers had broken their fast. Nan had thought to start it immediately but Diggin came to her on behalf of the other men.

"My lady, we wish to get in a few practice rounds before competition begins."

Nan looked to Tristan. "I defer to you, my lord."

"You may have an hour. No more," he said.

"Thank you, my lord." Diggin bowed and trotted off to spread the news.

Tristan looked around at the activity in the butts. "They certainly seem eager."

"Everyone enjoys competing when they have skills to show. I think you need to award some type of prize for the winner."

"Such as?"

"Whatever you wish. It could be something small, such as your cook making a special sweetmeat." Nan frowned. "Thinking about that, 'twould be more of a punishment."

"You do not like the food at Leventhorpe?" he asked, his brows raising.

"Nay," she said, unable to lie as she laughed.

"What else would you propose?"

She thought a moment. "The winner could be excused from sentry duty for a week. That would cost you nothing. Or you could award a few shillings. Even a crown if you're feeling particularly generous. Something to spur them on."

Gillian had joined them. "I could make the winner a new tunic," she suggested. "I am handy with my needle."

"What a wonderful idea," Nan said. "Don't you think so, Tristan?" She nudged him with her elbow, wanting him to recognize his sister's contribution.

"Aye, that would be most appreciated, Gillian," he said.

His sister gave him a sweet smile. "Only if you want me to."

Nan glared at him and Tristan finally seemed to understand how he should respond. "Then that will be our grand prize for the winner of the bow and arrow competition. The one who wins the crossbow contest will be given a crown."

"Thank you, Tristan!" Joy filled Gillian's face. "I am happy to be a part of today. I will go look now at what materials I have so I can tell the winner what color his new tunic will be."

After she left, Nan said, "You have made her happy by including her. You should do that more often. Seeing the guilty look on your face, I hope that you will take my advice to heart."

"No one speaks their mind to me as you do, Nan."

She shrugged. "What are friends for?" she asked casually.

"Is that what we are—friends?" His eyes bore into hers.

Nan thought back to last night in his bedchamber. How he'd warned her to leave.

And how much she had wanted to stay.

"I would hope we are, my lord."

Drew interrupted them, asking Nan about the targets to be used. She showed him what she wanted done but the entire time they spoke, she sensed Tristan's eyes burning into her back. She returned to his side and they continued watching the men as they warmed up for the competition.

Finally, she said, "I often wear a bracer on the inside forearm of my bow arm. The bowstring can smack hard when released. The bracer helps guard against bruising."

"I am familiar with the practice," Tristan replied.

"It would be a good gesture if you gifted each of your soldiers with a bracer. Most are carved from leather and they can be decorated to show the lord that archer serves. You could use the Therolde family colors or crest."

He nodded thoughtfully. "'Tis an excellent idea, Nan. Thank you. I will see about it soon."

"While you are thinking about that, I have another suggestion."

A crooked smile played about his lips. "Now what?"

"Barnaby has expressed a strong interest in becoming your bowyer and fletcher. He is a competent archer and would like to make all of the bows and arrows for Leventhorpe instead of you purchasing them from others. He's spent several hours quizzing me about the process."

"He has? I don't think I've heard Barnaby say more than three words together since he came to Leventhorpe." Tristan whistled shrilly and the arrows ceased flying. "Barnaby. Come here."

The young soldier hurried over as everyone watched.

"Continue," Tristan said, and the action started once more.

"Aye, my lord?" asked Barnaby, an inquisitive look on his face.

"Lady Nan says you have pestered her about bows and arrows. So tell me, what have you learned from her and why would you wish to make them for Leventhorpe?"

Barnaby grinned. "It starts in the wood, my lord. Yew is the best to use, though ash and elm can work, too. A bowyer must create a pair of curved elastic limbs and join them with a riser. The bowstring connects those limbs. 'Tis best to use hemp, according to Lady Nan, because it's the strongest. If in a pinch, animal guts and sinew also work well." He thought a moment. "Oh, and the strings need to be soaked. In glue. That protects them from moisture."

Barnaby went on to explain how the bowstrings had nocking points marked along them, which allowed archers to mark where their arrow should be fitted to the bowstring before shooting. He happily explained how to fletch an arrow and the benefits of using flint or bone as the arrowhead over horn and metal.

Finally, he wound down. "I have always been good with my hands, my lord. I could easily be both bowyer and fletcher for you."

"You seemed to have learned a remarkable amount in a short time, Barnaby."

The soldier blushed. "Lady Nan is an excellent tutor."

"That she is," Tristan agreed. "I will consider your request."

"Thank you, my lord."

Barnaby returned to his companions, who flocked around him to see what Tristan had wanted from him.

"If you would allow it, Barnaby could come to Kinwick. We have both a bowyer and fletcher. They would be happy to teach him what they know. It wouldn't take long. As you can tell, he's interested and passionate about the subject."

"That sounds reasonable."

"Good. I will write Father about him. In fact, when I leave Leventhorpe, Barnaby can take my missive directly to Kinwick. That way Mother and Father will know I have gone to Ancel and Barnaby can stay for a week and learn what he needs to know."

Tristan scowled. Nan thought he did so because he might actually miss her. They stood so close, almost touching. She could smell the scent of leather and horse on him and something else that was uniquely him. She wished she could shake some sense into this man but having three stubborn brothers, Nan knew that would be impossible. Whatever lay between them was something Tristan would not act upon. She decided that he understood what she wanted was love. Since he could never offer her that, he knew enough to stay away from her.

Bloody fool.

This time she was the one who whistled. The shrill sound pierced the air and brought the motion in the butts to a halt.

"We will start in the next few minutes. All practice ceases now." Nan signaled for David and Drew to begin setting up the targets as they had discussed.

"I have never heard a louder whistle," Tristan marveled. "From a man or a woman."

"Hal taught me how to whistle. He told me it was a skill which would come in handy. Father says my whistle is so loud that I could bring all the soldiers and horses on a battlefield to a halt."

"That was quite extraordinary, my lady," a voice nearby said.

Nan turned and saw Gillian approaching, a stranger next to her. He looked to be just under two score, with dark brown hair and a thin, cruel mouth. He wasn't tall and not very broad but nevertheless he somehow exuded an aura of power. She sensed Tristan stiffen beside her.

"Thank you," she said coolly. "And you are?"

He laughed. "I suppose I should introduce myself. I am Lord Petyr Medford. The Baron of Wycliffe. I am a neighbor of Lord Tristan's." He faced Tristan. "Good morn to you, my lord."

Nan immediately recognized the name. This was the nobleman who traded in illegally gotten goods, including horses. The men who had murdered Tristan's knights and tried to steal his horses had admitted as much. Yet no proof existed that they had been deliberately sent by Lord Petyr, only that he might have purchased the stolen animals from them had they made their way to his doorstep.

"Greetings, my lord," Tristan said, the cold of winter evident in his words. "What brings you to Thorpe Castle? We so rarely see you."

"I came because I've heard tale of a woman who can shoot an arrow better than a man." He smiled at Nan, his teeth even and white. "If I'm not mistaken, that might be you, my lady. An expert archer. And whistler."

Nan kept her head though she wanted to lash out at this stranger. "I know a thing or two about archery. I am Lady Nan de Montfort." She offered him her hand but did not curtsey.

Lord Petyr took it and kissed the leather glove she wore. "Might your father be Lord Geoffrey? And your mother Lady Merryn?"

"They are."

"I have met them at court. Lovely people."

"Thank you."

The nobleman glanced around. "It looks as if you're about to hold a competition." He looked back at Nan. "Are you entering, my lady? I would be delighted to see you in action with your bow."

"Nay. This is a contest for the men of Leventhorpe," Tristan said. "To see what they have learned from the lady. She will judge the contest."

Lord Petyr studied her. "So the rumors *are* true. You truly are an archer." He gave her an appreciative smile. "Mayhap once the winner has been announced you might be kind enough to give me a private demonstration of your skills. I would certainly be interested to see you in action with your bow. Once your stay is completed at Leventhorpe, you might consider coming to teach my men as you have Lord Tristan's."

Nan was happy to say, "I am sorry, my lord, but I have committed to go to the Earl of Mauntell's estate soon. My brother is anxious for me to tutor his men—not yours." She gave him an unapologetic smile.

"We're ready, my lady," called Drew.

Relief filled Nan. "Excuse me." She moved away from the nobleman. For some reason, he made her flesh feel as if ants crawled upon it.

She addressed the group of men, having come to know each of them by name over the past week.

"You have labored long over the last several days. Many of you possess skills you never knew you had. Both contests today will name winners." Nan motioned to Tristan. "My lord, if you would care to share the rewards with your men?"

Tristan stepped forward. "Originally, Lady Nan suggested the winners be provided with a special sweetmeat from Cook. Then she thought better of it since she wanted you to at least try to win."

The soldiers chuckled. Nan was pleased with Tristan's demeanor. Though she knew he took his responsibilities seriously, her father had taught her that showing yourself to be human was a way to bond with others.

"Instead, the victor in the crossbow will claim a crown and a meal I'll purchase for him at the village tavern in North Colnbourne. The bow and arrow winner will receive a crown and a new tunic sewn by

Lady Gillian." Tristan looked to his sister and gave her an encouraging smile.

She held up a bolt of dark material. "I will sew a tunic from this hunter green wool for our winner." She paused. "Unless it is Morys. In that case, my brother will need to buy an extra bolt."

The men laughed heartily. Morys, who was almost as broad as he was tall, stepped forward and took a bow.

"Let's begin," Nan cried.

For the crossbow, they started with the mounds as their targets and then as contestants were eliminated, they moved to cloth targets affixed to coiled, straw mats on portable easels. Morys claimed the championship in the final round.

"Better save up your coin, my lord," the soldier teased. "I can eat my weight easily—and then some."

Next, Nan had David and Drew set up targets marked with five colored rings, which she preferred when bow and arrows were involved.

"We have not used these targets before so they will test your mettle," she told the contestants. "The center circle of the yellow band is worth ten points and if you hit the ring around it, you receive eight. The red band will be worth six and the blue one four. The white band will earn you two points, while the outer black band gives you one."

David stood to the left and Drew to the right so they could help tally the points after each round.

"I hope you can remember all the totals, my lady," Tristan said to her.

Nan chuckled. "If I don't, there will be at least a dozen men out there who will."

She proved correct, as the men kept score. After David or Drew would call out the point earned, Morys would echo it and then remind everyone who was in first place at the moment. The tension and excitement grew as it came down to the last three archers. It didn't surprise Nan when Diggin claimed victory over the other two. The soldiers of Leventhorpe lifted him on their shoulders and paraded around the butts.

"When can I expect my new tunic, Lady Gillian?" Diggin called out as they circled around the range.

"Once I measure you, in two days' time, Diggin," she said, and another cheer went up from the men.

They finally returned Diggin to the ground and Tristan held up a hand. The soldiers fell silent.

"I am more than proud at today's outcome. Every man here has bettered himself. I know you have worked up a hearty appetite."

"And a thirst," a voice called out.

"That, too," Tristan agreed. "There's plenty of food and even more ale awaiting you in the great hall. Wash the grime away and I will see you there for a celebration."

The soldiers broke across the range and ran like children to the troughs in the training yard.

"You have done well, Nan," Tristan said softly. "Very well, indeed."

"Thank you."

He looked to Lord Petyr, who'd remained a silent bystander throughout the matches. "You may join us in our festivities, my lord."

Nan noticed that he did not say the nobleman was welcomed. She bit back a smile at the omission.

"I appreciate your kind invitation," Lord Petyr replied.

They returned to the keep, where the lavish amount of food laid out surprised Nan. She had no idea Tristan would make sure they celebrated today's contest in such a manner. She gave him an appreciative smile. He bowed his head in acknowledgement.

Once he helped seat her on the dais, Tristan sat next to her. Nan hated that Gillian would have to share her trencher with Lord Petyr, but she told herself that it was only for a single meal. Soon, Gillian would be sharing every meal with the man she adored.

Nan only wished she could do the same.

A giddiness filled her as Tristan made sure she received the choicest pieces of meat and the best of each course produced before them.

His thigh brushed against hers, causing a frisson of pleasure to run along her spine. Her belly felt as if butterflies warred within it and her head felt light. She caught Tristan smiling at her and knew, in that moment, that she had done something terrible.

Nan had fallen in love with him.

CHAPTER 15

WHY HAD SHE *done such a foolish thing?*
Nan berated herself. She had known she was physically attracted to Tristan. The two occasions they'd kissed had brought her enjoyment and caused her to yearn for more. She enjoyed being in the nobleman's company, as he was intelligent and had a quick wit. But to fall in love with him?

It was unthinkable.

How he had invaded her heart remained a mystery but any invasion could be repelled. She was a de Montfort—and de Montforts never lost anything.

Except their hearts.

Nan cursed under her breath. She refused to allow herself to be in this position. She would refuse to be in love with him. England was full of thousands of men. Hopefully, a few dozen from so many might prove worthy of her. She was charming and witty and beautiful.

Tristan had told her so.

How she could want to crawl into his lap and kiss the life out of him and still want to claw his eyes out at the same time puzzled her. She glanced up at his profile and her breath caught in her throat. Tristan was handsome beyond description. She couldn't think around him. She needed to escape the merriment and spend time alone trying to sort out her feelings. Even now, there was a call for music and dancing. Men began pushing aside trestle tables. Nan looked and saw Gillian had already abandoned the dais for David's company while a serving wench tugged on Drew's elbow, encouraging him to come dance with her as a tune began to play.

This wasn't something Nan could discuss with her cousin or even her closest friend. She would talk it through in her own company and keep her sentiments a secret from everyone.

Rising, she said, "If you will excuse me, my lord. I have had more than my fill to eat and need to check on Nightfoot. His knee proved tender yesterday and I want to see if any swelling has occurred. If so, I will prepare a poultice for it."

Tristan came to his feet. "If you would like, I can accompany you to the stables."

"Nay, I urge you to stay with your guest. Enjoy the music. Try dancing. It might do you some good."

He glanced over his shoulder at Lord Petyr and back to her. "You will let me know how Nightfoot fares?"

"Aye." She looked to Lord Petyr and gave him and Tristan a small curtsey, which seemed ridiculous to her the moment she did so since she still wore her pants and gypon.

Nan left the noise of the great hall and exited the keep. Outside, the bailey stood empty. Everyone at Thorpe Castle who wasn't a soldier had attended the morning's competition and now all except for a few soldiers along the wall walk on duty made merry in the great hall. She hurried to the stables, where she didn't see a single stable hand present. They, too, had left work for the celebration.

Glad she had the place to herself, she made her way to her horse's stall. On the way, she passed Skybourne, whose head peered out as he nickered softly. Nan stopped to pet Tristan's horse. He bumped her shoulder affectionately.

She laughed. "I have no treat for you today, Skybourne. I promise I will have something for you the next time I visit."

Stepping to the next stall, she entered it. Nightfoot seemed to look at her with sympathetic eyes. Here was a male who would give her unconditional love. Nan wrapped her arms about the horse's neck and pressed her cheek against his warm flesh as the tears came. She cried a few minutes, holding the horse tight, then abruptly stopped.

"What am I doing?" she asked aloud.

She told herself it was ridiculous to weep over someone in this manner. Tristan was a good man—but he wasn't the one meant for her. She might be fortunate to find a husband someday. If she did, she knew it would be one of her own choice. A man who would open up not only his arms but his heart to her. A man whose kisses would cause her pulse to race and her insides to quiver. If not, she had a wide circle of family to care for. She was woman who enjoyed staying busy and always found something to occupy her time. Love might not be in her future but she had a purpose in life.

Determination filled her. She had wasted her last tears on Tristan Therolde. She would finish at Thorpe Castle and move on. Nan stroked Nightfoot's forehead and kissed the bridge of his nose.

"Thank you, my friend," she told the animal, who nudged her as Skybourne had.

Nan stepped outside the stall and closed its gate. Turning, she gasped as she bumped into someone who grabbed hold of her arms to steady her.

It was the Baron of Wycliffe.

Nan took a step back and pushed against the stall. The nobleman dropped his hands but remained too close for comfort.

"How is your horse?" he asked. "I heard you tell Lord Tristan his knee was giving him trouble."

"My horse is fine. I will keep a close eye on him, though."

"I'll bet you keep a close eye on everything around you, my lady. Just as I do." His eyes slid from her face and slowly dragged down her body and back up again.

"I need to—"

"Don't tell me you need to go back to the keep, Lady Nan," he said in silken tones. "When you could stay and spend time with me. Mayhap give me that demonstration I asked about?"

"Nay," she said firmly, leaving no room for further discussion.

Lord Petyr's lips pursed in amusement. "That's what I like about you. Another woman would tell me she didn't think so and give me a pretty smile. You speak plainly, with no pretense."

"I don't need you to like me, my lord. I do need you to step out of my way."

Instead of moving, the baron placed flattened palms against both sides of her head, his body almost grazing hers. Nan's heart raced, sensing the danger as he studied her.

"Shouldn't you return to the great hall, my lord? I am sure you will be missed by your host."

"I told my host too much rich food upset my belly and that I would be in the garderobe for some time." He paused. "I wonder if you are betrothed," he mused.

Fear mingled with anger surged through her. "Whether I am or not is no concern of yours. You are no acquaintance—much less a friend of mine."

"Are you friends with Lord Tristan?"

Nan's chin rose a notch. "I am."

The nobleman tilted his head. "Do you really believe a man and a woman can be friends, Lady Nan?" His voice was whisper soft, like a caress.

"Aye. My closest friend is Drewett Stollars, a squire I have known since we were children. I am also friends with my male and female cousins."

"And Lord Tristan," he added.

"And Lord Tristan," Nan echoed. "We met at Cousin Elysande's home. She is countess to the Earl of Sandbourne."

"I have heard of them both," the baron said, his face now perilously close to hers. She could feel his warm breath on her skin.

Nan had had enough of his games. She lifted her hands to push him away but as she did, he quickly moved against her, trapping them, as he pressed his body into hers and forced his tongue inside her mouth. Revulsion filled her. Her knee slammed into his groin as she sank her teeth into his wandering tongue. His muffled yelp brought a smile to her face as he jerked away. Her arms now free, Nan pushed her palms against his chest will all her might. The nobleman sprawled onto the floor, blood dripping from his mouth.

"You little whore," he said, his eyes black and menacing.

Nan kicked him in his balls for good measure and left the stables. She brought the back of her hand to her mouth and wiped hard, trying to remove the sensation of his lips on hers. She could still taste him, which brought a wave of nausea. Suddenly, she began retching, everything she had eaten at the feast spewing from her. She passed a rain barrel outside the blacksmith's shed and rinsed her mouth, hoping all traces of Petyr Medford were now gone.

Entering the keep, she saw Tristan descending the stairs. The moment he spied her, he rushed to her.

He captured her elbow, his fingers pressing into her flesh. "What's wrong? Are you all right?"

Nan tried to slow her breathing as she told him, "I am fine. But your guest may have stumbled inside the stables."

Tristan's eyes grew murderous. "He *followed* you? *Touched* you?"

"He did. He'll think twice about doing so if he ever encounters me again."

"That man will never be welcomed at Leventhorpe again," Tristan swore.

"An excellent idea, my lord." Nan fled up the stairs and to her chamber. For the first time since she arrived at Thorpe Castle, she latched the solar's door so that no one could enter from the outside.

Finally, she felt safe.

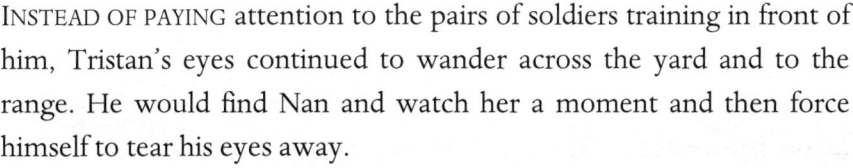

INSTEAD OF PAYING attention to the pairs of soldiers training in front of him, Tristan's eyes continued to wander across the yard and to the range. He would find Nan and watch her a moment and then force himself to tear his eyes away.

Anger still melted within him at Lord Petyr's untoward behavior yesterday. Tristan had gone immediately to the stables, only to see Lord Petyr mounted on his horse. The nobleman rode by him with a friendly wave but Tristan saw the blood on the baron's face and surcoat. Pride in Nan swelled within him.

She had not joined in any activities the rest of the day. He had allowed the soldiers a day of fun and they had stayed in the great hall until late, drinking and singing. Today, many walked around with heavy heads but no one complained.

Tristan looked again to the butts and saw Nan laughing, Drew by her side. Jealousy rippled through him, causing him to lose his head. As Nan moved to help a soldier with his stance, Tristan found himself headed toward the squire.

"Drewett. A word."

Drew set down the target he held and came toward him. "Aye, my lord?"

"'Tis time for you to return to Kinwick."

"What?" Drew looked at him in confusion. "Why?"

How could Tristan explain the envy and resentment he felt when looking at this man and his easy relationship with Nan? His head told him to back away and apologize for the odd outburst but his heart made him press onward.

"I order you to return to Lord Geoffrey. I have no further need of your services." Tristan knew his crazed behavior now would ruin any chances of the squire returning to serve him once he became a knight and yet he couldn't help himself.

Determination filled Drew's eyes. "You cannot order me home, Lord Tristan. I do not serve you, but the de Montforts. I won't go for I am to protect Nan at all costs." His eyes softened. "I always have—and will continue to do so. Though we got off to a rocky start, she is my closest friend. Nan is like family to me, more than my own ever was or could be."

"So you refuse to obey my command?" Tristan said, not disguising how infuriated he was.

"Aye." The squire stood his ground.

"Even though I am the liege lord at Leventhorpe and you stand upon my lands?"

"Aye."

Though admiration filled him, Tristan took a step toward the younger man. "I want you to leave. Now. I will force you if I must."

"If Drew isn't wanted here, neither am I," Nan said.

He saw the disappointment in her eyes and hated that she viewed him this way. Tristan wanted to apologize to them both for his outlandish behavior. Instead, he stormed off without further explanation. He couldn't remain in the training yard. He didn't want to return to the keep.

The stables.

He would find comfort in his horse. Ride until all the madness left him and his temper cooled.

Tristan strode to the building and entered Skybourne's stall. The horse munched on hay and looked at him quizzically.

"What on earth has gotten into you?" a familiar voice asked.

He turned and saw that Nan had followed him. Her fisted hands sat on her waist, emphasizing how small it was. Her black pants hugged her hips snuggly, causing a wave of lust to rush through him.

She marched over to him. "You're like a man gone mad," she exclaimed. "Drew has been nothing but helpful during our stay at Leventhorpe. Why you would lash out at him—".

He didn't allow her to finish her sentence. Tristan grabbed her shoulders and yanked her to him. His mouth came down on hers hard, almost punishing her for questioning his judgment. His tongue pushed inside and slid along the velvet of her mouth. It had been so long since he'd kissed her. Tasted her sweetness. Held her body close to his. Inhaled the rich floral scent that surrounded her.

Nan didn't respond at first. She stood frozen as a statue, allowing him to take and take from her. Then Tristan felt her sag. He enfolded her in his arms. He couldn't get her close enough. He couldn't kiss her deeply enough. He tightened his grip on her, afraid she would run away.

His hand slipped to her breast and cupped it, his thumb dragging across her already-hardened nipple. She sighed into his mouth. Her fingers gripped his shoulders and then moved to stroke his face.

He wanted her. It seemed he always had. She was the forbidden fruit that would remain forever out of his reach. Tristan wanted to toss her down into the hay and cover her body with his. He wanted to explore every curve, taste every part of her.

But he couldn't.

Nan de Montfort deserved a man far better than he was. One who would love and cherish her. Give her children. Make her the center of his world.

Tristan couldn't be—didn't want to be—that man.

Nan might believe in love and she might find someone who shared that belief. A man who would love her long and sweet, until his dying day.

Tristan tore his mouth from hers. "I'm sorry, Nan. I truly am."

With that, he stormed away.

"Oh, no, you don't."

Suddenly, a hard shove against his back caused him to pitch forward. Off-balance, he fell to his hands and knees. Before he could right himself, a heavy blow landed against the small of his back, knocking the air from him. Tristan rolled to face his attacker.

Nan hovered over him, smashing her booted foot into his stomach. He gasped for air as she moved her foot to rest against his throat.

"Don't move," she warned.

He nodded, unable to answer as he fought to suck in air.

"I can't for the life of me understand you, Tristan. Drew and I came to Leventhorpe willingly, wanting to help you in any way we could. We have made a difference here, the both of us. Your men are more responsive and more disciplined. They are working hard to become the soldiers they know they can be. And out of nowhere, you go into a rage and wish to banish Drew when he's done nothing but support your efforts to improve your estate."

"I resent . . . your closeness," he managed to say and pulled in a deep breath.

"God's wounds!" Nan growled. "You're an idiot, Tristan Therolde. Drew and I love each other as brother and sister. I have told you so but your thick-headed skull refuses to listen. We grew up together. His family did all but abandon him. We de Montforts took him in and made him one of our own. He is my brother. My friend. My confidant. My protector. We would go to the ends of the earth for one another."

She lifted her foot and moved away from him, pacing angrily along the stalls. Tristan pushed himself to a sitting position and listened to her swearing, better than any man of his acquaintance. He rose to his feet, knowing he needed to apologize for his outburst.

Finally, she turned and faced him. "I've done my best to try and be *your* friend, as well. Just when I think I have an inkling and might understand a small part of you, you do something outrageous to throw me off-balance." She crossed her arms. "Your jealousy of Drew has ruined any prospect of friendship between us, Tristan. I will stay here to finish what I set out to do. With Drew. You will refrain from being a fool and asking us to leave. Is that understood?"

Tristan couldn't help but admire her spirit and fortitude. Nan de Montfort was worth ten men.

"I understand, my lady," he said contritely. "I will keep my tongue from running wild. You and Drewett are welcome to remain at Leventhorpe until it is time to leave for your brother's estate."

"Thank you." With that, Nan left the stables.

Forever taking his heart with her.

CHAPTER 16

Nan went to the training yard after breaking her fast. Tristan had not come to the evening meal the night before nor this morning. She had been grateful for his absence. Her heart and mind warred within her. She longed to understand this man and hadn't a clue where to begin. She'd tried before with Gillian but the girl had become so upset when discussing her deceased brothers. Nan hadn't the heart to try again by asking Gillian to help decipher her brother's actions. Gillian was so happy with David now. It wouldn't be fair to drag her into Nan's troubles.

She went to stand near Drew, wishing she could talk over matters with him but knowing it to be impossible. How could she tell her best friend that she'd fallen in love with a man whose moods changed so rapidly, a man who tempted her beyond her wildest dreams and yet smashed those very dreams, grinding them under his boot until they turned to dust? If Drew knew, he would kill Tristan. So would her brothers. And by the Christ, she must never let her father learn of what had passed between her and Tristan. Geoffrey de Montfort could be the most generous man in all of England but if anyone wronged him or his family, he would be unstoppable.

She glanced around the range and then to the adjacent training yard. Her eyes stopped as they fell on Sir Dawkin. He had been at Thorpe Castle since he was a boy. If anyone could clue her in as to what troubled Tristan, it would be Leventhorpe's captain of the guard.

"Drew, continue rotating the men. Stick to longbows only today. I have something to do."

Her friend nodded, not questioning her, and Nan set off. She crossed to where Sir Dawkin stood on the raised platform watching the soldiers at work.

"My lord, may I have a private word with you?"

The old man glanced down, studying her for a long moment with his one good eye. Nan did not blink. Finally, he said, "I wondered how long it would take for you to come to me."

He signaled for another knight to join him. Nan thought the man a poor archer but having observed him, she knew he swung a sword better than any other soldier in the yard. Sir Dawkin instructed the soldier to take over until he or Lord Tristan returned to supervise the men's exercises. Then Dawkin eased down from the platform with some difficulty. Nan couldn't help but wonder how he'd lost his leg. Mayhap that would be part of the story she sought from him.

"Shall we walk?" He extended a hand and they fell into step together, Nan adjusting her pace to match his much slower one.

They left the castle grounds, strolling out the gate and along the road until they reached a meadow in full bloom. Not a word passed between them during this time. She practiced patience, knowing this man might be the only one who could answer her many questions. Worried about how far they'd come and not knowing how much longer he could walk, she suggested they sit on the flat boulder to their right. She and Gillian had come to the spot twice during Nan's visit to Thorpe Castle, spending time getting to know one another.

After they sat, the captain said, "I suppose you want to know about Lord Tristan. And what happened at Leventhorpe."

She nodded.

He sighed. "Let me go back a ways. To his parents. The earl and countess were not suited for one another. In some marriages, a couple may come to some type of agreement. Those two never did. The lady did right by him, though, and produced a child every few years. Lord Tristan was the first, followed by three boys and then Lady Gillian. Another boy the year after the girl. Then a babe came six years after the last one had appeared."

Sir Dawkin rubbed his eye. "They saw their children had clothes on their backs and knew what was expected of them but never offered any outward signs of affection. The countess referred to the last babe as a mistake and claimed no more children would result from their union."

He looked at her. "The children liked one another, though Tristan was the one who really seemed to care for his siblings and watch over them, being the oldest. His brothers tended to be competitive and fight among themselves. Master Tristan was always the voice of reason. They all were sent to different estates to foster, except for Lady Gillian, who remained home with her mother. The boys returned each summer. Some children in a family remain close to their siblings despite being apart most of a year but the Therolde children did not. The earl pitted the boys against one another and they became strangers to each other and their parents, though Master Tristan would talk to me sometimes about how things would be different once he became the earl. He spoke of how he wanted to bring his family together under one roof and make a new start. A happy one, where all were supported—and loved."

Nan finally spoke. "I have noticed how formal and distant Tristan and Gillian are with one another. Their upbringing explains that, in part." She frowned. "But I know she seeks his approval and longs for a closer relationship with her brother. Why won't he allow it?"

"Oh, Tristan was always her favorite of all the five brothers. She worshipped him from afar. The other boys paid scant attention to her since she was a girl but every now and then, Tristan would take her around the estate on his horse. And then the babe came," Sir Dawkin added. "Lady Gillian did dote on her youngest brother. She was the one who cared for him. Though a wet nurse fed the boy, 'twas Lady Gillian who mothered the infant. The countess had little to do with him."

Sir Dawkin paused and looked out across the meadow. "Sometimes, one or more of the boys did not come home for their summer break. They would stay where they fostered or even travel to another lad's home. Can't say I blame them. But that year, the earl wanted all of them home. Even sent for them to come back early."

Dawkin gave her sad look. "Because of the troubles."

Immediately, Nan knew what the knight spoke of. "The peasants' rebellion," she said, her belly knotting, guessing what was to come.

"Aye. Seven years ago at this time of year is when it began. All the children had arrived back at Thorpe Castle except for Master Tristan. He was expected within a day or so." Sir Dawkin finally turned back to her. "You see, Leventhorpe hadn't been a particularly happy place. I don't believe the earl was a cruel man. Just not a thoughtful one. Complaints turned to resentment and that grew over the years. When trouble broke out in Essex and Kent, the people on the estate were ripe for the picking."

"Is that how all of Gillian's brothers died? She'd mentioned them once before in passing and when I asked her about them later, she grew quite upset."

"They did. Thorpe Castle turned into a bloodbath that night, my lady. No one should ever have to see what happened here that day, not even seasoned soldiers."

Sir Dawkin fell silent. Nan allowed him to gather his thoughts without interruption, knowing how difficult it must be to share with her what he had lived through.

After a long time, he said, "The soldiers in the barracks had their throats slit to a man. I was on duty at the wall walk and escaped that fate but I knew something foul was adrift. I rushed to the keep. Lady Gillian was up with the babe, walking him around the great hall. He was a fussy one from the start and had been ill for several weeks. I'd even overhead the countess say she hoped the child would die because he'd proved to be so much trouble.

"Anyway, I grabbed Lady Gillian by the arm and rushed her from the keep. There was no time to alert the rest of the family. I took her to what I thought would be the safest place—the stables. I didn't think the animals would be harmed.

"I was wrong."

His words were as a stab wound to Nan's heart. She had recognized the stables were new. A sick feeling washed over her.

"I hid her in the loft, telling her not to come down for any reason until I returned for her. I urged her to keep the babe quiet and then returned to the keep to help the others." Sir Dawkin shook his head in sorrow. "By then, I was too late. The serfs and servants had rounded up the family and taken them downstairs to the great hall. Slaughtered them like lambs. A few remained behind to loot the keep and I tangled with them." He pointed to his face. "You see how that turned out."

Nan took his hand and squeezed it. No words came to her.

"Lost my eye and leg that day but clung to life. Barely. Lord Tristan arrived several hours later."

She couldn't imagine the carnage that had awaited him. Seeing his family butchered. His parents. Four brothers.

"What of Gillian . . . and the babe?" she finally asked.

"They burned the stables, the animals left inside to perish. Lady Gillian only spoke of it once to me, hearing the horses scream. You know, she's never ridden on her own since then." He swallowed. "The babe died before the fire broke out. A brave girl, Lady Gillian was. She crept down the ladder as flames danced around her, carrying the poor dead babe. The path to the exit was blocked by the fire. She took an ax and pounded through a few boards, just enough to squeeze through and escape before the building collapsed, with her dead brother still inside. She fled to the woods. Master Tristan found her three days later, cowering there, unable to speak."

Tears spilled down Nan's cheeks.

"I can tell Lord Tristan cares for you," the old captain said. "I've seen the way he looks at you when he doesn't think anyone watches him." He squeezed her hand. "If anyone can help him, 'twould be you, my lady."

Nan hugged the old man. "Thank you for sharing this with me. It helps me to understand Tristan, knowing what he's suffered through." She gave him a weak smile. "He's told me he doesn't believe in love, Sir Dawkin."

"He's never had any given to him, my lady, though I do think he loved those boys. Lady Gillian has tried to love him but Lord Tristan's pushed her away. I'm sure he's done the same with you. But he needs saving, Lady Nan."

"I know. I'll try," she promised.

They walked back in silence to the castle. Everything fell into place. Why so few servants were present at Leventhorpe and only a handful of tenant families existed on the property. The soldiers Tristan had were either old ones who looked for a place to serve after the rebellion or young ones who needed a place to learn.

It also explained why Tristan had locked away his feelings. He'd never been close to his parents nor felt any kind of affection from them. Sir Dawkin said Tristan had loved his siblings but after seeing their murdered corpses, he had closed off his emotions. He couldn't risk his heart, caring for anyone—because they might be taken away from him at any moment.

She also ached for Gillian and everything she had gone through as a young girl. Nan decided to seek her out now. She bade Sir Dawkin farewell and expressed her thanks for what he'd shared with her then returned to the keep. She found Gillian in the great hall, sewing by the fire. The room stood empty.

"Might I have a word with you?" Nan asked.

Gillian put aside what she worked on. "You've been crying."

"Aye. For you. And Tristan." Nan took a deep breath. "I know what happened that day. Sir Dawkin told me."

The girl's jaw fell open. A stricken look appeared on her face. She leapt to her feet, ready to flee the room.

Nan embraced her, holding fast. "I am here, Gillian. I am here for you."

Sobs racked Gillian's body. The harder she cried, the more tightly Nan held on to her. Finally, her weeping subsided. Nan released her and Gillian fell into her chair. Nan sat next to her, taking her hand.

"You know everything?" Gillian hiccoughed.

"Aye."

"It was horrible, Nan. Sometimes, I think I only dreamed it but it all happened. I couldn't even enter the great hall for a year after it occurred. I didn't speak for months. And poor Tristan. He came home on his birthday and . . . that . . . is what awaited him." She wiped her tears with her sleeve. "We never speak of it. Never. Why did Sir Dawkin tell you about it?"

"Because I asked. I care for Tristan, Gillian. I think he cares for me and I wanted to understand why he continually holds me at arm's length. I come from a family where love is abundant. Celebrated. I need to love and be loved by the man I wed. Tristan has told me he does not believe in love."

Gillian's face fell. "He guards his heart, Nan. And he has worked so hard over the past few years. No servants were left afterward. No tenants. Tristan is the one who scrubbed floors and washed all the bedclothes. He harvested wheat from the fields. He has done his best to buy livestock and convince new tenants to move to Leventhorpe. Soldiers, too."

"When did Sir Stephen and Sir Toby come?"

Her lips trembled. "Two years after . . . everything. They remained where they'd fostered with Tristan and completed their service, both earning their knighthood. Immediately, they set out for Leventhorpe because of their loyalty to my brother."

Nan's throat grew thick with emotion. "And then he lost them, too. What a tragedy."

Gillian nodded, her eyes misting with tears. "They had become as my new brothers. They talked to me and teased me when I returned from Shercastle each summer. Tristan thought it best for me to leave Leventhorpe once I finally began to speak. He wanted me away from the hardship here. That was when I went to Lady Magdalen." She hiccoughed again. "Losing Toby and Stephen hurt both me and Tristan. Especially him."

"Have you told David any of this?"

Her eyes widened. "Nay. I would never do such a thing."

"You need to," Nan urged. "David should know. You shouldn't

have to fight these terrible memories alone. He will love you and support you and be strong for you when you can't be for yourself."

Gillian bit her lip. "I suppose you are right."

"I am," Nan said with confidence. "Go find him. Now. Tell him everything. Leave nothing out."

"And what will you do?"

"Find Tristan."

CHAPTER 17

TRISTAN HAD AVOIDED Nan last night and continued to do so today. He was embarrassed at his behavior yesterday—and yet couldn't wait to put his hands on her again. To avoid making a fool of himself or worse, having her make good on her promise to do him bodily harm if he did try to touch her again, he decided to skip going to the training yard, knowing she would be in the butts.

The time drew near when she and David Devereux would be leaving Leventhorpe. Tristan decided to speak with the young knight about the horses he had purchased at Sandbourne and how they were adjusting to their new home. Mayhap that would take his mind off Nan de Montfort. A stable hand told him the nobleman was in the pasture so Tristan made his way there and saw David standing next to the fence, leaning his elbows on it as he watched the activity on the other side.

As Tristan approached, David turned. "Greetings, my lord. Have you come to take a look at your horses?"

"Aye."

David spent a good half-hour telling him what he had done with both the horses and Tristan's staff. How often the horses were fed and the different types of exercises and training they'd been put through. When they were moved from the stables to the open space. Adjustments he had made inside the stables and the various stalls. Tristan listened carefully and saw how thorough Devereux had been in working with both the animals and his people.

"Do you have any questions I might answer for you?"

Tristan shook his head. "Nay. You have done a remarkable job. I hope to return to bargain with your mother every spring and add to my stable. It would relieve me to know you might come each year and do as you have these past two weeks to help my new purchases settle in."

"May I speak frankly, my lord?"

He saw the knight was ready to voice what lay in his heart regarding Gillian.

"Feel free, Sir David."

"I would be happy to return to Leventhorpe every spring so I could bring Lady Gillian with me. You see, we have fallen in love and wish to wed."

Love? Why did that word keep coming up with the members of this family? Tristan calmed the anger that sprang to the surface. He knew he should be happy that his sister had found a good man who cared for her. She deserved it after everything that had happened.

When he failed to reply, David said, "I am asking for your permission to wed Lady Gillian, my lord. You would be welcome at any time at Sandbourne and I would not keep her from visiting you here at Thorpe Castle. In fact, I would encourage visits between the two of you. Gillian cares a great deal for you, my lord."

Tristan smiled wistfully. "My sister would be happy at Sandbourne. I know your parents will look after her, as you would. You have my approval, Sir David. I will draw up papers regarding Gillian's bridal price."

The younger man broke out in a huge grin. "Thank you, my lord," he repeated several times as he pumped Tristan's hand enthusiastically.

"I assume you have spoken to Gillian about this."

"Aye, we have. She will be pleased to receive your blessing, Lord Tristan. She thinks the world of you."

If only he had been able to restore her world. Tristan had tried these past few years but he knew many areas were still lacking at Leventhorpe.

"Will you excuse me, my lord? I'd like to find her and share the good news."

"Of course."

David Devereux raced off. Tristan wished he remembered what it was like to feel eager. To have hope. To think he would find someone to share everything with. Build a life together.

But the one woman who had sparked any interest from him was one he needed to let go. She would be gone in two days. He would never see her again.

Misery filled him. He began walking and found himself at the edge of the woods. He decided to go visit Hugo. It had been a good while since he'd seen the Leventhorpe falconer, who had been on his own for many years after his wife died giving birth to their first child. The child hadn't survived a day and Hugo kept much to himself ever since. He had not even known a rebellion had occurred on the estate until weeks after it ended. Mayhap Tristan could plan a hunt for tomorrow, using the falcons. Anything to get his mind off his woes.

He arrived at the falconer's space, which included a small cottage and a large clearing where the raptors were housed in cages. Hugo greeted him and they talked about the horses he had recently purchased from Lady Elysande. The falconer was eager to come see them. Tristan also broke the news about Stephen and Toby's deaths.

"You've had a rough time of things, my lord. But I'll bet your luck'll change. These new horses could help."

"My luck might not but my sister's has." Tristan told him about David Devereux and how the knight wished to wed Gillian.

"Let me know when the nuptial mass is, my lord. I don't get up to the castle often but I would enjoy seeing Lady Gillian in her wedding finery, a smile on her face. It's been missing from her for a good while."

"It has, Hugo. It has."

Tristan heard something rustle and looked to the woods. A figure approached. As it came closer, he recognized who arrived.

Nan.

She stepped into the clearing. "Greetings, my lord. Hugo."

"You know Hugo?" he asked, surprise filling him.

"Aye. I have taken a few walks through your woods and met Hugo last week. He showed me your new eyases and how they'd become accustomed to the lure."

Hugo beamed. "Lady Nan knows quite a bit about raptors. From Joseph, her father's falconer, and her sister-in-law. We had a fine time together."

Tristan remembered Nan telling him about her sister-in-law, who was a falconer. He watched Hugo slip his leather glove off and allow Nan to put it on. She held it out to one of their largest birds, who hopped onto her arm. Hugo slipped her a bechin to give the peregrine, who downed it greedily. He sat silently as the two talked about the falcons, watching Nan's animated face, realizing how much he would miss seeing it every day.

Finally, she returned the falcon to its cage and gave Hugo his glove back.

"Thank you for letting me visit, Hugo."

"I enjoy your company, my lady. Do come again."

She hesitated. "I'm afraid I will be leaving soon."

"Then if you ever come to Leventhorpe again, please stop by to see me."

"I will," she promised. Glancing to Tristan, she said, "Are you returning to the castle?"

He stood. "Aye. Allow me to escort you."

As they made their way back, he smelled rain in the air. The shadows in the forest grew darker as the sun faded away. They came out of the woods as thunder rumbled nearby.

"It looks as if we'll be caught in a downpour," Nan said, glancing up.

Just then, the first drops began to fall and then the bottom fell out of the sky.

"We should take shelter," Tristan suggested. He pointed to his right. "That cottage up ahead is empty."

Nan took out running, as graceful as a doe. He could only stare at her in longing for a minute before he raced across the wet grass. She reached the door first and threw it open, Tristan on her heels. He closed it behind them. A little light came in from the lone open space cut out, which served as a window.

She did a quick turn around the cottage. "No kindling. I suppose that means no fire for us. We'll simply have to wait out the thunderstorm." A drop slid from her hair down the bridge of her nose. She giggled and brushed it away.

Nan was soaked to the skin—and yet had never looked more beautiful to him than in that moment.

She rubbed her hands up and down her arms absently as she paced the small room, trying to warm herself.

"You're shivering," he said.

Turning to face him, their eyes locked. Neither moved. Then Nan shrugged and began to move again restlessly. She paused in front of the tiny window, standing far enough away so that the incoming rain didn't pelt her.

Without realizing he moved, Tristan suddenly stood behind her. He slid his arms around her waist and drew her against him, locking his fingers together to make sure she stayed put.

"Tristan," she said, her voice low, warning him.

But he ignored her words. She felt too good, all warm and womanly. He bent and brushed his lips against her neck. Her head tilted, giving him better access, and his lips burned a path along her neck. Her jaw. Up to her ear. Her fingers grabbed onto his forearms, tightening with each kiss. He lazily ran a tongue around the shape of her ear, enjoying the small, surprised cry she emitted.

"Tristan," she warned again, but he was having none of that. He pulled her hard against him, so that she could feel his manhood rising.

"This is what you do to me, Nan," he murmured into her ear. "Only you."

He spun her in his arms and found her mouth. The heat between them now burned brightly. She seemed to melt in his arms. Tristan kissed her over and over, thrilling each time she made some tiny sound of approval in the back of her throat. He had never wanted a woman the way he wanted Nan.

Breaking the kiss, he stared at her beautiful, heart-shaped face. "I can't get enough of you," he whispered.

Laughing, she pulled his mouth back down to hers and took the lead. This time, she was kissing him and Tristan hung on for the wild ride. He became the one making satisfied noises, murmuring against her lips.

They stumbled and fell to their knees, still kissing as if they needed to as much as they needed to breathe. His hands roamed her body, lighting his own afire. Somehow, they wound up on the floor of the cottage. His hand slid under her tunic and to her breast. It filled his palm, seeming to grow, as Nan's hips lifted against him. He dragged his hand down her body, against her flat belly, the skin smoother than silk.

Continuing to kiss her, he tugged her pants down until they sat at her knees. He needed to taste her. All of her.

Tristan broke the kiss, panting, seeing her eyes glazed with passion. He lifted her gypon and kissed her belly, running his tongue around her bellybutton. Her hips bucked again and he moved lower, fastening his mouth against her most intimate place.

"Tristan?"

He heard her voice, small and unsure, and knew he ventured where no man had gone before with her. His tongue plunged into her wet heat. Nan gasped, her fingers tightening in his hair. Then a deep moan came from her, sparking wild desire within him. He sampled her treasure chest until she writhed beneath him. When she came, she cried his name over and over as she rode the wave of pleasure.

Tristan licked her a final time and looked at her. She lay dazed, unmoving. He gently kissed her belly once more and then lifted her hips to pull the pants back to her waist, hovering over her.

He might not be able to offer Nan what she wanted from him, but he could try to make her happy in his own way. He knew he would never find any kind of happiness if she left.

"We will need to wed," he told her. "Soon."

A smile more genuine than any he'd ever seen lit her face. Tristan leaned down and kissed her softly.

Then she frowned. "Why? Do you finally admit that you love me?" Nan asked.

His belly clenched in fear.

"Do you love me?" she repeated, her tone growing sharp. When he remained silent, anger sparked in her eyes. "Nay, you can't love anyone, can you? Oh, Tristan, what can I say to make you trust me?"

He wanted to trust her. To love her. But all he saw was a heap of savaged bodies, blood spilling from them, soaking the rushes they laid upon. He refused to give his heart to anyone. Not even Nan. Especially not her. For if he ever lost her, he would lose himself. 'Twould be worse than death.

She shoved him away and rolled to her feet. Instead of glaring at him angrily, he saw pity in her eyes.

"This ends now," she declared.

Tristan rose to his feet. "But we must wed, Nan. After what we just did. 'Tis only right." He looked at her pleadingly. "This could be how it is between us," he said softly. "We can pleasure one another. I can give you children. A home. You would be my countess."

"You didn't ask me to wed you, Tristan. You announced we would do so." She shook her head. "I am sorry. So very, very sorry. More than I could ever explain to you. I could never marry without love or trust between my husband and me." Her mouth trembled. "That means I can never marry you."

Nan went for the door and opened it, ready to leave. Tristan slammed it shut and whipped her around to face him. He backed her against the door and began kissing her, thinking if he did so for long enough that he could convince her to change her mind. He needed her. He couldn't let her walk out that door without agreeing to wed him. To stay with him. To be a partner to him.

To heal him.

He cupped her face between his hands and lifted his lips a fraction from hers. "I am mad for you, Nan. I must have you in my life." He kissed her softly once more, his hands sliding down and tightening on her shoulders.

But Nan didn't respond this time. She became as frozen as a block of ice in his arms.

Tristan tried to kiss her again but she ordered him to stop. He pulled away, his hands still fastened to her shoulders, unwilling to break the link between them.

"This is the hardest thing I have ever done," she told him, her face grave. "Because I have fallen in love with you." She swallowed, pain reflected in her eyes. "But I am asking you to release me."

Determination filled him. "I owe it to you to marry you, Nan. Besides, I must wed someone, someday, so that I may pass Leventhorpe along."

Her eyes narrowed. "You make it sound like some business transaction. I'll not barter my virginity merely to be your countess." She shook her head sadly. "Nay, Tristan, I don't need you—or any other man—under those circumstances. I refuse to compromise on something so important to me. Release me. I beg you."

He saw nothing he could do or say would alter her stance, other than uttering the words he dare not say. Ones he refused to believe in. Ones that would punish and haunt him.

Tristan pressed a tender kiss to her forehead and forced his fingers to let go. Wordlessly, he took a step back and watched as Nan slowly turned away and opened the door. She left, closing it quietly behind her. He sank to the ground and did something he never remembered doing before, not even during those dark days seven years ago.

He wept.

CHAPTER 18

Nan trudged back to the castle. Her heart seemed to weigh more than her entire body, causing her to labor over each step that put distance between her and Tristan.

Something had stopped her from telling him that she knew why he had closed himself off from the idea of love. She didn't blame him. Nan couldn't imagine arriving at Kinwick and finding her entire family brutally murdered. To lose everyone important to her in one fell swoop would cause her to question everything about life.

And love.

She didn't know if Tristan had it in him to love again. To open his heart and allow himself to feel once more. He might believe it wasn't worth the risk. In the end, she had decided not to reveal that she knew the root of his pain. If he did ever learn to put away his past and reach out, she would be waiting—for Nan knew in her heart that no man would ever come close to how she felt about Tristan Therolde. She would rather spend a lifetime alone, wife to no man, than allow a substitute to take his place. It wouldn't be fair to anyone who wished to wed her for her heart now, and always would, belong to another.

Arriving in the bailey, she saw the soldiers had been dismissed from their training exercises for the day. She found Drew so she could tell him that they would leave in the morning for Bexley.

"What has that fool done now?" Drew asked before Nan uttered a single word, anger darkening his features.

"What do you mean?"

"I mean what has that bloody dolt done or said to cause you to be so upset?" He shook his head. "I'm sure he's gone into a rage again, threatening to banish me from Leventhorpe. Can't the bastard see that there's nothing romantic between you and me? His judgment is clouded by the jealousy he can't seem to let go of."

Nan couldn't reply. The ache ran deep inside her. What had just occurred between her and Tristan had drained her physically and emotionally. She was weary of fighting her feelings for Tristan. Afraid she would weaken and give in to her desire for him. She wondered, for a brief moment, if her love alone could be enough to sustain them. Mayhap, for a short while. But marriage was a lifetime commitment. She refused to have a husband who did not love her. Not when she saw how rich the lives were of the happy couples in the de Montfort family.

"Never mind. Come here." Drew enfolded her in his strong arms.

Nan began weeping, something she despised. She saw it as a sign of weakness. Or, in this case, foolishness. She could cry a river of tears and it would not change things between her and Tristan.

"I know something strong binds you to this man, Nan. Why he cannot surrender to it as you have is beyond my understanding. I'm afraid, though, that he's become like poison to you."

"You're right, Drew," she agreed. Getting away from Tristan would be the only thing that might save her. Angrily, she rubbed her sleeve against her eyes. "I've come to tell you that we're leaving in the morning."

"I thought we had two days left," he protested, releasing her.

She shook her head. "I've made up my mind. I want to leave."

Drew nodded. "I understand." He looked at her a long moment. "He's an idiot to give you up but, if that's the case, so be it. I'll make sure we're ready to go at first light." He embraced her once again and said, "I am sorry, Nan. I wish I could change things for you. Departing Leventhorpe will be for the best."

With that, Drew left.

Nan needed to find David next. Her cousin would probably be upset that their time at Thorpe Castle would be cut short but he would be lucky enough to come out of this visit with a bride.

As the rain ceased, she found him approaching the keep, saving her a trip to the stables. He called out a greeting and then a look of concern crossed his face as he drew near.

"What's wrong, Nan?"

"If I tell you I wish to leave for Ancel's in the morning, would that be a problem?"

He sighed. "I was afraid it might come to this."

Nan blew out a frustrated breath. "Does everyone seem to know?" she huffed.

Her cousin gave her a wry smile. "Aye. The people here will be disappointed that Lord Tristan has not opened his eyes and accepted what they all know. That he is in love with you, Nan, whether he admits it or not."

Her mouth tightened. "He says he doesn't believe in love." She hesitated. "I know something—something about his past—and just how difficult it would be for him to love anyone."

"Mayhap, he will change his mind," David said encouragingly. "In the meantime, leaving tomorrow suits me well. I'll have a last few bits of advice for the stable hands but the sooner I escort you to Bexley, the more quickly I can return to Sandbourne and share with Mother and Father that a wedding is to take place and that all our family should gather in celebration."

Nan smiled despite feeling so low. "Elysande will enjoy planning a wedding and be grateful that Gillian wishes to hold it at Sandbourne."

Naturally, Tristan would attend the nuptial mass of his sister and meet all of Nan's extended family. Would it be possible for him to be surrounded by such love and happiness and not have any of it rub off on him?

She would take that small bit of hope and lock it away, deep in her heart. It might be the last chance she had with Tristan.

Once she returned to the solar, she threw off her rain-soaked clothes and spread them out to dry. She unbound her damp hair and combed through it before dressing in her cotehardie. Though she knew she should rebraid her hair, she made a bold choice to leave it down so that it could dry. She was not above trying to entice Tristan. Let him see what he would miss out on if he let her slip through his fingers.

Nan went to the great hall and found that David sat in her usual place upon the dais. She supposed she couldn't begrudge him sharing a last meal with Gillian. She seated herself next to Tristan, who nodded without speaking. He remained silent as each course was brought out to them. She ate simply because it gave her something to do. It wasn't her place to fill the silence, much less the void that had grown between them.

Finishing her meal, Nan rose. "If you will excuse me?"

Looking up, he said, "I hear you are leaving at dawn. Would you care to play a game of chess with me tonight?"

She had seen the unused chess set in the solar. "If you wish."

Tristan rose and accompanied her to the solar. Nan readied the board and placed it on the table. She took a seat on one side and he sat opposite her.

For much of the game, she avoided looking at him and concentrated on the pieces on the board. Tristan, on the other hand, did not seem to take his eyes from her, moving his pawn or queen with a quick glance and little strategy. Nan won the game with no effort.

"Why did you ask me to play when you cared so little about focusing on the game?" she asked, afraid to hear his reply.

He swept the board away from them and leaned strong forearms in front of him.

"I would like to ask if you will reconsider what we discussed earlier today. Will you marry me, Nan?" he asked politely, his features blank, showing no emotion.

Just as courteously, she replied, "Thank you for your kind offer, my lord, but I choose not to accept it."

His eyes burned into hers. "Why? You must marry someone, Nan."

She sniffed. "Not really. I could become a nun."

"You can't be serious," he scoffed.

"I did not say I would. I merely said I could." She took a deep breath. "Some noblewomen choose not to wed. I might be one of them. I have enough family as it is. 'Tis a large group. Loud and loving, as a family should be." She paused. "And not one of them behaves as you do with Gillian."

Without thinking, Nan reached out and fastened a hand to his wrist and saw him flinch at the contact. "Don't you see how you are hurting your sister by not opening up and showing your affection for her? She craves attention from her brother and is harmed when you ignore her repeatedly. If you keep this up, you will lose her—and regret it."

Tristan gave her a wintry look. "I don't see where that is any of your business."

"What if I were your wife? Would it be my business then?" she demanded.

When he remained silent, her fury grew. "Oh, I see. You think we should wed so that I can be your brood mare. Just like one that you purchased from Elysande. You'd get an heir off of me and, mayhap, plenty more to spare."

She rose and began pacing about the room, his eyes following her. Nan finally stopped in front of him.

"Don't you understand, Tristan? I am not a woman you can shove into a corner and only bring out when you want a plaything. I want what my parents have. What my siblings have. I want a man who desires me. Excites me. Yearns for me. Loves me. I want a husband who shares everything with me, from his favorite foods to how he passes his day to his bed. I want to be his full companion in everything, a partner who is equal in every aspect. I want both our opinions to count. I wish for both of us to support one another and believe in the other and defend one another. I want a man who would fight to the death for me—because I would do the same for him. I want to live every day to its fullest with the man I love, awakening beside him each morning and knowing we have that day to share with one another.

"And I would know that the next day when we awoke entangled in one another's arms that we would love each other even more than we did the day before. That each day our love would multiply and we would grow richer for it."

Nan's fingers grazed his cheek. "That is what my parents have. What my siblings have found with those they've wed. I deserve no less. I will settle for no less."

Her hand fell to her side as she eyed him sadly. "I love you, Tristan, but you have convinced me that I could never experience everything I want with you." She shook her head. "You stubborn man. You have broken my heart. I only wish you would listen to what yours is telling you."

Crossing the length of the solar, Nan exited the rooms and hurried down the corridor. She had almost given in to him and his wishes. The passion between them burned brightly. She had wanted to climb into his lap and kiss him until they were both breathless before she led him to the bed in the next room. She longed to have his hands on her and wanted them to belong to one another through the act of love.

But she hadn't given in to that temptation. For if they wed under these circumstances, she would never receive the life—and love—that she desired. One day, it would catch up to her if she did and she would realize how unhappy she was.

At the foot of the stairs, Gillian awaited her, distress on her lovely face.

"David tells me that you are leaving Leventhorpe in the morning. Why do you have to go, Nan? I know my brother cares for you. 'Tis obvious to everyone."

She took the girl's hands and gave her a sad smile. "Because I want with Tristan what you and David share. I will never get that from him, Gillian. He'll never open himself up to me. I can't live like that. I won't live like that. I believe it's better to end things between us now and move on."

Nan released Gillian. She needed to leave the keep. From the time she was young, she had roamed Kinwick. Being outside always renewed her. Refreshed her. The solitude of the woods called out to her, ready to comfort her. She was most at home when alone in nature.

Leaving the castle grounds, she strode down the road and across the meadow until she reached the forest and entered. The cool air and stillness wrapped around her, as a hand sliding into a glove. Nan found a fallen log and sat upon it, ready to think about her future. She refused to give in to tears. For what good would they do? They only made her feel ill and weak.

How would she live without Tristan?

No answer came. Nan let her thoughts wander and decided keeping busy would be the only solution. She would go from here to Ancel and Margery at Bexley. They would offer her sanctuary and comfort and give her a renewed purpose as she worked with their soldiers. She found great satisfaction and enjoyment from tutoring others in the weaponry she had practiced with over many years.

She rarely came into the woods with no bow and arrow. Being here now without them caused her to feel naked and exposed. As she sat listening to an owl hooting, she realized the sun was falling. She should head back to Thorpe Castle. Standing, she had the impression she wasn't alone and grew wary, especially with no weapon to defend herself. She did know how to protect herself with her fists and feet, though. Hal had made certain of that.

Then Gillian emerged. Nan gave a sigh of relief.

"What are you doing here?" she asked, regretting her harsh tone as Gillian winced.

"I saw the direction you headed and wanted to speak with you." Tears welled in Gillian's eyes. "Oh, Nan, I'm sorry you're so unhappy. So is Tristan. He loves you, I know he does. Give him another chance. Please. I know he keeps everyone at a distance but if anyone can break through the walls he has surrounded himself with, it's you, Nan."

Though she wished it could be true, Nan said, "Mayhap 'tis better if I go away. Either Tristan will forget me and move on or he will miss me like crazy and come after me." She shrugged.

Gillian's smile lit up her face. "That could actually work." She hugged Nan. "I couldn't pick a better sister than you. I will pray to the Virgin that Tristan comes to his senses."

"Come, the sun is starting to set. We need to return to the keep," Nan urged.

Gillian linked her arm with Nan's. "Your plan gives me hope."

They began walking and came out of the woods. Without warning, strong hands yanked Nan away from her friend, slinging her to the ground. Instinctively, she grabbed her blade from her boot. Springing up, Nan advanced on the man who moved menacingly toward her and swung her arm around, stabbing him in his temple. His eyes bulged. His lips moved but no sound emerged. Then he crumpled. As he fell, she jerked the knife from him. Tossing it to her other hand, Nan bent and unsheathed her attacker's sword.

She spun around and saw another soldier almost upon her and jammed it into his belly. Once. Twice. He fell and she turned wildly, weapons in both hands now, ready to kill anyone else who threatened her or Gillian.

And saw the dagger held to Gillian's throat.

The stranger who restrained Gillian calmly said, "I will kill her. My lord doesn't have a need for her. Put down your blades or else." The man wore the look of experience. Nan had no doubt he would follow through with his threat.

Her thoughts jumbled. Even if she laid down her weapons, he might still kill Gillian. But if she didn't, Gillian's death was certain. Nan would never be able to look David in the eye and tell him she was the cause of his beloved's demise. Her responsibility now was to see that they both lived.

And to find out whoever was behind this attack. Someone wanted her. Nan had to find out who—and kill him.

"Your move, my lady," the soldier said, his grasp tightening on Gillian. The tip of the baselard now rested against her throat, pricking it slightly, causing her to moan in fear.

Nan dropped her weapons and held her hands wide in surrender.

CHAPTER 19

Nan saw how Gillian trembled as a thin stream of blood trickled down her neck. Her friend's eyes began to glaze over as terror seized her.

"Gillian," Nan said firmly. "Look at me."

Gillian blinked rapidly several times as she fought to focus. Her gaze finally met Nan's.

"Stay strong." Nan hoped she sounded confident as Gillian gave her a weak smile.

The man eyed her warily as he dropped one shoulder. A satchel slid from it. He removed the blade from Gillian's throat and grabbed on to the satchel before he tossed it in front of him.

"Open it," he commanded, returning the dagger to its original position.

Nan stepped forward and knelt. She unfastened the leather ties holding it shut and dumped the contents onto the ground, seeing several coils of rope.

"Bind her legs," the stranger said, keeping Gillian close against him.

She took a piece of the rope and wrapped it around Gillian's ankles, using the special knot Hal had taught her to keep it in place.

"Now her hands." The soldier gripped his prisoner's waist tighter. "Hold 'em out."

Gillian did as instructed, her arms shaking badly. Taking a second coil, Nan looped it around her the girl's wrists and knotted it in place with the same distinct knot.

The one that would allow her friend to escape.

She only hoped they would be taken to the same place and left together. Only then would Nan be able to reveal to Gillian how to slip the knot. She doubted the girl knew anything about the trickery. The fool kidnapping them certainly didn't. It helped that he'd kept his eyes on Nan the entire time and not what she was doing.

"Sit!" the man barked at her.

Nan plopped on the ground, her eyes never wavering from his. He started to release Gillian but the girl swayed. The soldier grabbed her elbow to steady her.

"Take a length of rope and tie your own ankles. Firmly. No tricks."

She reached over and took another piece of rope from the pile. Keeping her eyes on him, she wound it around her ankles, making sure she knotted it in back just in case he saw what she did. Hal had made Nan tie this knot a thousand times over the years. She could do it in her sleep.

Glaring up at him, she asked, "And would you like me to secure my wrists, as well?"

His eyes narrowed in anger. He jerked Gillian, forcing her to the ground, and then strode to where the remaining strands of rope sat on the ground. Nan held her wrists up together as he lifted a coil.

"I don't trust you," he growled and flipped her to her belly, quickly yanking her arms behind her back and winding the rope around her captured wrists.

Nan did her best to strain against the rope so that it might have a slight bit of slack in it once he finished.

He left her facing the ground. She felt his forearm holding her legs down and heard material ripping. She glanced over her shoulder and saw he tore a strip from the linen smock she wore beneath her cotehardie. He did it four times, trimming the cloth with his dagger. Rolling her over to face him, he wadded up one of the strips and brought it close to her face. Nan twisted her head back and forth to avoid it but he grabbed her chin and held on firmly as he stuffed it into her mouth. Taking a second fragment, he flipped her back to her belly and tied the piece around her head to keep the cloth in place before she could spit it out.

The soldier moved away and gagged Gillian the same way before he sat both women up and placed them back to back. Nan watched him kneel beside each corpse and root around until he found their coin purses. Emptying them, he placed what he stole in his own.

"Don't go anywhere," he said and then burst out in laughter at his wit.

She reined in her temper. It was foolish to waste energy being angry. What was important was to watch and wait and learn everything she could in order to escape.

Nan looked at the two bodies of the men she'd slain. At least when faced with danger, she hadn't hesitated. Though this situation seemed hopeless, she knew she could triumph—because she was a de Montfort. De Montforts never gave up and never gave in.

The man was gone for several minutes. She assumed he'd gone to fetch horses. More than likely, the plan would have been to overpower Nan and carry her to the horses. Now that their kidnapper was two men down and had an extra woman to manage, he was already having to improvise. She only hoped he would make a mistake because of the new circumstances he'd been forced into.

He returned riding one horse and leading another by its reins. A third horse had been tied to the second one. She realized that, although he would be leaving behind the bodies of the others, the horses were too valuable to do the same. They might also give away who their owners were and give Tristan a clue as to who had kidnapped them. Nan studied this man's face because she never wanted to forget it. Lifting Gillian, he placed her atop the second horse and tied her hands to the horn with the remaining rope.

"I'll lead your horse, my lady, but I would hold on if I were you. If you don't, you'll fall off. And I won't come back for you," he warned. "Best behave if you don't want to be trampled."

Nan fumed at how he taunted the poor, scared girl. She would enjoy seeking retribution against this bastard. Tears poured down

Gillian's face as she wrapped her fingers tightly around the horn.

He latched on to Nan's elbows and pulled her to her feet. "You'll ride with me. Even bound hand and foot, you're the kind who would try to escape." Picking her up by the waist, he took her to his horse and set her down, leapt into the saddle, and then yanked her up so that she sat sideways in front of him.

"My advice is that you conduct yourself like a lady," he said into her ear. "Sit still and do nothing to anger me, else I'll leave your pretty little friend behind. I'm sure you know what happens to a woman alone on the road. Especially a defenseless one tied hand and foot."

Again, Nan thought of ways she would kill this monster.

He walked the horses, keeping a steady pace. Nan stared out at the countryside they passed but every now and then, she would glance to make sure Gillian was still in the saddle.

They rode by one castle that stood in the distance. She took in every detail so she would know where they'd been taken and the best places to hide as they made their way back to Leventhorpe. A second estate appeared with its castle on the right. Their captor led the horses toward it. A sick feeling grew in Nan's belly. Without being told, she now understood where they would end up.

The gates opened as they approached and they trotted through. As they cleared them, a stout man with worry written across his face met them.

"What took so long?" he demanded. "And two of them? Where are—"

"Dead," their abductor interrupted. He pointed to Nan. "She killed both of them."

The soldier who'd met them eyed her with suspicion. "A woman?"

"Aye. She's as deadly as any soldier I've ever seen."

"Well, come on," the other urged. "The baron isn't happy. And his mood will grow even more foul when he hears that two of his men aren't coming back."

They were taken to the keep. Since she and Gillian couldn't walk, the two men slung them over their shoulders. Nan watched the ground under them pass by as they entered the keep and ascended a flight of stairs. As they trod down the corridor, the men stopped in front of a door.

"Put yours in here for now," the man who carried Nan ordered the second one.

She heard a door swing open and footsteps shuffling. She only wished she could have made eye contact with Gillian and tried to give her friend some hope before they were separated. The footsteps returned and the door closed.

"Guard the door," her abductor ordered. Then the bouncing began again until they reached the end of the hallway. Knocking on the door, she heard a muffled voice bid them to enter.

The man crossed the threshold into what she guessed was the solar. He stopped after a few steps and eased her from his shoulder so that she faced him. Her belly ached from the jarring she'd been subjected to, not to mention the strain in her shoulders and back from being bound for so long.

"Set her in the chair," a voice behind her said.

Her kidnapper lifted her at the waist and plopped her into a chair several feet away. He flashed an amused smile at her as he moved away.

Nan now faced the man behind her and Gillian's abduction.

The Baron of Wycliffe.

He eyed her with interest, his lips curling in a smile that Nan wanted to slap from his cruel mouth.

"I had to bring another woman along," her kidnapper said.

A flash of irritation crossed the nobleman's face. "Why, Roland? I only wanted Lady Nan."

The man she now knew as Roland shrugged. "It seemed the thing to do. I found them together and didn't think it wise to leave the other behind. This one had already killed John and Fitch. She seemed to care about the girl and I needed something to use as leverage to control her."

Lord Petyr's jaw dropped. "John . . . *and* Fitch?" He glanced at Nan and back to Roland. "You are telling me Lady Nan killed both men?"

"Aye, my lord. So fast neither of them had time to react."

A gleam entered the nobleman's eyes as he appraised her. Without taking his gaze from Nan, he said, "Where is the other woman?"

"In a bedchamber three down from the solar," Roland replied.

"Is she similarly bound?" asked Lord Petyr.

Roland nodded.

"Lady Gillian will be no threat. Free her ties and warn her to remain within the chamber. If she tries to leave, advise her 'tis Lady Nan who will suffer harsh punishment for her actions."

"I left a man in front of her door," Roland told the baron.

"He's to remain until I dismiss him. Let him know."

"Aye, my lord." Roland exited the room, leaving her alone with the baron responsible for having her brought here.

Nan glared up at him as he came to hover over her. He reached out a hand and ran it through her long locks, making her regret that she hadn't braided it earlier. Wishing to tempt Tristan into somehow loving her seemed so long ago.

The nobleman pushed his fingers through her hair again. She refused to flinch at his touch. His hands slid around and untied the knot at the back of her head. Pulling away the linen strip, he dropped it to the ground. Then he removed the wad of material from her mouth. Nan longed to spit in his face but her tongue felt thrice its size and the inside of her mouth was as dry as a desert. She tried to swallow but only coughed instead.

"You must be parched, my lady," Lord Petyr said smoothly.

He went to a table and poured wine into a silver cup and brought it to her. His fingers clasped the back of her neck, holding her steady, as he raised the cup to her lips. Tilting it slightly, she drank greedily. Moments later, he returned the empty cup to the table.

More than anything, she wanted him to untie her aching wrists. They had been bound behind her back for over two hours, mayhap longer. She hurt from her neck and shoulders to her back and arms. Besides her agony, she was aware how this position thrust her breasts out. Nan felt defenseless as Lord Petyr's gaze dropped to them now.

"So lovely," he whispered as he ran his fingertips lightly along the curve that protruded from her cotehardie.

Nan remained frozen in place as he repeated the action along her other breast. Her cheeks flamed in humiliation.

Finally, she found her voice and rasped, "I will take pleasure cutting every finger from your hands and then your hands from your arms and then your arms from your body. And I promise that will only be the beginning."

He brushed the back of his hand along her cheek. "You are magnificent. Conquered and still unbowed. Oh, we will enjoy our time together, Nan." He paused. "I had thought merely to make you my whore since I already have an heir but now I think I will enjoy the challenge of taking you to wife." He thought a moment. "We shall wed in the morning."

This time, Nan spit in his face. His shock turned to laughter as he wiped the spittle away with the back of his hand. "I like your spirit but you will need to be broken, my dear. I will mold you into what I need."

"You cannot force me to wed you," she proclaimed. "I will refuse to say the words."

"You will." His eyes darkened. "Or I will slit Lady Gillian's throat. She means nothing to me." His evil smile sent a chill through her. "I would deflower her first. In the center of the great hall. In front of all of my men as they cheered me on. You would be there to watch the spectacle, my dear. Then I would let every man present line up to take their own turns with her, until they'd used her up. Who knows how many hours she might last?"

Bile rose in Nan's throat. She forced it down. Looking at this fiend, she knew he would carry out his threat without a second thought.

"And if I agree to wed you?" she asked.

The nobleman stroked her hair. "I would let Lady Gillian go," he said and then grinned. "After her brother paid a ransom for her release, of course. I wonder if I should make that ransom your bridal price?" he mused. "I suppose I must give Lord Geoffrey something for having taken you to wife."

Nan thought that Tristan would kill this stupid man, as would her father and her brothers and the other men in her family who loved her. Lord Petyr Medford deserved to die a thousand times over. And Tristan would have to wait in line because Nan wouldn't think twice about taking this man's life if Tristan didn't arrive by the time this so-called marriage was supposed to take place. Even if it meant killing the baron in front of the priest and facing eternal damnation because Nan was determined never to wed this fiend.

"So be it." Nan dropped her head, trying her best to look defeated.

Silence lingered until he said, "Here, let me loosen your bonds."

The baron grabbed her about the waist and brought her to her feet. Her breasts grazed against his chest, causing a ripple of revulsion to run through her. Pulling a knife that hung from the belt he wore, he spun her around and sliced through the rope that held her fast.

Nan had wanted to attack him immediately but savored the sweet relief of being unbound for a moment. Then as she tried to raise her arms, a burning sensation engulfed her. She cried out in agony as the blood began to flow through her arms again and found she couldn't even lift them. Lord Petyr returned her to the chair and strode into his bedchamber while Nan tried to shake her arms and hands enough to regain feeling in them so she could remove the rope around her ankles.

Before that happened, the nobleman returned with something in his hand. He captured her wrists and wound a length of silk around them, tying it tightly.

"I know you are in pain from being restrained, so I will only bind your hands in front of you tonight." He sighed. "The hour is late, my lady. Unfortunately, as I have grown older, I have found my cock won't always rise when I am this tired, even in the presence of one as lovely as you are. So you may hold fast to your virginity a final night. I will get the sleep I crave and after our wedding tomorrow, I plan to have you. Over and over. I will fuck your brains out until you are worn into submission."

Angry tears gathered in Nan's eyes but she held her tongue. He bent and pressed a hot kiss against her brow, probably knowing she would bite his lip off if he came close to her mouth.

"Good night, my sweet Nan. Until tomorrow."

The nobleman crossed the room and closed the door to his bedchamber.

Nan sent a swift prayer to the Virgin Mary.

The bastard didn't even have the foresight to lash her to the chair. Smiling, Nan bent from the waist and lowered her fingers to her ankles—and the knot she herself had tied around them.

CHAPTER 20

TRISTAN WAITED PATIENTLY for Nan to return to the solar.
Until his patience wore thin.

She had left him at least an hour ago. Mayhap, she lurked in the corridor, waiting for him to leave. He couldn't let her depart Leventhorpe with things so bitter between them. He had no idea what he would say to her but he decided to find her and try to make amends—if she'd let him.

Leaving the solar, he did not find her in the hallway. Thinking she might have taken refuge in Gillian's bedchamber, he rapped on the door but received no response. Normally, Tristan would respect his sister's privacy. But this time, he pushed the door open, only to find the room empty. He went down to the great hall but neither woman was present amidst those gathered there.

Stepping outside the keep, he saw it was growing dark. Concerned, he went to the stables, thinking Nan might have taken solace by visiting her horse. Again, he did not find her.

Tristan crossed the bailey and saw David heading toward him.

"Have you seen Gillian?" the knight called out as he closed the distance between them.

"Nay. Neither her nor Nan. I am growing worried," Tristan admitted. "Nan and I . . . had words. She took off. I wanted to find her and . . . apologize."

"Mayhap they are together," David uttered, but his tone said otherwise.

Just then, Drewett Stollars appeared, on his way to the barracks.

They stopped him but the squire had seen neither woman.

"We'd best look for them," Tristan said.

"My lord!" a voice called.

He looked up and saw Sir Dawkin approaching. The captain of his guard shuffled toward them awkwardly as he tried to hurry. It struck Tristan anew how much this man had sacrificed for Leventhorpe.

"'Tis time to close the gates for the evening but I've just been notified by the gatekeeper that Lady Gillian and Lady Nan are still outside the castle walls. I think you need to find them and bring them inside."

"Nan does like to walk. Especially when she's upset," Drew said, flashing Tristan an angry look.

"And Gillian has accompanied her several times on her walks the past two weeks," David added. "They have strolled through the meadow and into the forest, so Gillian has told me."

"Then we search there first," Tristan proclaimed. "Stay here, Dawkin. Close the gates behind us. I'll return if we need more men."

They debated a moment whether to take their horses or not and favored walking instead, especially since night had now fallen. All three men hurried through the outer bailey and out the gates, which slowly closed behind them at Sir Dawkin's instruction.

"If they aren't in the forest, they could be with Hugo, our falconer," Tristan suggested. "I know Nan has gone to visit him a few times."

"We should check the meadow first," David said, worry now evident on his face. "It's closer."

They reached the meadow and crossed it, seeing no sign of either woman.

"I'll walk the perimeter of the woods," Tristan said. "David, you enter here. Drew, accompany me a little further down before you venture in. I'll continue on to the large oak and go from there. We should convene in this spot after half an hour."

David gave a curt nod and moved away from the other two. Tristan and Drew walked several minutes before Drew stopped.

"I see something ahead. On the ground." The squire drew his

sword and Tristan did the same.

They crept closer until they came upon two bodies at the edge of the forest. Drew rolled one over while Tristan went from one to the other.

"Do you recognize either man?" Drew demanded.

"Nay. I have never seen them before. They are not Leventhorpe men."

"Then what are they doing on your lands?" Drew asked. "Wait." He bent and picked up something.

Tristan saw it was a baselard. His eyes roamed the ground and saw a sword also lying nearby.

"God's teeth!" Drew ground out as he gazed at the dagger.

"What?"

Anger flashed in Drew's eyes. "This is Nan's blade. I gave it to her. I had Ancel inscribe it."

He held it out and showed Tristan the inscription engraved upon it. He also saw the blood staining the weapon. Retrieving the abandoned sword, Tristan saw it, too, had blood on its blade.

"Nan would never go anywhere without this in her boot. And if she withdrew it and used it, she is the one who killed these men," Drew said. "But she would never willingly leave it behind."

"Unless forced to," Tristan said dully.

"I'll fetch David. Stay here," the squire said.

As he waited for the two men to return, nausea spread through him. All Tristan could visualize were the bodies of his murdered family strewn about the great hall, their blood soaking the rushes beneath them. Panic seized him.

What if the same had happened to Nan?

Tristan could no longer deny his feelings. He thought he had kept her away from his heart, but Nan de Montfort had wriggled under his skin until she possessed him, body and soul. He'd only pretended to himself that he didn't love her when, all along, she was the very reason he breathed. His life would have no meaning, no purpose, without Nan in it.

David and Drew returned and Tristan knew the squire had explained the situation to the knight.

"I fully admit I have been a damned fool. I love Nan. I need her in my life. I have to get her—and Gillian—back."

"Who would wish to take them? Does someone bear you a grudge?" David demanded, his anger evident by his stance. "Who are your enemies?" His voice broke. "I love Gillian more than words can say. I cannot lose her. I can't."

"I know of no enemies but that does not mean they do not exist," Tristan said. "Let's go back to Thorpe Castle for horses and men."

As they ran toward the castle at full speed, he tried to think of who might want him harm. The best way to hurt him would be through injuring Gillian. Or Nan.

Tristan decided they would start their search with his closest neighbor, Sir Archibald, and move on from there. Then he stopped in his tracks.

The women hadn't been on the road. They'd been either in or near the forest so it couldn't be highwaymen who attacked and took them. Only one man in the area had met Nan and knew she staying was at Thorpe Castle.

Lord Petyr Medford.

He remembered how the baron had been more than interested in Nan. How something ugly had passed between the two, enough to make him swear never to allow the nobleman on Leventhorpe lands again.

But would the nobleman go so far as to steal Nan—and Gillian—away?

Tristan's gut answered in the affirmative. He came to a halt. His companions did the same.

"You know?" Drew asked.

He nodded. "I think I do."

They reached the gates to the castle, which swung open, and the three men rushed inside. Sir Dawkin met them.

"Gather every soldier in the training yard," Tristan ordered. "Even those atop the wall walk."

The captain left to do his bidding. Tristan shared his suspicions with his companions.

"But why kidnap them?" David asked. "Would he seek ransom?"

"Lord Petyr is very influential throughout Essex. He is not a man who accepts rejection. From what little I know, he cornered Nan in the stables during his recent visit to Thorpe Castle and made an unwelcomed advance toward her."

"Holy Mother of Mary!" cried Drew, balling his hands into fists.

"I came across her right after the incident occurred," Tristan explained. "Nan did not elaborate, only saying she had taken care of the matter. I never had an opportunity to press the baron because when I went to confront him, he rode by me swiftly and left the castle grounds. I assured Nan that Lord Petyr would not be welcomed at Leventhorpe ever again." He shrugged. "If he took a fancy to her and she turned him down, it might be enough for him to . . ." Tristan's voice faded.

"For him to want to possess her," David finished. "I know men such as that. They are vile to their core. I agree, my lord. I believe this nobleman ordered Nan brought to him. Gillian probably accompanied Nan to the woods and unwittingly became part of the plot."

"Come," Tristan said and they followed him to the training yard.

Torches had been lit. Every soldier in service to Leventhorpe filled the area. He climbed onto the platform and scanned the crowd.

"Lady Gillian and Lady Nan have gone missing. I believe they have been taken by men sent by the Baron of Wycliffe."

A rumbling rustled through the yard.

"Lady Gillian is the only family I have left. Words cannot describe how dear she is to me. And you all know Lady Nan from these past two weeks. She fought hard. We found the bodies of two men who attacked her and my sister. Lady Nan's weapons were drenched in their blood."

The murmurs grew in volume. Tristan let them play out for a moment.

"I have had a hard time accepting a fact that many of you seem to recognize. For years, I have closed my heart from any kind of emotion, even while my sister did her best to understand me and try to love me. But meeting Lady Nan has changed everything." His voice broke.

Tristan saw the sea of faces before him, hanging on his words, and couldn't disguise the raw pain rushing through him. "I bare my soul to you tonight. Nan de Montfort is the woman I love. The woman I want to make my countess. She is the one who brought me back from the blackest pit of darkness that invaded my soul. My life means nothing without her in it. Nothing.

"I ask for you to ride with me now to seek their return. Gather your weapons and saddle your horses."

As one, the soldiers surged forward from the training yard, eager to do their liege lord's bidding.

Sir Dawkin stepped up. "We will get them back, my lord, and give you the happiness that you deserve. These soldiers are loyal to Lady Gillian and they truly respect Lady Nan. There's not a man here who doesn't recognize how good she is for you."

Tristan prayed his captain would be proven right this night.

CHAPTER 21

As Nan began to labor over the knot, she abruptly stopped and sat up.

What if this was a test?

Lord Petyr Medford might be more clever than she realized. If she freed herself too quickly, he could be waiting to pounce. She forced herself to sit perfectly still, eyes closed, waiting to see if he would reappear. Her thoughts drifted first to Gillian. She hoped her friend's terror had calmed since the baron had instructed his man to free her from the ropes. Nan told herself that, soon, she would find Gillian and they would make their escape. Together.

Though he was the last person she wanted to think about, Tristan's handsome image invaded her mind. Nan longed to touch his face. Brush her lips against his. Feel his hands caressing her body. She bit her lip, silently begging herself to concentrate on other things. Anything besides Tristan Therolde. Then pictures of Kinwick and her loved ones rushed through her head. A few tears escaped and cascaded down her cheeks.

This wouldn't do. She needed to clear her mind. Nan decided to count in her head. She began counting by threes, trying to soothe herself. Gradually, it began to work.

Then she heard a slight noise, followed by an almost imperceptible breeze. She forced her face to remain a blank and her breathing to continue to be even and steady. Petyr Medford had opened his bedchamber door and now stood next to her. She could feel his body's heat. Smell the wine that had been on his breath when he'd drawn near her earlier. Nan continued to breathe slowly, in and out, over and over.

Then a small rustle sounded as the nobleman turned away and left her. She counted to one hundred before she opened her eyes again.

His door was shut as before. Nan was almost glad she had cried so he could see the evidence of how distraught she was. If he thought she had given up hope, he would stay in his bedchamber.

Now, it was time to go to work.

She labored carefully over the knot. When Hal had first showed it to her years ago, he had let her tie it and then undo it dozens of times until it became second nature. He had warned her a time might come when she found herself in a bad situation. Because of that, she needed to practice in a different way. That was when Hal had lashed her wrists together and told her to free her feet, which had been shackled with the trick knot. It proved harder to do with her wrists incapable of movement, but Nan had practiced enough until, once again, she could easily free her ankles from the rope. Thank goodness for a brother who'd taught her such a useful skill.

The knot finally gave way and she wound the loosened rope around until it could be slipped over her feet. She stood, looking about the room for a way to free her hands since she'd had to leave behind her baselard. Lord Petyr had fastened the silk cord firmly. Her search proved fruitless. Nothing in the solar would help her cut through the restraint. She would have to find Gillian and have her help release the binding.

Tiptoeing to the door, she found the solar unlocked and unguarded. The least the baron should have done was put a guard at the door. Did he expect so little from her? For once, Nan was glad she was a woman since men such as Petyr Medford underestimated the fairer sex.

Then she remembered that he had placed a sentry at Gillian's door, which Roland had said was three doors' distance from the solar. How was she supposed to get past an armed man? The guard would see her the minute she left this space.

Unless he was distracted. Nan knew she had to venture far enough outside the solar to catch a glimpse of the soldier and where his gaze fell. If he looked down or in the other direction, she might be able to slip inside another chamber, either across from the solar or next door to it. If she could do so, she might be able to find a way to free herself before confronting the guard.

Nan's lips moved in a silent prayer, begging the Virgin to intercede on her behalf and keep her safe so that she and Gillian could escape from the fiend who held them against their wills. She had never prayed with more fervor than in this moment. Finishing, she opened her eyes and leaned her head out as her body hugged the doorframe.

By the Christ!

No one stood guard in the hallway. Nan's heart pounded fiercely as she slipped from the solar and gently shut the door. She would find Gillian and then return and take care of Lord Petyr Medford. A plan was beginning to formulate in her mind.

Nan went to the bedchamber and hoped Gillian had not been moved elsewhere. She opened the door and slipped inside as quietly as she could. No candle burned in the darkened room.

She hesitated a moment and then softly said, "Gillian?"

"Nan? Is that you?"

"Where are you?"

"On the bed."

"Stay there. I am coming to you."

With her feet free now, Nan stepped slowly, thrusting her tied hands in front of her to feel for any obstacles that might be in her path. She finally bumped into what she hoped was the bed.

"Nan?"

"I'm here." She used her hands to push up so that she could sit upon the mattress.

Arms went about her. Gillian buried her face in Nan's neck. Nan could feel the hot tears dripping along her skin.

"How did you get free? Where are we? Why were we brought here?"

"My brother, Hal, taught me a trick knot. I used it when I secured the rope about your wrists and ankles, hoping they would place us together. I could have told you how to free yourself and then help loosen me."

Gillian's hands slid down Nan's arms. "Oh! Your hands are still tied together."

"Aye. Roland, the man who took us, had me tie my own ankles. I used the special knot then but Lord Petyr was the one who tied my hands."

"Lord Petyr? *He* is the one that ordered us taken?" Gillian hiccoughed.

"He is."

"But why?"

"Later, Gillian. For now, we need to find a way to break my restraints and then escape."

"But how, Nan? I know it must be late and the castle bedded down for the night. But even if we could flee the keep, there will be sentries along the wall walk. Someone would see us."

"I will figure something out, Gillian. I need my hands free, though. See if you can untie me."

She lifted her hands in front of her and Gillian's fingers found them in the dark. After some minutes, Nan felt the cord begin to loosen.

"That's right, Gillian. Keep up whatever you are doing," Nan praised.

At last, her friend pulled the binding away. Nan slipped the cord inside her cotehardie and rubbed her aching wrists.

"We need to go back to the solar."

"No!" Gillian cried.

"Hush," Nan warned. "No one was guarding your door when I came, but that could have changed."

"The one you called Roland told me that a guard would remain outside my door all night." Gillian sniffed. "And that if I tried to escape, he promised he would . . . hurt you."

"They said that to frighten you."

"Well, it worked, Nan. I am still terrified, despite you being with me. Why do you want to go to the solar? Won't Lord Petyr be there?"

"He is fast asleep by now. I need to keep him there and hold him hostage while you ride for help."

Gillian grabbed her hands. Nan felt Gillian's nails digging into her skin. "I can't, Nan. I'm scared."

Nan took a deep breath. "After going through what you have tonight and coming through it, you'll never be frightened of anything again. David awaits you, Gillian. You and he will have an amazing life together. But to live it, we need to secure Lord Petyr and you will need to bring help."

Gillian's hands eased. Nan sensed the calm descend upon her friend. "You're right, Nan. I want to be brave. Like you."

She touched Gillian's cheek. "Remember, David already loves you as you are."

"You really believe I will see him again?"

"I promise." Nan's voice was resolute. She needed to bolster Gillian's courage. It would take both of them to pull off what she wished to accomplish. "We will need to bind Lord Petyr so I can manage him. We can take the silk cord he used on me but I'll need more. Help me strip the bed. We can tear the bedclothes and use that to secure him."

They worked quickly in the dark, feeling their way and gathering long bits of material to use as Nan revealed her plan. If they needed more, she thought they could do what Roland had, this time using pieces from Gillian's smock, if necessary.

Nan opened the door again and saw the dimly lit corridor was still empty. She thanked the Virgin for watching over them as they returned to the solar. The candles in the first room she'd been held in burned low. Nan saw Gillian wavering between fear and determination and gave her an encouraging smile. Her friend returned it and Nan saw that Gillian's resolve increased.

Opening the door that led into the bedchamber, Nan held her breath. The first thing she heard was steady snoring. She glanced to the bed and saw the curtains had been drawn aside and the nobleman had been too lazy to pull them around the bed again. That would make it easier. She had feared having to ease the curtains away to reach him. As they sneaked inside the room, she was grateful that two candles still burned. That allowed her to hunt for the baron's sword. She found it and silently withdrew it from its sheath as she crept toward the bed.

A naked Petyr Medford slept on his belly, his hairy back thick as a rug. Nan pressed the tip of the sword to the base of his neck and spoke to him.

"My lord, you need to awaken. Now."

Part of his face was buried in his pillow but the one eye she could see opened—and then widened as he recognized her.

"Keep still or I will drive your own blade through your neck and out your throat, pinning you to the bed. And you know I have no qualms about killing. Ask John. Or Fitch."

He blinked rapidly, trying to comprehend his position. She could almost see the wheels turning inside his head, looking for a way to outwit her.

Nan motioned to Gillian to toss the bedclothes aside. She did so, wrinkling her nose at the sight of the man's hairy buttocks and skinny legs.

"First, place your hands behind your back, wrists together."

The nobleman did as she asked, though Nan caught a few of the curses he mumbled.

"Use the silk cord that Lord Petyr used on me, Gillian," she instructed as she slipped it from her cotehardie and placed it on the bed. "Loop it around his wrists several times." To the nobleman, she warned, "Do not move. Do not breathe."

Watching Gillian, she nodded her approval. "Tie a knot and loop it again. Good. Tie another knot. We don't want him to get loose."

Gillian concentrated, knotting the cord twice more for good measure before she grinned at Nan.

"Do the same with his ankles."

Gillian took some of the torn bedclothes and did the same with the nobleman's ankles and then his knees. Nan began breathing more easily now that the nobleman was trussed. Flipping him over, she held the sword just below one nostril.

"Give me a reason, Lord Petyr. Even the smallest one will force me to slice off your nose before you take your next breath."

A mixture of fear and anger flashed across his face. The anger won out and he stared defiantly at her.

In return, Nan let her eyes roam down his body. She snorted and then met his gaze again, lowering the sword.

"You thought to put that shrunken little cock inside me?" She laughed softly. "I am surprised that you even have an heir, my lord."

Wadding up a larger piece of cloth that she'd held in reserve, she started to place it in his mouth. He clamped his lips together.

"Allow me," Gillian said. She stepped closer and grabbed a fistful of his hair in each hand and yanked.

The baron's mouth flew open to protest. Nan quickly shoved the wadded material inside, muffling his roar. He tried to use his tongue to push it out but she quickly secured a strip around his head to hold the gag in place.

"Now what?" Gillian asked.

Nan already had changed her thinking on how they would win their freedom. "Find ink and parchment and write a note to Tristan to tell him where we are. One of Lord Petyr's men will ride to deliver the missive."

"I could ride to Leventhorpe on my own," Gillian volunteered, still looking unsure.

Nan shook her head, knowing from Sir Dawkin that Gillian hadn't ridden alone since before the peasants had revolted. That alone made her loath to let the girl out of her sight. After pondering the situation, she doubted Lord Petyr's men would allow Gillian to leave Wycliffe unscathed. Nan couldn't afford having Gillian used as a pawn against her, forcing her to release the baron. And if by some miracle they decided to let her friend pass through the gates of Wycliffe unharmed, something unthinkable might happen to her while she was on the road.

"Nay, the roads are far too dangerous for a woman alone to ride that far."

"But what if they refuse to send a rider to Tristan?" Gillian's voice trembled with doubt.

Nan steeled herself. "Then we'll start sending out pieces of Lord Petyr, one at a time. A tooth. A finger. A toe. An eye. Believe me, Gillian, Lord Petyr will be able to convince them to do our bidding."

CHAPTER 22

ROLAND COULDN'T SLEEP. Tension still filled his body as he relived parts of this day over and over. He wondered how soon it would be before the bodies of his companions might be discovered at Leventhorpe. He realized he should have lashed both of the corpses to their horses and brought them back to Wycliffe so that nothing could link the baron to the missing women. That had been impossible since he would have had no place to put the tawny-haired noblewoman for the return trip, and Roland had needed her to keep Lady Nan in line.

He understood now why Lord Petyr was so taken with the dark-haired creature. If her archery skills were anything like her knife skills, Lady Nan would be a formidable opponent. The fact that she was breathtakingly beautiful only added to her allure. He found himself growing hard simply thinking about her, envious that such an impressive woman now belonged, body and soul, to Lord Petyr. Of course, if the baron wanted her as his bedmate he had better not close his eyes during or after their love play. After seeing Lady Nan roll swiftly into action tonight, Roland had no doubt the lady would gut the nobleman the moment she saw he was vulnerable. He didn't envy Lord Petyr trying to control such a vixen—but if he could, it would be worth every moment.

Sitting up, Roland decided he needed a woman to release what troubled him. He left the barracks where dozens of soldiers slumbered around him, wondering if the new kitchen maid would be willing to tumble with him in the middle of the night. Though her face held nowhere near the beauty of Lady Nan's, the wench had given him a few bold looks and a saucy smile when she served him this past week. He felt she would be open to love play with him, especially if he flattered her. Roland had found that was the key to getting his way with any woman and this new one would be like them all.

He entered the keep and, instead of making his way to the great hall where the servants bedded down each night, he found himself climbing the stairs as a delicious idea came to him. He wouldn't dare steal Nan de Montfort from the solar. Roland liked his head attached to his body too much to try something so foolish.

But her companion was available tonight.

The baron hadn't wanted Lady Gillian and seemed put out that Roland had brought the lady to Wycliffe. Knowing the shrewd nobleman, Roland suspected he would ransom her back to her brother. And if the lady returned to Tristan Therolde a little worse for the wear? So be it. She shouldn't have been traipsing through the Leventhorpe forest without a male escort.

The thought of plowing into her virgin womb caused his heartbeat to quicken. Roland reached the top of the staircase and started down the corridor—and then stopped in his tracks.

Where was Baul?

He had left the soldier to guard Lady Gillian's door after Roland had threatened her not to leave the bedchamber. Surely, Baul hadn't had the same idea as Roland and now rode Lady Gillian himself. Or had he?

Keeping his anger in check, Roland crept down the stone passageway until he reached the room where the noblewoman was being held hostage. He lifted a nearby torch from its sconce. Holding it in one hand, he opened the door with the other.

Roland found it hard to breathe. Lady Gillian was gone. The bedclothes had been ripped asunder. Had she somehow enticed Baul into the room and knocked him senseless and tied him up? Nay, he doubted it. That would have been something Nan de Montfort would have been more than capable of doing. Gillian Therolde had seemed too timid to even leave the bed he'd left her upon, weeping pitifully.

Roland searched the small chamber and saw no sign of the soldier. His gut wrenched painfully. It told him that Lady Nan was somehow involved in her friend's disappearance. He left the room and returned the torch to its place and then headed for the solar. Without knocking, he quietly opened the door and found the room empty, a single candle flickering. Still, that didn't prove anything. The baron's bedchamber door was closed. For all Roland knew, the noblewoman was tied to his liege lord's bed this very moment, her virgin blood spilled upon the sheets as Lord Petyr sampled her delights.

And if she wasn't? That meant that two women were missing. Though Baul had been the careless one, Lord Petyr would blame them both.

Roland had to find them before the baron awoke.

He slipped from the solar, his head spinning as he tried to think of where they might have gone. Would they hide inside the keep or try to leave it? Would they be bold enough to slip into the stables to saddle horses to make their escape? He didn't see how they could possibly leave Wycliffe. The gates were locked for the night. The gatekeeper would never have opened them for any reason. The two women were trapped within the castle walls. He simply needed to be clever enough to locate them before sunrise.

As he passed a bedchamber, Roland thought he heard a muffled cry coming from inside it. He retraced his steps and pressed his ear against the door. Anger sizzled through him. He opened the door and heard the cry again—one of a woman being pleasured. In the dim light spilling from the corridor, he saw her silhouetted as she rode a man, her head tossed back and her abundant breasts jutting out. Her lover's voice now chimed in, moaning as he reached his climax.

Roland strode to the bed, his fingers digging into the woman's arm. He jerked her away, tossing her to the floor. She hit the stones hard and cried out in pain. Baul sat up, ready to swing at their attacker.

"Tell your slut to leave," Roland said, his tone deadly as he recognized the very kitchen maid he'd thought to relieve himself with.

Baul swung his legs from the bed and pointed at her. "Go. You heard what he said."

"But we—"

"Not now. Leave us."

The woman pushed herself to her feet and retrieved a smock. She threw it over her head and lowered it before leaving the chamber.

When she was gone, Roland demanded, "What possessed you to leave your post?"

Baul shrugged. "You saw how the lady cowered, Roland. Especially when you told her you'd cut out Lady Nan's tongue if she tried to leave the bedchamber. I knew she was so terrified that she wouldn't go anywhere."

"You rutting with that whore may have cost both of us our heads. Lady Gillian is gone from her chamber," Roland revealed. "Lady Nan might have also found her way out of the solar, as well. We've got to find them. Now."

Baul shot to his feet. "Where do we look?" he asked, fear in his eyes.

"Everywhere," Roland said. "Leave no stone unturned inside this keep. I will look outside." He stepped close to the soldier, crowding him until their noses almost touched. "And you'd better hope we find them both before Lord Petyr realizes they're gone."

Roland strode from the room. "How would Lady Nan think?" he asked under his breath as he rushed down the stairs and out into the dark night.

TRISTAN AND HIS men rode to Wycliffe en masse, arriving a few hours before dawn. He'd promised himself if he found Nan here that he would slay Petyr Medford on the spot and then beg her forgiveness for being such a fool for so long.

He signaled for his soldiers to halt and approached the gates on his own.

"Gatekeeper!" he hollered. "I am Tristan Therolde, Earl of Leventhorpe. I demand entrance at once!"

A man with thinning hair looked down at him, a torch held high in his hand. He looked frightened to be confronted by an angry nobleman. "You aren't expected, my lord. Especially not in the middle of the night. I must seek out our captain of the guard. He will be the one who decides whether or not to give you permission to enter."

The gatekeeper disappeared from his view. Tristan groaned in frustration.

David Devereux trotted his horse up next to Tristan, followed by Drew Stollars, who came to Tristan's other side.

"A gatekeeper cannot make that kind of decision on his own, Lord Tristan," said David. "Hold your temper and exercise patience. Anger can make you lose focus. What is important is to get Gillian and Nan back unharmed."

Tristan sighed. "You're right." He studied the knight beside him. "I will tell you now that I want no fighting between us. I am the one who will kill Petyr Medford. If he's touched Nan or Gillian, I plan for him to suffer before he dies."

"Agreed."

A small entryway cut into the wall swung open and a large man stepped out. He approached them warily, his sword in hand.

"Lord Tristan?" he asked.

"Are you the captain of Wycliffe's guard?"

"Aye. I cannot let you and this small army of men inside our walls, my lord. You are armed and look ready to fight. I will awaken Lord Petyr so he may determine whether we open the gates or not to you and your men. I know of no trouble between you and my liege lord but I cannot let my guard down in such a way. I hope you can understand my position."

Tristan refused to accept this answer. "Lord Petyr holds both my sister, Lady Gillian, and my betrothed, Lady Nan de Montfort, inside Wycliffe's walls. They were taken from Leventhorpe tonight, against their will. Open now, Captain, or suffer the consequences."

The knight's eyes flickered in alarm. "Your betrothed?"

"Aye. Lady Nan and I are as good as wed, so she cannot marry another. You know the laws of the Church."

"I do." He frowned. "You may enter, my lord. But your men must stay outside our gates."

Tristan was loath to enter on his own.

"At least allow Lady Gillian's betrothed, Sir David Devereux, and my squire, Drewett Stollars, to accompany me," he countered, indicating the men next to him.

After a moment's hesitation, the captain said, "Only the three of you. Leave your horses." He fled back inside the castle the way he came.

Tristan turned his horse in order to face his men. In a loud, commanding voice, he told them, "We three are going inside the castle's walls. Sir Dawkin will lead you in an attack on Wycliffe if one is necessary." He motioned to his captain and Dawkin rode toward him.

"If we are not back with both Nan and Gillian within an hour, begin the assault," he instructed.

"Aye, my lord." Dawkin nudged his horse and returned to the assembled army.

The gates slowly opened, enough to allow the trio to walk through them single file. The captain waited inside for them. Tristan saw a man up ahead running toward the keep and wondered if he went to warn Lord Petyr of their arrival. It didn't matter. Tristan was committed to this course of action.

He only prayed Nan would go along with it.

"I'M FINISHED," GILLIAN said, entering the bedchamber. "Do you care to read it?"

"Nay. I trust you said enough to bring Tristan here. Sand it and seal it. Hurry, Gillian," she urged.

Though it was still the dead of night, she didn't like the girl out of her sight. If someone entered the solar, he might capture her and threaten to harm Gillian unless Nan released Lord Petyr.

Gillian returned moments later, the missive rolled up and sealed with wax.

"What do we do now, Nan?"

"Wait. I'm sure a servant will come to wake Lord Petyr or even bring him food to break his fast. When that happens, we'll show whoever arrives that his liege lord is our hostage and demand a rider leave for Leventhorpe immediately."

A door outside the bedchamber crashed open. Nan stepped toward the bed and rested the tip of the sword against Lord Petyr's throat, motioning Gillian to come stand close to her. Moments later, Roland threw open the bedchamber door. He rushed inside, only to gape at the nobleman lying trussed on the bed and held hostage with a blade to this throat. Though it disgusted Nan to see the baron naked, she had wanted whoever came through that door to see how dire the situation had turned.

Nan slipped the scroll from her friend's fingers and tossed it toward Roland. It hit him in the chest and fell to the floor. He retrieved it and stared at her.

"That missive is to be delivered to Lord Tristan Therolde at Thorpe Castle," she directed. "You seem to know where that lies so you might as well take it—else your baron will meet with an accident."

"Mayhap you should begin by cutting out Lord Petyr's tongue," Gillian said. "'Tis what this man told me would happen to you, Nan, if I did not obey."

The baron groaned loudly.

"There's no need for me to ride anywhere, my lady," Roland said. "An army from Leventhorpe arrived at the gates of Wycliffe moments ago. At the head of it is your betrothed—and Lady Gillian's betrothed, as well. They will arrive at the solar any moment now."

Lord Petyr's eyes cut from Roland's to hers. Nan knew instantly what strategy Tristan used. She looked down at the restrained nobleman, trying to look innocent instead of triumphant.

"Oh, did no one tell you that Lord Tristan and I are betrothed? It must have slipped my mind. I knew there was a reason we could not wed in the morning."

He growled behind his gag, trying to speak.

Nan smiled sweetly and looked to Roland. "Then you better let them in."

Before the soldier could leave the chamber, she heard shouts from the distance. 'Twas Tristan calling her name at the top of his lungs.

"In the solar," she cried loudly.

Roland slid through the doorway, making his escape. Immediately, Tristan, David, and Drew rushed into the bedchamber, followed by an older man who wore an air of authority. He glanced at the scene and then left without a word.

Tristan's eyes widened as he studied Petyr Medford a moment, then a brilliant smile crossed his face.

"I see you have the situation in hand, my love."

His words warmed Nan to her core. More than that, they gave her hope—of a shared life with this man.

"Lord Petyr thought to force me to marry him by threatening to kill Gillian," she told the three men.

She saw David's hands ball into fists as his face flushed an angry red. Drew quickly grabbed David's elbow to hold him back. Gillian ran to David and threw her arms around him. Drew released him and Gillian led David from the bedchamber.

"When were you going to tell him that you could not legally wed him? That you were betrothed to me?" Tristan's eyes danced with amusement.

Nan shrugged. "I thought you might show up before the nuptial mass began and inform him yourself, my lord." She withdrew the sword tip from the baron's throat and took several steps away from her trussed hostage.

"Well, I have and will make it clear now in case he is too thick to understand."

Tristan strode toward her and captured her hand in his. He brought it to his lips in a kiss that seared her skin. Entwining their fingers together, he stared down at the helpless nobleman.

"Lord Petyr, you have offended me beyond measure by kidnapping the woman I love. Nan de Montfort means everything to me. Everything. She is the reason I rise in the morning with the sun. No man has ever loved a woman as much as I love her."

He squeezed her hand. Though Tristan kept his eyes focused on Lord Petyr, Nan knew every word was meant for her ears. She squeezed back.

"And no man ever will. You took from me what is mine. Mine alone. You threatened Lady Nan's life and that of my beloved sister. For that, you owe me a debt that can never be repaid. Not in horses or cattle. Not in gold or land. Instead, my gift to you . . . is your life. A lesser man would disembowel you and set you ablaze for what you have done but I am choosing to show you mercy."

Nan frowned. She thought Tristan would kill Lord Petyr for the wrongs he had done to her and Gillian. Surprise—and hurt—filled her at him being so generous to such an enemy.

"Your gift to us? Never come near us again. Never speak to us or of us. Never set foot anywhere that might be in my sight. For if you do, I will kill you, my lord." Tristan smiled. "Or mayhap, I will let my wife do so. I know she is not as forgiving as I am."

By this time, Lord Petyr had fouled himself, quaking in fear. The smell sickened her.

"I think we are done here," announced Tristan.

Nan dropped the baron's sword and it clanged upon hitting the ground. She saw Drew give Tristan a nod of respect and he withdrew from the room. Tristan pulled her from the chamber and they silently passed through the solar. In the corridor, David and Gillian were locked in a heated embrace.

Tristan pulled Nan to him and kissed her thoroughly until she was breathless. Someone cleared his throat. She and Tristan pulled apart.

Drew said to both couples, "We'd best be off."

No one stopped them as they left the keep. Only a few servants watched in silence from the doorway of the great hall. They crossed through both baileys. Wycliffe's captain of the guard awaited them and signaled for the gates to open when they approached. The moment Nan stepped through them, she felt the nightmare had finally come to an end.

As dawn broke on the horizon, she looked out and saw what had to be every soldier from Leventhorpe waiting outside, mounted on horses, weapons in hand. A rousing cheer went up as the army caught sight of the two women. Tears came to her eyes, thinking how all of these men had come to her and Gillian's rescue. Nan gave a brash wave, causing more cheers to break out. She saw Sir Dawkin's pleased smile. He nodded graciously and pivoted his horse to face the men.

Tristan swung into his saddle and lifted her to his horse, placing her in front of him. His arms went around her. Nan felt as if she were deep inside a cocoon, one of warmth and protection.

And love.

As the soldiers turned their horses to return to Leventhorpe, Tristan nuzzled her ear.

Though she longed for him to do more, she turned and looked up at him, asking what weighed on her heart. "What has changed, Tristan? You have fought me every step of the way. From the moment we met, you told you didn't believe in love. Even when I admitted that I had fallen in love with you, you rejected me. I need the truth before we ride away from this awful place.

"Do you truly love me? Or did you do and say what you needed to in order to save my life?"

He pressed his lips to her brow. Nan felt his tears against her skin.

"I meant every word I said in there, Nan de Montfort. I love you with all my heart. I give it—I give everything I have and am—to you. You have taught me so much. I now understand that love doesn't make a man weak. He is stronger because of it. I think I loved you from the moment I met you, something I did not believe possible. It took you being placed in grave danger for me to realize what was most important to me. You. And how much I need you. How much we need one another. How much we can love."

Tristan had finally opened his heart to her, something Nan didn't know was possible. Now that it had come to pass, she knew each day would be better than the one before because it would be lived in love, with this man by her side.

"I know you may be disappointed in me, sweetheart. I entered Wycliffe intending to strike down Lord Petyr. But... something stopped me. Because of something that happened to my family and what I saw that I can never forget, no matter how much time has passed. The baron's children are innocent of any wrongdoing. I couldn't let them suffer—couldn't make them orphans—for his foolish actions."

Nan knew he spoke of finding his family butchered upon his return to Leventhorpe and how he had immense responsibility thrust upon his shoulders at a young age.

"It takes a very strong man to grant mercy as you did, Tristan. I am not disappointed in you. Nor angry with you. If anything, it makes me love you even more."

"Then will you marry me, my love? I want you as my countess. My wife. My partner in life and love, from today until the end of time."

"You know I will, Tristan. I love you. I always will." She smiled. "Until beyond the end of time."

His arms tightened about her and his horse took off. As they headed toward Thorpe Castle, her new home, peace filled Nan.

CHAPTER 23

BY THE TIME they arrived at Thorpe Castle, Nan was ravenous. The soldiers of Leventhorpe went to discard their armor and weapons and returned to the great hall. Servants dashed about, bringing food for everyone. Nan ate her fill, content to stare out over what would be her new home. Already, she had many ideas she would like to implement inside the keep, from scenting the rushes to hanging new tapestries. She could hear Alys now, teasing her for finally being interested in domestic issues, something that had never held Nan's interest at Kinwick.

She looked at the trencher in front of her and decided if she took another bite, she might burst. Instead, more than anything, she desired a bath. Washing away not only the grime but also Lord Petyr's touch was important to her. It still surprised her how forgiving Tristan had been of the nobleman but she did understand why he would not want to leave the baron's children as orphans, having them find their father's bloodied corpse as Tristan had his own family's dead bodies years before. Nan thought she needed to let her future husband know that she had learned of the deaths of his family during the peasants' rebellion, but didn't want him to think she had gossiped with others about him.

Gillian sat to her left on the dais, next to David. David would leave after the meal and ride to Sandbourne to bring his parents back to Leventhorpe. Together, she and Gillian had made a quick, easy decision that they both should marry together at Thorpe Castle in a single ceremony as soon as possible. Drew would ride for Kinwick, as well, in order to notify her parents. Riders would be sent from Kinwick to Alys and Edward's estates, while Tristan would send one of his men to Ancel since Ancel lived the closest to Leventhorpe. Nan hoped that within a week all her family would arrive so that the two marriages could take place.

They went out into the sunshine of the warm day to see David and Drew off.

Drew pulled her aside and embraced her. "I am happy for you, Nan, and I can see how happy you are. I worried that Lord Tristan would not come around and admit his feelings for you."

She chuckled. "That makes two of us, Drew. I suppose it took the thought of losing me for Tristan to understand what we share between us."

He smiled. "You're a love match, just as the earl and countess are. At least Lord Geoffrey has already met your husband-to-be. Now, he'll have to pass Lady Merryn's inspection." The squire paused. "Before I forget." He pulled out a blade and handed it to her.

"My baselard! You found it!" she cried. "It certainly proved useful."

"We saw your handiwork," Drew said dryly.

"Thank you for returning it. 'Tis the best gift I have ever received and it's all the more precious to me because it came from you. Be safe, Drew," she cautioned him. "I will miss you." Already, the thought of being parted from her dearest friend saddened Nan, knowing she would remain at Thorpe Castle after her marriage while Drew returned permanently to Kinwick.

The two men mounted their horses and waved goodbye. Nan watched until they were both gone from sight.

"I don't know about you," she told Gillian, "but I long for a bath."

"I have been thinking of one, as well. I'll let the servants know to bring hot water to us both."

Nan returned to the solar, glancing at it with new eyes. She would spend many years in these rooms.

With the man she loved.

Buckets of hot water arrived and the bath proved to be exactly what she needed. Nan scrubbed her limbs vigorously, trying to wash away any trace of the events that had occurred. She dried herself and combed out her hair, waiting to braid it until it dried.

Someone rapped upon the chamber door. She answered and found Tristan standing before her.

"May I come in?" he asked.

Nan chuckled. "Well, it *is* your solar." She stepped aside to allow him entry.

"*Our* solar," he corrected as he shut the door. "Or it will be soon. Are you feeling refreshed?"

"Aye."

He reached out and ran his fingers through her unbound hair, sending a delicious thrill through her. "I like when you leave your hair down." He rubbed a lock between his fingertips. "I hope you will leave it loose every night," he said huskily.

"I can do so since it pleases you," she said, her pulse quickening with his nearness.

"Are you tired? I thought you might wish to sleep after your bath."

"Nay. In fact, I'm bursting with energy," she admitted, hoping he had kisses—or more—on his mind.

"Can we talk? There are things I wish to speak to you about."

Tristan's tone was serious. Nan wondered what he wished to discuss. "I hope you aren't regretting expressing your feelings toward me."

"Not at all," Tristan said, a smile playing about his lips as he toyed with her hair. "Come."

He led her to a chair and sat, pulling her into his lap. She slipped her hands behind his neck and locked her fingers together. Being next to him like this made her wish they never had to leave the solar.

"I want to share something with you. What made me offer Petyr Medford forgiveness, though he didn't deserve it."

Now knowing what Tristan wanted to discuss with her and how painful it might be for him caused her to say, "I'm not interested in your past, Tristan. Only our present and future together."

He gave her a gentle smile. "I need to talk to you about it, Nan."

"Go ahead," she encouraged. "Tell me what you wish."

Tristan took a deep breath. "My family was like many. My parents met once—briefly—when their betrothal contracts were signed and then years later on the day they wed. They were civil toward one another but had no real affection between them. The moment we reached seven years of age, we were sent away to foster. All but Gillian. As the only girl, she remained home. My brothers and I returned to Leventhorpe during the summers and I looked forward to seeing them each year. I was the oldest and they all looked up to me. I was quite adventurous and outgoing, not the cautious man of few words that you now see.

"Seven years ago, my father sent a missive, asking that I return to Thorpe Castle earlier than usual. I fostered far from home in the West Country and none of us there had any idea of the seeds of rebellion that had begun to spread east of London. I left at once and rode for home, reaching Leventhorpe on the day I turned ten and nine. Cook had always spoiled me amongst all of the children and I looked forward to the lente frytoures that I knew she would make for me once I arrived." He smiled sadly. "No one could fry battered apple rings as she did."

Nan already ached, hearing the wistfulness in his voice and thinking of how tragedy had changed him.

"As I drew close to the castle, it struck me as odd that no serfs labored in the fields. Then the scent of something burning reached me, so acrid that my nose and throat began to burn. I galloped to the gates, only to find them open and no soldiers stationed along the wall walk. The bailey was deserted. I turned my horse in the direction of where the fire had occurred and found myself at what had been our stables."

She stroked his back lightly, trying to comfort him.

"The structure had burned to the ground, though embers still smoldered. The stench of burned horseflesh stayed in my nostrils for a week." Tristan swallowed. "I heard . . . noises. I found two horses that had escaped, probably when a side or the roof collapsed. But they were burned so badly, they had no chance of survival." He shuddered. "I quickly put them out of their misery."

"Oh, Tristan." The words escaped her unintentionally.

"I picked through the rubble, afraid to go anywhere else. It was so silent, Nan. No sound at all beyond a gentle breeze. No birds sang. Nothing."

He remained taciturn a few minutes. Nan let him be, knowing the rest of his tale would unfold when he could manage to speak of it.

"I came across something. At first, 'twas hard for me to reconcile what it might be. Then I realized it was the remains of . . . a babe."

Her fingers stilled from stroking him.

"My mother had been with child the summer before. The babe was to come about three months after I left Leventhorpe. I knew . . . I knew . . . that this was that child."

Nan laid her head on his shoulder. His arms tightened about her. Once again, they sat for some minutes without speaking.

Finally, Tristan said, "I hunted through the debris desperately after that. My mother had made it plain that she was unhappy to be with child again, especially after birthing five boys and a girl. I knew Gillian would be the one to care for this babe. Already, her maternal instincts were strong at a young age." He finally looked at her, tears filling his eyes. "And if the babe had been in the stables, I knew Gillian had been, as well."

"But you didn't find her," Nan murmured.

"Nay. I didn't know if she had hidden the babe there and been unable to return for it." He swallowed hard. "But I knew I couldn't put it off any longer.

"I went to the keep."

She knew what he would find when he arrived. She wanted to tell him to stop but, at the same time, Nan realized Tristan had never spoken of these events with another soul. Releasing this was something he needed to do.

"On the way, I came across a few scattered bodies on the ground. I was only beginning to understand that a rebellion had occurred but I was so dazed that I didn't know who started it or why. I thought I would find my family huddled together in the solar, weeping at the losses that had occurred.

"I was wrong."

Nan's hand slid down to rest against Tristan's heart. It pounded beneath her fingertips. She closed her eyes, hating that he would now relive the horror of that moment.

"The door to the keep stood open, as the gates had been. I called out. No one answered. I started up the stairs to the solar but something stopped me. I retraced my steps and went into the great hall instead." He drew in a long breath and expelled it slowly.

"My family was there. My father. My mother. All four of my brothers. Their bodies mutilated. Blood... everywhere. I had never seen such savagery. I stood there for who knows how long, staring at their brutalized corpses. Then I heard a low moan. It finally pulled me from my confusion. I found Dawkin lying nearby, horribly injured."

"He'd tried to defend them?"

"Aye. To save his life, I had to saw off his leg. His eye had already been plucked from his face. I nursed him back to health even as I took time away each day to dig the graves for the dead. My dead. And the other bodies I found. The soldiers' barracks was a virtual slaughterhouse."

Nan kissed his cheek softly.

"I also knew I had to find Gillian. Dawkin was able to tell me that she had escaped with the babe but I knew I hadn't found her bones in the stables. It took three days before I found her in the forest, huddled in a tiny ball, shivering."

Their eyes met. "I have had nightmares about that day ever since. Those rebelling peasants and their murdering ways defined the man I became. A man who isolated himself. One who found he couldn't trust anyone because he never knew who might turn on him. I cut myself off from every emotion and held everything inside me. I believed I could never love again because it would hurt too much. I refused to let my guard down. I never let anyone close to me again, not even Gillian, who craved my attention. I was lucky enough that once Stephen and Toby earned their knighthoods that they came to be in my service. And then I lost them, too."

He paused. "I saw myself alone for the rest of my life. Until you came along, Nan, and changed everything."

Tristan cupped her face in both of his hands, his thumbs caressing her cheeks, wet from the tears she wept.

"You made me yearn to be different. To break away from my past. To want and receive love. Your optimism reminded me of everything lacking in my life. You began to pull me from my shell, little by little. You became like a breath of fresh air—and then you became the very air I needed to breathe, my love.

"Because of you, I want to explore life—and love. With you. No more hiding from my past."

Tristan's lips touched Nan's and he felt he had come home. He pressed soft kisses against her mouth, each one healing him. With this woman by his side, Tristan knew everything would be transformed for the better. She parted her soft lips and he deepened the kiss, sweeping his tongue inside her mouth. One kiss melted into the next until he finally broke away. They both gasped for air.

"I love you, sweetest Nan," he said earnestly. "I cannot wait to speak our vows and make you mine."

Love shone in her eyes as she told him, "I am yours, Tristan, for the taking. Love me."

He frowned. "But—"

She cut off his reply, her hands gripping his gypon and pulling his mouth back down to hers. They kissed hungrily. His arms enveloped her and held her close. Nan wiggled her bottom against him. His manhood sprang to life.

This time, she broke the kiss. "Come. The bed awaits us."

Nan scrambled off his lap and captured his hand, tugging hard. He allowed her to pull him from the chair.

"Are you sure?" he asked.

Her smile lit up the room. "I will always be sure—when I am with you." Those sapphire blue eyes sparkled at him with certainty.

And a bit of mischief.

Tristan scooped her up and took her into the bedchamber, his pulse racing. He gently placed her on the bed, the cloud of long, dark hair spilling about her. His trembling fingers undressed her slowly, admiring the creamy, smooth flesh as it was bared to him. When he pulled her boots from her feet, her dagger fell to the floor.

"I see Drew returned your blade."

Nan shrugged. "Every woman should carry one."

Finally, she lay before him, unclothed. Tristan's eyes roamed over her frame, taking in her full breasts and the beautiful curve to her hips.

"Prepare for every inch of you to be kissed, my lady," he promised.

"Nay."

Had she changed her mind?

"First, you must let me see you, my lord." A smile played about her lips. "Then we shall have this kissing come to pass—although it may be my lips kissing every bit of your flesh."

Tristan began tearing at his clothes. He had never undressed as quickly in his life. Nan giggled as she watched.

"Wait," she said as he started to climb onto the bed.

She rose to her knees and placed her palms against his chest. Lightly, she ran her hands along him, over his nipples. Then she tweaked them playfully. Before he could speak, her hands glided lower, brushing his belly, then coming to where his manhood jutted out. Nan clasped it in her hand and stroked it. Tristan shuddered. She pulled on it, bringing him down onto the bed with her.

They explored one another with slow curiosity, taking their time to learn what the other liked. Finally, he hovered above her, his fingers pushing into her as she writhed upon the bed. Nan gasped and quivered, her hips bucking as she came. He covered her mouth with his to muffle her cries and plunged into her, knowing it would hurt her but hoping the pain would be short lived. Once she got used to him, he began thrusting slowly, gaining speed as he kissed her with a passion unknown to him.

He climaxed with a pleasure so intense, he thought he might die from the sensations. Tristan collapsed onto Nan and quickly rolled until she rested atop him. He kissed her over and over, knowing he would never grow tired of the taste or feel of this woman.

The woman he loved.

CHAPTER 24

Nan awaited the arrival of her parents, standing beside Tristan as she had the day before when David had returned from Sandbourne with Michael, Elysande, and his brother. Greeting her relatives had only been half of the fun. The most satisfying part had been watching David reunite with Gillian and seeing him introduce his parents to her. Elysande greeted Gillian with a love that radiated from her, sweeping the younger Therolde into her arms as if she'd found a long-lost daughter. Knowing Gillian had been motherless for so long and seeing how quickly these two women took to one another touched Nan's heart.

The familiar de Montfort banner rounded the corner and a rider broke away from the pack. Hal galloped ahead and brought his horse to a halt next to where she stood. He leapt from the beast's back and captured her waist, lifting her high as he twirled twice in a circle as she laughed. Setting her back onto the ground, Hal wrapped his arms around her and held her tight.

Nan looked up at him. "I am so glad to see you."

He kissed her cheek, love for her shining in his eyes. "I couldn't be happier for you, Sister." Releasing her, he turned to Tristan and eyed him a moment before thrusting out his hand.

Tristan took it and as they shook, Hal said, "I hope you realize if you ever make her unhappy that the wrath of the de Montforts will descend upon you."

The old Tristan would have withdrawn and become aloof at such teasing. Instead, he boldly looked Hal in the eye and said, "Nan will never have a moment of unhappiness. I guarantee it."

Hal smiled his approval and slapped Tristan on the back.

Then Tristan said, "I know you've taught Nan many things over the years. What I wish for you to teach me is how to produce that earth-shattering whistle."

The two men laughed, already brothers-in-arms. Having Hal's blessing upon her upcoming marriage meant the world to her.

Nan turned and saw her father handing her mother from her horse. "Move your horse," she ordered Hal and he led the animal a few feet away. She threw her arms around her mother and said, "It seems as if it's been years since I last saw you."

Merryn de Montfort hugged her, the familiar scent of vanilla wafting toward Nan. She pulled away and took her mother's arm, leading her to a waiting Tristan.

"Mother, I would like to introduce to you Lord Tristan Therolde."

Tristan bowed deeply and took Merryn's hand, brushing a kiss across her knuckles. Nan saw her mother smiled warmly at the nobleman even as her eyes assessed everything about him.

"Enough of that!" Geoffrey said, claiming his wife's hand again and kissing it for good measure. "You have your own woman now, Lord Tristan."

"I do, indeed, my lord, if you and Lady Merryn approve of our match."

Geoffrey said, "We trust Nan. If she believes you are her one true love, then we welcome you with open arms. I will tell you that you are getting a beautiful, spirited woman as your wife." He grinned. "Then again, I'm quite partial to her." He embraced his daughter, kissing the top of her head.

As her parents continued speaking with Tristan, Jessimond finally made her way to Nan. She hugged the younger girl.

"What do you think of Tristan?" she asked her sister.

Jessimond cocked her head and looked Tristan's way. "He's very handsome, of course, but I knew you would always find a handsome man to wed." She glanced back at Nan. "But I see a change in you,

Nan. A good change. I think you and Lord Tristan are meant to be together. I will be honored to welcome him into our family."

"I would like it if you stayed with us at Thorpe Castle awhile, Jess. I'll admit that the keep has been sorely neglected for years. You have a good eye and are much better with domestic matters than I could ever be. Would you be willing to extend your visit and help me turn this place into a home?"

Jessimond's face lit up. "Oh, Nan, you know I will. Thank you for asking me." She wrapped her arms around Nan's waist. "Can I tell Mother and Father?"

"Certainly. You will need their permission to do so but I don't think that will be a problem."

"I'll ask Mother now." Jessimond hurried away and Nan saw that Elinor now approached.

"I am so glad to see you," Nan told her sister-in-law. "Are you keeping Hal on the straight and narrow path?"

"What do you think?" she asked as she hugged Nan. "Oh, I can see how joyful you are. I am delighted that you have found your own Hal to love."

"I never knew it could be like this," Nan confided, her voice low.

Elinor's cheeks pinkened. "You mean . . . you have . . ."

Nan grinned. "We most certainly have. Every day—for almost a week. And it's divine."

Both women chuckled.

Elinor looked around. "I have only told Hal but I wanted to share with you that you will be an aunt again," she confided. "'Tis early but I am certain that shortly after the new year appears, so will our babe."

She hugged Elinor again. "I hope I can say the same soon. It would be nice for us to have children that would be close in age."

"Nan," Tristan called. "Come inside. The others are waiting. Gillian has made sure refreshments are available."

Linking her arm through Elinor's, they entered the keep. Soon, conversation flowed rapidly as the de Montforts met Gillian and enjoyed catching up with the Devereux family. David's brother,

Tucker, had come with his parents, but their sister was too heavy with child to travel to the wedding. David promised Gillian that he would take her to meet her new sister in the near future.

Nan went and pulled her mother aside so they could speak privately. She led Merryn to a corner of the great hall and the women sat facing one another.

"What do you think?" she asked.

Merryn looked back to where Tristan stood, talking with Hal and Drew, who had accompanied the de Montforts to Leventhorpe.

"Physically, Lord Tristan is the same man that your father described to me after they met at Sandbourne. His disposition seems different than what it once was, though. Geoffrey told me Lord Tristan was quiet. Reserved. The man I see before us has changed."

Tristan glanced over at them and gave Nan a tender smile before he turned back and gave Hal his full attention.

Her mother took her hands. "I know it's because of you, Nan. You have opened his mind and heart. I see a man with a bright future. One who loves and is loved by the lovely woman in front of me." Merryn squeezed Nan's hands for emphasis. "You've always brought me such happiness over the years, Nan. To have seen you grow from a sweet babe to an inquisitive child to the talented, capable woman you now are has been one of my greatest pleasures of my life."

Tears filled Nan's eyes. "I love you, Mother. So much. I know I wasn't always the easiest child."

"I had hoped you would be interested in the things I am, as Alys was. It took me time to understand that you were your own person with your own interests." Merryn stroked Nan's hair. "I know we haven't always agreed on everything, but you have followed your heart—and look where it led you."

Nan sighed in contentment. "To the man I love. Oh, Mother, to have what you and Father have? I never thought this could happen to me. I love Tristan so very much." She paused. "I only hope you are not disappointed that we've decided to marry here at Leventhorpe instead of the nuptial mass taking place at Kinwick."

"I could never be disappointed in you, dearest Nan. I think the idea of Tristan and his sister marrying on the same day at their home is a blessing." Merryn looked to the group they'd separated from. "I think your future husband misses you. Let's rejoin the others."

Nan and Merryn strolled back and Nan went to stand beside Tristan. His arm encircled her waist, giving her a sense of serenity and security.

He bent and whispered into her ear, "I see the love between your parents and know the same is in store for us in the years to come."

Nan nodded, knowing it would be true.

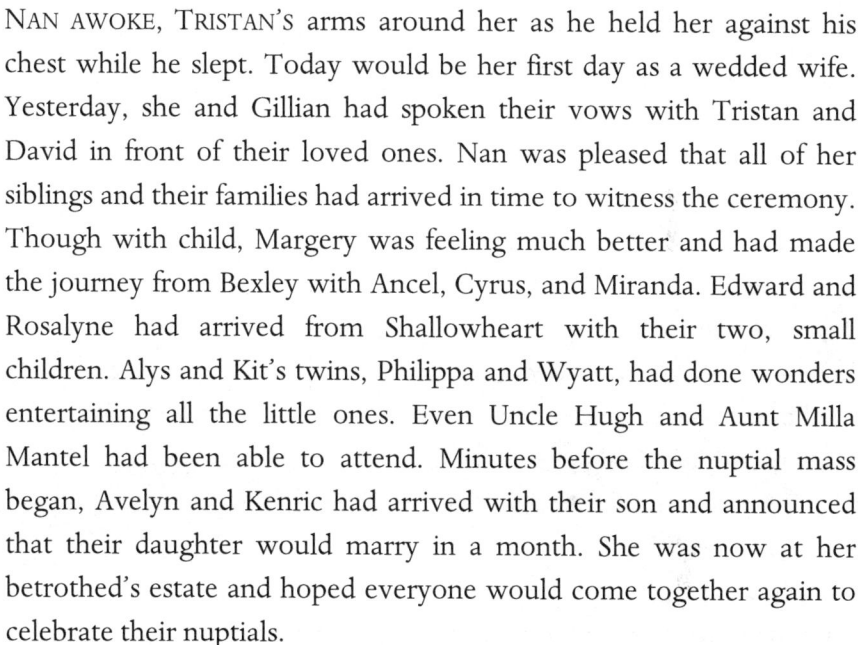

NAN AWOKE, TRISTAN'S arms around her as he held her against his chest while he slept. Today would be her first day as a wedded wife. Yesterday, she and Gillian had spoken their vows with Tristan and David in front of their loved ones. Nan was pleased that all of her siblings and their families had arrived in time to witness the ceremony. Though with child, Margery was feeling much better and had made the journey from Bexley with Ancel, Cyrus, and Miranda. Edward and Rosalyne had arrived from Shallowheart with their two, small children. Alys and Kit's twins, Philippa and Wyatt, had done wonders entertaining all the little ones. Even Uncle Hugh and Aunt Milla Mantel had been able to attend. Minutes before the nuptial mass began, Avelyn and Kenric had arrived with their son and announced that their daughter would marry in a month. She was now at her betrothed's estate and hoped everyone would come together again to celebrate their nuptials.

She stroked Tristan's arm with her thumb, marveling at their love play. Sometimes when they came together, he could be so tender and gentle that she felt like a treasured piece of glass that he didn't want to break. Other times, he became so fierce and passionate that Nan thought he was a flame which consumed her whole. Last night, he had taught her something new. She had ridden atop him, in charge of every move, feeling every bit as majestic and beautiful as he told her she was each day.

His lips suddenly caressed her neck as his fingers splayed wide against her belly. Slowly, they glided down to the curls at the apex of her legs and began a teasing dance that aroused her.

"You are already ready for me," Tristan whispered in her ear.

Nan chuckled. "I think I stay that way."

This time, their love play was lengthy, building from slow, long caresses until Tristan finally entered her. She urged him on, whispering endearments to him, until they both reached their peaks and lay exhausted in one another's arms.

"Your father said he wished to speak to us this morning," Tristan informed her. "Do you know why?"

"Nay. He said nothing of it to me. Mayhap he wants to invite us to Kinwick so you can see where I grew up."

They dressed and broke their fast. Nan had already told her husband that he would need to write to the bishop and seek a priest for Leventhorpe. She'd told him faith was the foundation on which they would begin to rebuild their estate and that she would expect everyone at Thorpe Castle to attend mass daily once a man of God had been permanently sent to them.

Helping one another dress, they finally arrived downstairs to a plethora of noisy conversations. So many de Montforts and their relatives occupied the great hall and their talk filled the room.

"There's Father," Nan said, spying him with his cousin, Raynor, and Kenric and Edward.

They went around the room acknowledging everyone until they arrived at where Geoffrey de Montfort was engaged in conversation.

He greeted them and then said, "Could we adjourn to your solar to discuss private matters?"

They agreed and he signaled to Merryn to join them. Once upstairs, the two couples seated themselves.

"Nan wrote to me of her idea to help build up Leventhorpe when she told us of your marriage," Geoffrey began. "I have spoken to others in the family and they are willing to ask for two of their knights to come to Thorpe Castle and join in service to you. That would be men from Kinwick, Wellbury, Ashcroft, Sandbourne, Shadowfaire, Brentwood, Bexley, and Shallowheart."

"Truly?" Nan did the figures in her head. "So many?"

"Family helps one another," her father said. "Leventhorpe suffered some terrible losses during the peasants' rebellion. Having talented soldiers will be a start to bolstering the estate."

"And we will each ask one family from all of our properties to relocate to Leventhorpe," Merryn added. "Of course, you will have to make it worth their while, giving them a large portion of land to farm and a cottage to live in."

Tristan shook his head. "I am dumbstruck at such an offer but we have more than enough land for that number of tenants. I've also spoken with Edward and Hal about raising sheep here and will continue to breed horses I purchase from Sandbourne." He looked from Geoffrey to Merryn. "I cannot begin to thank you for such support, my lord, my lady."

"Please. We are Geoffrey and Merryn now," Merryn said with a smile. "We are your family, Tristan, and hope you will always think of us in that manner."

"Little did I know when I decided to wed Nan that I would be marrying such a large group of people, as well," Tristan teased. He embraced both de Montforts, as did Nan.

"We have something else to discuss," Geoffrey said. "Nan, will you bring in Drew? He should be waiting outside the solar."

She rose and opened the door. Drew stood in the corridor, shuffling his feet. "Come in," she encouraged.

"Do you know why I'm here?" he whispered.

Nan shrugged. "It's a mystery to me."

"Have a seat, Drew," Geoffrey said.

The squire did, an apprehensive look on his face. "Am I . . . am I in trouble, Lord Geoffrey?"

"Nay, but we have important matters to discuss with you. First, I want you to know how much Merryn and I have enjoyed having you foster at Kinwick all these many years."

Gratitude filled Drew's face. "You have been as a father and mother to me, my lord. I couldn't have asked to go to a better place than Kinwick."

"You also have done well in regards to Nan. You have befriended her and protected her all her life. That has not gone unnoticed."

Drew grinned. "Nan and I are the best of friends. As close as brother and sister."

"What I suggest is that we go ahead and hold your knighthood ceremony tomorrow. Here at Thorpe Castle."

"My lord?" Drew looked confused, but Nan suddenly knew what her father was up to.

"You have proven yourself beyond measure and I think the sooner you become a knight, the better. But there's more to it," Geoffrey continued. "The choice will be yours to make. You may take your oath and do one of three things. Return to your home and serve your brother. Remain at Kinwick and take your place in my barracks.

"Or you may accept an offer from Lord Tristan and pledge your loyalty to him and his family and the people of Leventhorpe."

Drew's jaw dropped. Nan didn't bother to hide her smile.

Her friend now looked to Tristan. "You would have me in your service, my lord?"

"I cannot think of a man I would want more than you, Drewett Stollars," Tristan said. "Your experience and loyalty cannot be bought."

Drew looked back to Geoffrey. "All my life, I hoped and prayed that I would be given the chance to remain at Kinwick, my lord. But I see a world of opportunity awaiting me here at Leventhorpe. Lord Tristan needs good men." He looked back to Tristan. "I would be honored to become one of your knights, my lord." Then he glanced to Nan. "And you know I would give my life for you, my lady."

Nan leapt to her feet as Drew did the same and they threw their arms around one another in glee.

"We can stay together," Nan told him. "Why, you can tutor my children in swordplay!" she exclaimed.

"And archery," Drew added. "I've become quite adept at teaching those skills to others."

Glancing over Drew's shoulder through a blur of tears, Nan mouthed a thank you to her father and then caught the wink Tristan gave her.

Nan had wed a man she loved completely and would continue to share in a friendship with another man she respected. She looked forward to all the years to come.

EPILOGUE

Thorpe Castle—August, 1417

"Look—a butterfly!" Anne broke away, leaving the cool shadows of the forest and running into the nearby meadow.

Nan followed her six-year-old granddaughter, marveling at how curious Anne was about the world around her. Though she loved her two grandsons dearly, Anne was the first granddaughter born to one of her five children. Nan had been secretly thrilled that they named the babe in honor of her grandmother.

Emerging from the woods, Nan paused a moment. 'Twas at this very spot that she had taken the life of two men many years ago. She never crossed the place without thinking about those days and how terrified she'd been when she and Gillian had been taken against their will. Fortunately, in the almost thirty years since, she had never once seen the Baron of Wycliffe. Word somehow got out about what the nobleman had done and the power he'd wielded in Essex waned away. Men in this area had begun to look to Tristan Therolde for guidance and continued to do so decades later.

She watched Anne chase the butterfly until the insect flew too far and fast for the young girl to keep up. Anne returned to her side.

"Can we practice archery now, Grandmother? I'm getting better, aren't I?"

"You are, indeed, my precious. Come."

Nan took her granddaughter's hand again and they made their way back to the castle. When they reached the training yard, she signaled a page and instructed him to go to the keep to fetch Anne's bow and quiver. The boy grinned and took off, eager to please the Countess of Leventhorpe.

Anne watched the soldiers as they paired up for their combat exercises but Nan's eyes drifted to the platform where her husband stood. Even at five and fifty, Tristan still had a mane of tawny hair with only a few strands of white mixed into it. He stood tall and proud, every bit the man she had fallen in love with that summer when she first came to Thorpe Castle—but so much more. For that man had grown in confidence and leadership. More importantly, he had unlocked his feelings and let love inside, doting on his wife, his children, and now their children.

Anne danced around impatiently. Her actions must have caught Tristan's eye. He waved at the girl and she waved back with enthusiasm.

But his smile was for Nan—and she knew what it meant.

The page returned with the bow and quiver and Nan led Anne to the butts, passing Drew on their way. The knight, who had become Leventhorpe's captain of the guard years ago, worked with a left-handed squire. Nan was still thankful that Drew had chosen to come to Leventhorpe. She treasured their friendship and had enjoyed seeing their children play together. Drew's ginger hair was now threaded with silver, but he still had the same happy spirit and sense of optimism that he helped spread among their knights.

No one was at practice on the range and Nan enjoyed having the area to themselves. She could see already how much progress Anne had made in the week since she'd arrived for a visit with her grandparents. Nan enjoyed watching the young girl nock her arrow and send it flying toward its target. This time, though, a gust of wind came up just as Anne released the arrow. Because of that, it fell far from the mark.

Anne muttered a curse under her breath.

"What did you say?" Nan asked, fighting to keep the smile from her face and her tone stern.

Anne sighed in exasperation. "You heard me, Grandmother, and I know I'll be in even more trouble if I repeat what I said to your face."

"You're right about that," Nan readily agreed.

"But Father said—"

"So your father taught you this?"

Anne's eyes dropped to the ground. "Nay. 'Twas Mother," the girl confessed.

Nan thought she would have to have a talk with her oldest daughter—and then a good laugh.

"Gather your arrows and go again," she told Anne.

The girl scampered toward the target as Drew joined Nan.

"She's so like you at that age," he said.

"Even down to the cursing," she replied. "Apparently, her mother has been teaching her a few choice words."

Anne returned, beaming when she saw who had joined them. "Sir Drew, I'm getting better. Grandmother says so. Would you like to see me hit the target?"

"Aye, Anne."

"But I have to watch for the wind. It's died down now but it could come back."

"It could," he agreed. "But 'twill only be me watching you. Your grandfather sent me to tell your grandmother that he has urgent need of her."

Nan knew exactly what awaited her.

"I will see you both later," she told the pair and headed toward the keep, her heart pounding against her ribs in anticipation.

Over the years, Tristan had sent everyone from servants to stable hands to soldiers to his wife, instructing them to tell the countess that he had an urgent need to see her. Gradually, everyone at Leventhorpe had caught on and Nan would see the smiles that these messengers tried to hide.

She entered the keep and went straight to the solar, where she knew her husband would be waiting. Sometimes with clothes. Sometimes without.

Nan opened the door and quickly shut it. Tristan was not in sight. She crossed the room and entered their bedchamber.

Her husband sat against the pillows, anticipating her arrival—without a stitch on.

"What took you so long?" he asked playfully.

"I wasn't sure where you needed to see me," she teased back.

Growling, Tristan leapt from the bed and captured her in his arms. His kiss was hot and his hands everywhere, stripping her clothes from her. Once she was naked, he carried her to their bed and drew the bed curtains to ensure their privacy. Then they engaged in love play for the next hour. Touching. Tasting. Still hungry for one another as they had been from the beginning.

Lying in his arms afterward, Nan asked, "Do you ever think you will tire of me?"

Tristan brushed his lips against her hair. "I have loved you nigh on a score and ten years, my sweet Nan. I committed my heart, my mind, my body, and my soul to you."

Turning her so that they faced one another, he added, "Why don't you ask me that question in another score and ten? Mayhap then I will give you an answer. But until that time? I plan to worship your body each day and never let you go."

He kissed her tenderly and said, "I understand the power of love and the bond it has forged between us. Nay, my love, I could never tire of you. I will come back again and again to drink at the well of love inside you."

With that, Tristan kissed her again, making Nan feel like that young woman who'd first tasted his kiss all those years ago.

Life was good—and would be even better tomorrow—thanks to the love of this man by her side.

Knights of Honor Series by Alexa Aston
Word of Honor
Marked by Honor
Code of Honor
Journey to Honor
Heart of Honor
Bold in Honor
Love and Honor
Gift of Honor
Path to Honor

About the Author

As a child, Alexa Aston gathered her neighborhood friends together and made up stories for them to act out, her first venture into creating memorable characters. Following her passion for history and love of learning, she became a teacher who began writing on the side to maintain her sanity in a sea of teenage hormones.

Alexa's historical romances use history as a backdrop to place her characters in extraordinary circumstances, where their intense desire for one another grows into the treasured gift of love.

She is the author of *The Knights of Honor*, a medieval romance series that takes place in 14th century England during the reign of Edward III and centers on the de Montfort family. Each romance focuses on the code of chivalry that bound knights of this era.

A native Texan, Alexa lives with her husband in a Dallas suburb, where she eats her fair share of dark chocolate and plots out stories while she walks every morning. She enjoys reading, watching movies and sports, and can't get enough of *Fixer Upper* or *Game of Thrones*. Alexa also writes romantic suspense, western historicals, and standalone medieval novels as Lauren Linwood.

Alexa loves to hear from her readers. You can connect with her through FB, Twitter, and her website: alexaaston.com.

Facebook: facebook.com/authoralexaaston

Twitter: twitter.com/AlexaAston

BookBub Follow: bookbub.com/authors/alexa-aston

Newsletter sign-up: madmimi.com/signups/422152/join

Amazon Page: amazon.com/author/alexaaston

Made in the USA
Middletown, DE
28 August 2018